GIRLS
IN THE
LAKE

HELEN PHIFER

Bookouture

Published by Bookouture in 2019

An imprint of Storyfire Ltd.
Carmelite House
50 Victoria Embankment
London EC4Y 0DZ

www.bookouture.com

ISBN: 978-1-78681-926-0
eBook ISBN: 978-1-78681-925-3

For all the writers who paved the way and taught me that anything is possible if you work hard enough and never give up. I thank you for the endless hours of entertainment and chances to lead so many different lives.

CHAPTER ONE

Ethan tried to open his eyes and immediately shut them again, groaning as the boat lurched violently to one side. His stomach contracted; he shouldn't have drunk so many lagers last night, not to mention the vodka chasers. He didn't even remember how he'd got down below deck and into the cabin. He patted his body; at least he was fully dressed. But where was that girl he had been talking to? The one with the white-blonde hair and pretty eyes. They'd been chatting and laughing most of the night. Trust him to have got so drunk that he never had the chance to even kiss her. It wasn't often he met someone new, not in a small town like Windermere where everyone knew everyone. She'd mentioned she was from Devon and had only been here in the Lake District a couple of weeks working at a local hotel. If only he could, for the life of him, remember which one.

His thoughts were interrupted by the sound of something bumping against the side of the boat. He sat up, his head exploding with pain at the sudden movement. More slowly, he slid off the bed and went into the narrow bathroom to relieve himself. He didn't even look in the mirror. He didn't want to know what a state he must look.

Knocking on the other cabin door as he passed, he listened for a response, suddenly imagining the girl he liked in bed with James. Not that he could blame her: James was the one with the fancy boat, the penthouse apartment and more money than he actually knew what to do with. There was no reply. Opening the door, an empty, messy cabin bed stared back at him.

Up the steps and out on deck, there was no sign of anyone amongst the mess of empty champagne glasses, lager cans and vodka bottles. He shivered. The autumn sun hadn't risen yet and there was a gale-force wind blowing across the lake, whipping the water into a frenzy and making the boats unsteady on their moorings. Looking around, the only sign of life was a flock of goldeneye ducks swimming past the marina, looking to take shelter from the approaching storm.

He was just thinking how glad he was that James hadn't been too drunk and he had put the boat back on its mooring, when he heard that thud again. One of the small dinghies must have come loose. He didn't want to have to climb down and drag it away, but there was no one else around and it wasn't fair to let James's boat get damaged just because he had a hangover and couldn't face it. It wasn't the sort of thing you did to your best friend, even if they could afford to get the damage fixed without blinking an eye. Stumbling as the boat rolled to one side again, he grabbed hold of the rails, his head leaning over, and he stared down into the inky waters of Lake Windermere. The glow from the lamps along the quay gave just enough light to see there was something in the water; in the shadow of the boat it looked as if a clump of reeds had got tangled in the anchor chain. Leaning further over, he blinked a couple of times and focused his vision, realising too late that they weren't reeds at all.

It was a woman, floating face down in the water, her long, blonde hair fanned out around her shoulders and snagged onto the anchor chain. A scream so loud it echoed around the marina left his mouth. Heart pounding, he jumped down from the boat and onto the jetty. If he could get her out of the water, he might be able to resuscitate her. Pulling his phone from his pocket as he ran, he dialled 999 and asked for the police and ambulance, giving his location. Dropping to his knees, he reached for her, but she was too far away. Desperately he looked around for something to try and grab her with, or someone to help. Why had no one come to see why he was screaming? Where was Pete? – he practically lived down here! It might take the police forever to get to the marina.

Pulling off his jeans, which he knew would weigh him down, he plunged into the freezing water, hitting it hard. In a couple of strokes he was close enough to grab the girl around the waist. He turned and tried to swim, taking her towards the jetty, but she wouldn't move. He tugged and tugged but her hair was knotted around the thick, rusted chain that held the anchor. He grimaced. He knew deep down that it was too late for the girl, her body cold and rigid in his arms, but he had to carry on. He couldn't leave her there. Grabbing the length of her hair that was caught around the chain, he tried to untangle it with trembling hands. But the shock of the freezing water was cutting off the feeling in the tips of his fingers. He had no choice but to pull it as hard as he could, and finally, she was free and he was able to drag her towards the jetty where, at long last, he could hear the shouts and pounding feet of the police as they ran along the wooden causeway to help him. He'd never been so relieved to see a copper in his life.

Hands reached down and grabbed the girl, pulling her out of the water. Then they leant over and pulled him out too. He fell onto the rough boards on his hands and knees. His teeth were chattering, and he couldn't speak. A blanket was wrapped around him as a strong pair of arms lifted him to his feet.

'Well done, son, that was pretty damn brave of you. Let's get you to the ambulance to get checked out and before you catch your death.'

Ethan didn't argue, letting the officer lead him towards the ambulance that had just pulled up onto the walkway. He looked back at the girl, horror flooding through him as it dawned on him that he knew her: he'd spent last night laughing and sinking vodka shots with her. It was the beautiful girl with no name. The one he'd hoped would be lying next to him when he'd woken up less than twenty minutes ago.

CHAPTER TWO

Beth's body hit the surface of the water like a brick. Then she was sinking under, her arms and legs tied together, the weight of her clothes dragging deeper and deeper though she struggled. Her lungs burned, craving air, and the pressure screamed in her ears. Somewhere nearby the hum of a boat's engine getting closer caught her attention. Someone coming to help, or to finish the job? She screamed into the abyss, her lungs filling with water and making her cough and sending a flurry of fear-filled bubbles to the surface. That was it, her last breath. Wasted.

*

She woke with a start, sucking in air as if breathing for the first time. She was in bed. Thank God. She blinked hard to push away the nightmare that had haunted her for weeks, and wiped the sweat from her face with the corner of her quilt. Her phone was vibrating on the bedside table. Reaching out, she grabbed it before it woke Josh, who was sleeping soundly beside her.

'Adams,' she whispered, still panting a little.

'Sorry to bother you, Doctor Adams, it's Helen from the control room at Penrith. Someone's found a body in Lake Windermere.'

She was out of bed and on the landing in an instant.

'Where?'

'Bowness Bay Marina on Glebe Road.'

'I can be there in fifteen.'

'Thank you. Someone is calling the duty DS as we speak. You answered before he did, so you might want to give it ten minutes before you leave so we can get hold of him.'

She smiled, thanking her and ending the call. It would only be a few seconds before the phone on Josh's side of the bed began to ring. So much for trying not to wake him. She padded along the corridor to the bathroom to splash some water on her face and brush her teeth. By the time she was dressed Josh was on his way out of the bedroom, his hair ruffled, his eyes crinkled against the bright bathroom light.

'Got to love an early call out,' he grunted.

She laughed. 'I never realised just how much of a miserable bugger you are in the morning.'

Josh smiled. 'I didn't realise how annoyingly perky you were this early, so swings and roundabouts.'

She shrugged. 'At least we're alive to complain, not like the poor soul they've just pulled out of the water.' She crossed the hallway and kissed his bristly cheek. 'I'll see you there, Detective Sergeant Walker. Maybe for the sake of everyone at the scene you should make yourself a quick mug of coffee and a slice of toast.'

She turned and ran down the stairs. Going into the kitchen, she grabbed a Mars bar out of the cupboard. Josh followed her in and she threw it across the room towards him.

'At least eat that; the sugar will give you a boost and maybe improve your mood.'

She'd known he wouldn't bother making toast and coffee. Like her, he'd want to get to the scene as fast as he could.

She looked out of the huge picture windows; it was still dark outside and the sun wouldn't be up for another hour. She looked down to the shadow-steeped view of the water, the wind scudding across the white-topped waves, simultaneously admiring its beauty and shivering at the memory of her dream.

Opening the cupboard by the front door, she pulled on her thick, insulated jacket and grabbed the heavy case she kept in there for emergencies. Josh watched her and smiled as she passed him his almost matching North Face jacket. Then she sat on the bottom step, waiting for him to leave first. He walked out of the front door, not turning to wave or say goodbye. There was little point: they were both heading to the same scene.

Beth went to her car and waited, turning the heating on full, until Josh's car was well ahead of her through the gates and out onto the deserted country road. It wouldn't look good if they arrived in the same car at this hour; their relationship was new and they'd both decided to keep it quiet for the time being. There was no need for anyone to know about them. It was their business.

CHAPTER THREE

Beth drove cautiously even though the winding roads were deserted, aware that she was still tired, her senses not quite clear after the nightmare and the rude awakening. She indicated as she turned the car into the marina. It was a lovely place, especially in summer with all the boats moored up and bobbing around in the breeze. She'd spent several happy, warm evenings sitting outside the pub nearby drinking a chilled glass of wine and admiring the view.

Seeing the blue flashing lights ahead, she blinked several times; it was time to focus her mind on the job in hand. It wasn't the first time she'd been called to a drowning; in fact, it was probably one of the most common causes of death in the Lake District after road traffic accidents and deaths on the fells. Almost every year, especially in the summer months, someone would underestimate exactly how cold or deep the water was and get themselves in trouble. The lights ahead led to an ambulance. She parked near a walkway down to the marina between the pub and the row of gift shops. There were several police vans nearby and the entrance to the slipway had been taped off.

She parked on the opposite side of the road, glanced over and smiled at Josh. They had been living together for a month or so now, but very few people knew. She liked her privacy, and Josh was technically still married to Jodie, though they had separated after he found out about her affair. Beth's life had changed beyond belief since the man she'd once loved tried to kill her. She'd lived as a recluse for the past seven years after her ex-partner, Robert

Hartshorn – the man she once thought she would spend the rest of her life with – had plotted, then tried to kill her in the home she'd shared with him then. Thankfully, she'd survived, albeit mentally scarred and terrified of her own shadow, but she hadn't given in. Just a few weeks ago, when she'd been involved in an investigation where girls had been murdered and their bodies hidden in other people's graves, Robert Hartshorn had resurfaced as the main suspect and he had tried to kill her again. Both times that Robert had attempted to kill her, Josh had been the one to save her – Beth owed him everything.

As she dressed in the protective clothing from the back of her car, bending to shield herself from the wind, she thanked her lucky stars she was alive and that Robert was safely behind bars. She could handle a few nightmares and was very slowly beginning to feel safe again. Being with Josh helped; he made her feel safe.

She took her time, knowing that Josh would want to be first on the scene. He always did. Checking her watch, she gave him five minutes to assess the incident, and then she grabbed the case and walked down to where the officer was standing with a crime scene log book, guarding the entrance. Signing herself in and walking towards the marina, she could see the body laid out on the wooden planks of the jetty, and she shuddered against the fine mist of rain as it blew across the lake towards her, tiny flecks of icy water kissing her skin. What a cold, gloomy day to die, she thought, but death was death and, as sad as the reality was, it kept her in a job. At times she'd wondered how on earth she could do this job day in, day out, but what kept her going was knowing that she could use her forensic pathologist skills to help the families left behind get answers. That made it all worthwhile.

'Morning, Doctor Adams.'

The voice startled her. So lost in her thoughts, she hadn't realised Josh had appeared beside her.

'Good morning, Detective Sergeant.'

She gave him a little smile, glad that their personal relationship had no bearing whatsoever on their professional lives, which was how she liked it.

The officers, Josh and the paramedics all stood back leaving her to walk alone along the narrow jetty to where the naked body of a young woman was laid out. Pausing in front of her, Beth felt as if time had frozen; the cold chill in the air made her shudder. The only sound was the water lapping against the sides of the many different yachts and motorboats, all moored up in uniform rows on jetties like the one she was standing on. Daylight was beginning to pierce the dark clouds, although the sun wouldn't rise for at least another hour. It was just her and the dead girl, no one else mattered. They'd all stopped what they were doing to let her do her job and for that she was thankful.

Jerking herself back to the moment, she took in the body in front of her, the glazed eyes staring up into the sky. Whoever this woman was with her porcelain, blemish-free skin, blue eyes and full lips, she was stunning. Beth bent down to examine her closely. There were some superficial skin bruises on her extremities and some abrasions on the right side of her face but the white, frothy foam coming from the woman's mouth was consistent with drowning.

Turning around, Beth raised her voice. 'Do we know exactly where she was in the water?'

The officer who had been first at the scene took a step forward and answered. 'The guy who found her and pulled her out said she was on the port side of that boat.' He pointed to the large, very expensive motor cruiser next to them.

'Which way was she facing?'

'Face down.'

'No, sorry, I meant which way was her head pointing: towards the lake or the marina?'

He shrugged. 'I didn't ask, but he's over there in the back of the ambulance still.'

Josh, who was standing next to him, shouted against the wind. 'I'll go and check.'

Beth smiled at the officer. 'It's okay, I just need to know to see if the marks on her body and face can be accounted for.'

She looked back down at the girl and felt her heart contract in sorrow for the loss of a life so young. Turning the girl's head to the side, she noted there was no rigor, indicating she hadn't been in the water too long before she'd been found. That was a relief, of sorts.

Josh returned, walking closer so he didn't have to shout. 'He said her head was facing out towards the lake; he also said her hair was caught on the anchor chain and he had to forcibly pull it away to get her free. He woke up to the sound of thudding against the side of the boat, came above deck and looked over to find her floating face down in the water.'

'Ah, that would explain the injuries and also why she didn't sink. Normally when someone drowns, the body sinks to the bottom as the water pressure compresses the gases in the chest and abdominal cavities. This results in the body displacing less water and sinking deeper, becoming less buoyant the deeper it goes.'

Picking up the woman's hands, she studied her slender fingers and nails; there were no defence marks on them, nothing to suspect foul play, although Beth couldn't rule it out until she'd performed the post-mortem. She continued working her way around taking the relevant samples and the victim's body temperature.

'So, any initial observations?'

Beth turned to Josh. 'Why is she naked?'

'The witness said she was on the boat with him and four others until the early hours. They were drinking heavily. Her clothes are all discarded on the deck in a pile. It's likely she decided to go for a midnight swim and didn't realise how cold the water was?'

'Maybe. It doesn't look suspicious to me at this moment in time; however I still need to do a full post-mortem cataloguing the bruising and abrasions, then check they correspond with the witness statement before I can give you a definite answer.'

He nodded. 'Thanks, Beth.'

She stood up. 'My pleasure. Poor girl, they say drowning is a peaceful death. I don't think falling into a freezing cold lake and swallowing the water until your lungs feel as if they're going to burst could ever be peaceful.'

Snapping the locks on her case shut, she turned to Josh. 'You know where to find me if you need anything. I'll see you at the hospital.'

Then she left, heading back towards her car with a heavy heart.

CHAPTER FOUR

They finally got clearance to move the body about an hour after Beth had left. Josh could hardly bear to look as the girl was placed into the black body bag, the sound of the zipper sealing her fate forever.

'What a bloody shame,' he said to Patrol Sergeant Karen Taylor, who was standing on the opposite side of the jetty. 'Long time no see, how are you?'

She shrugged. 'I'd be better if I wasn't freezing to death standing here.'

Josh walked over to her, curious. 'Why are you here?'

'I'm on my way to Kendal, they're short-staffed. I heard this come in and thought I'd swing by on my way. You know how it is, Josh, I like to keep you lot on your toes.'

He smiled and laughed. 'How am I doing up to now?'

She shrugged. 'Not bad. Are you sure it's accidental though? I mean you'd have to be totally off your trolley to strip naked and jump into the lake at this time of year.'

'The doc seems to think it is, but I agree with you that it seems like a mad thing to do. There are no obvious signs of foul play and judging by the number of empty alcohol bottles on the boat she came off, I'd have to say her judgement may have been a little distorted. The post-mortem will tell us for sure.'

'How is Beth by the way?'

He wondered if she knew about their relationship – gossip spread faster than the flu in the station. Then again, Karen was usually stationed at Barrow, so how could she possibly know? 'She seems okay, better than I thought.'

'Good, the poor woman has had a terrible time. I suppose you've already heard about the suicide at the prison.'

He shook his head.

'Oh, you've been busy here. That monster ex-boyfriend of hers, Hartshorn, topped himself; they found his body in his cell last night.'

A hundred thoughts rushed through his mind. Did Beth know? Had anyone warned her before she got to work? His hands itched to ring her and find out if she was okay, but they were supposed to be keeping their relationship low profile. It would look too obvious.

'I didn't know. I was called out to come straight here.'

'Well, send her my best. Seeing as how you have everything covered here, I'm off to a cosy warm office in Kendal. I'll see you later.'

She walked away, back to the white Ford Focus parked near the police tape. Josh liked her, she was a good officer and didn't take any crap, but he couldn't help wondering if she had just come here fishing for gossip. Either way, it didn't matter. He walked to his car and got inside, not realising how cold his hands were until he tried to unlock his phone. He needed to speak to Beth. When his fingers warmed up sufficiently to slide across the screen and give him access to his recent call list, he pressed his finger against Beth's name and hoped she wasn't already in the mortuary. It went straight to voicemail and he left her a message to call him as soon as she could.

CHAPTER FIVE

Beth arrived at the hospital mortuary much earlier than usual due to her morning call out. As she walked in, she saw Abe, her 'trusty sidekick' as he called himself. His real job title was Anatomical Pathology Technician and he was already in scrubs dealing with two undertakers and a body in a bag on a steel gurney at the rear doors. Beth wondered who it was. It couldn't be the girl they'd pulled from the lake here already.

She waved at Abe and, as he turned to look at her, for the first time in forever his brilliant-white smile faltered. Immediately she knew something was wrong. After Josh, Abe was probably the second closest thing she had to a friend, since she'd spent the last seven years living in fear and wrapped in a protective bubble of loneliness. Things were different now; she still found it hard to socialise, but at least she made the effort. After surviving two attempts on her life by the same twisted killer, she had vowed to herself that she would no longer live in fear and try to enjoy the life she'd been given.

Whatever bad news Abe had, she could handle. But she needed coffee first. Trying her best to ignore the churning in her stomach, she made her way to the small staffroom and set the coffee brewing while she went in search of something to eat. Her stomach was in knots in anticipation, but perhaps she could persuade herself she was just hungry.

The staff canteen at Furness General Hospital was full, and a few of the doctors and nurses stared over at her as she entered. She smiled at them and they quickly turned away; the celebrity status she'd earned after the last case she'd worked on showed no sign of dying out. She had nothing to hide; none of it had been her fault. Josh had told her time and time again that pretty soon another story would come along and her five minutes of infamy would pass, and people would forget about the tragedy and horror she'd endured.

When it was her turn in the queue, she ordered two fried egg, tomato and mushroom toasted sandwiches. Beth and Abe rarely ate meat on the days they performed post-mortems. The woman handed over two boxes, and she made her way to the till to pay just as a group of police officers piled in, joining the queue and sending a sigh of relief through her body. Now they would become the focus of everyone's attention, which suited her far better. As she walked past, a couple of them nodded; one of them said: 'Morning, Doc.'

'Morning, officers, enjoy your breakfast.'

Smiling, she was out of there as fast as she could walk and made her way back along the long corridors to get to the mortuary. As she keyed in the number on the keypad she was hit by the strong smell of fresh coffee and smiled with delight. Now all she had to do was to eat her breakfast and try to find out why Abe was acting so strange.

He was in the staffroom waiting for her. She sat down and slid a box across the table towards him. 'I wasn't sure if you'd eaten yet; if you don't want it you can warm it up for lunch.' She winked at him.

'Thanks, Beth, you shouldn't have.'

He passed her the bottle of tomato sauce and she smothered her sandwich in it. He shuddered.

'Why don't you have some food with your ketchup? It's gross you know, watching it drip out of the sides of your toast.'

Beth choked, trying not to laugh and splatter fried egg everywhere. 'I thought you had a stomach of steel! I've told you, when your cooking skills are as dire as mine you need all the ketchup you can get.'

'You're not that bad a cook.'

'You haven't had the pleasure of an actual meal. Sandwiches, pasta and packed lunches I can do.'

They ate in silence and when Beth was satisfied Abe was done, she stood up and poured out two mugs of coffee.

'Now we've both eaten and are ready to face the day are you going to tell me what's going on?'

He moved his head up and down slowly.

'Why are you acting strangely?'

'I am?'

She arched one eyebrow at him.

'They brought a suicide victim in from the prison late last night.'

'It's been a while since we've had one of those; why is it making you so edgy?'

She took a sip of coffee, then another. Feeling her brain begin to kick into action as she put Abe's behaviour and a prison suicide together, she came to a revelation that made her blood run cold.

'It's him, isn't it?'

'Yes.'

She stared down into the mug she was holding, a multitude of emotions rushing through her veins towards her brain. Guilt, despite the fact she had nothing to be remorseful about, closely followed by a surge of relief. She hid her face behind her coffee cup. She needed time to process this information and decide how she was going to handle it. Abe stood up and left her alone, taking his mug into the mortuary with him, and for that she was thankful. A few minutes, she just needed a few minutes and then she'd be good to go.

CHAPTER SIX

Sitting at his desk sipping the mug of coffee his colleague, DC Sam Thomas, had made him to take away the chill he was feeling, Josh scanned through the scene photographs from the marina. He was erring on the side of accidental death, but the final call would be down to Beth.

He was waiting for DC John Paton to get back from the hospital, where the witness who'd pulled the victim out of the lake had been taken. Looking down at his notebook, Ethan Scales seemed like a decent lad; he worked out of the Freshwater Marine Biology site on the shore of Lake Windermere, and the boat belonged to a friend of his. It sounded as if they'd been doing what most twenty-year-olds do, drinking and having a good time. His phone began to ring, so he answered it and stood up.

'We're here. I've taken him to interview room A and gone to make him a brew.'

'Cheers, John, I'll be down now. I don't need a drink, I've already got one.'

The call ended and he smiled. DC Paton hated brewing up at the best of times and only ever did it when he had to. Josh grabbed his notepad and pen off his desk in one hand, coffee in the other and he made his way down to the custody suite, where his witness would be waiting for him.

*

Knocking on the grey steel door of the small room, he opened it and walked in. The lad sitting at the table looked up him, and Josh got the impression he was still in shock by the paleness of his complexion and wide eyes. He sat opposite him, reaching out a hand.

'I didn't get the chance to introduce myself properly earlier. I'm Detective Sergeant Josh Walker.'

Ethan took his hand and shook it. 'Ethan Scales.'

Josh smiled. 'First of all, thank you for doing what you did. It takes a brave man to jump into that lake at this time of year.'

He shrugged. 'I had to. I thought, or I suppose I was hoping, she was still alive and I could save her.'

Another knock and this time Paton entered, carrying two steaming mugs in one hand and a KitKat in the other that looked as if it had been kicked around the canteen floor for a couple of hours. He put the drinks down, passing one to Ethan along with the chocolate biscuit.

'Thanks. I'm so cold, I can't get warm.' He wrapped his hands around the mug, dismissing the biscuit. 'Am I under arrest, do I need a solicitor? I don't understand what's going on.'

Josh shook his head. 'Oh, God no. Of course not. As far as we're concerned, you're the hero of the day. This is just a formality. I'm afraid we need to take an official statement to pass to the coroner's officer. It's easier to do it here where we can get it sorted without any interruptions. Of course, if you feel you need a solicitor we can arrange for the duty one to attend.'

'No, I don't. I heard the noise, looked in the water and saw her. I jumped in, dragged her out and prayed I'd be able to resuscitate her. I'm so sorry I couldn't.' He bent his head, and Josh reached out and patted his hand.

'You did everything you could. Should we get this over with so you can get home, have a hot bath and get some sleep?'

Ethan lifted his head, the expression of pure misery on his face making even Josh feel bad for him.

'Yes, please. I feel like shit. I'm never drinking again.'

Josh smiled. How many times had he said the very same the morning after?

'Can you tell me what happened earlier on in the evening, the events leading up to you discovering the body? I need to get a clearer picture of who was there, how much the victim drank, did anyone take any drugs?'

Ethan looked at him, distress visible in his face.

'I don't do drugs; as far as I know neither did anyone else. Well James could have, I can't speak for him, but he sometimes dabbles, nothing too heavy. I prefer to stick to the booze.'

'No one is in any trouble. I'm not interested in a bit of drugs for personal use, I just need to understand what happened to end up with one of the party dead. Did she jump into the water for a dare? Did she tell anyone she was going to go for a swim?'

Ethan shook his head. 'There was me, James Marshall, Marcus Johnson, who left really early before anyone got drunk, and the two girls. I'm sorry, I don't know either of their names. One was the girl I pulled from the lake, the other was her friend. She didn't speak a lot of English, she was French, on an exchange visit or something like that. Look I'm sorry, I can't tell you much more. We drank far too much. It was all free. James always has cases of wine and spirits onboard. I remember we started off on champagne, but soon progressed to vodka shots. I have no recollection of getting to bed. I don't know what time James left. I do know that I wouldn't have let her go into the water for a late-night swim, and no one dared her to. I wouldn't let anyone go into the water, it's freezing and dangerous. For what it's worth, neither would James. I don't know what she was thinking to be honest with you. I keep asking myself and it doesn't make any sense.'

Nodding, Josh was inclined to agree: this felt like nothing more than a tragic accident and he was pretty sure Beth's findings would support his hunch.

'Was she happy? She didn't seem upset over anything?'

'She was laughing and having a good time with the rest of us. I couldn't say if she was upset. I didn't know her well enough to figure out anything more than I liked her. A lot.' He began to blink back the tears that were welling in his eyes.

CHAPTER SEVEN

James Marshall looked at his phone; he had nine missed calls from Ethan. He rolled over in his bed and was surprised to see a woman lying next to him. Christ, he didn't remember bringing her back to his apartment. Why hadn't they stayed on the boat? It was far easier to get rid of a one-night stand when they didn't know where he lived. He stared at the long, blonde hair and tried to remember her name. He thought back to who was on the boat with him last night: Ethan, Marcus and two women; one of them hadn't spoken very much English. The blonde one who had been from down South somewhere he'd left behind with Ethan, who had been fawning over her. If he remembered right, this girl was a French exchange student, over here on work experience. Her English was good, which was a shame because it would be far easier to fob her off with a quick kiss and a taxi fare home if she didn't understand what he was saying.

He threw the covers back and strode naked into the ensuite, stopping for a moment to admire his tanned, toned body in the mirrored walls. He flexed his arm to make his bicep bulge, grinned and blew himself a kiss. He was vain, as his mother and grandmother liked to tell him on a regular basis, and so what if he was. He knew he was good-looking with his line of straight, white teeth and his thick hair brushed to one side like a member of a boy band. He worked hard to look this way, plus a little help from an orthodontist and a plastic surgeon. He'd been fortunate enough to be born to wealthy parents; why wouldn't he make the most of the money at his disposal? He liked the gym, but he also liked to party.

Showering, shaving and dressing in a suit, he tried to ring Ethan back but it went straight to voicemail. Ethan didn't normally ring so many times, not unless it was important, and James hoped that he hadn't done something stupid like crash the boat. Going back into the bedroom, he stared at the naked woman now stretched diagonally, taking up the whole of the bed. She was attractive and if he didn't have work he'd have screwed her one more time. He would probably see her again if she asked. For the life of him he didn't know whether the sex had been any good; he'd been too drunk to remember. He picked up her clothes then bent over her, shaking her shoulder. She let out a moan and for a moment he felt himself go hard, then she began to cough, followed by a loud belch as she cupped her hand over her mouth and stumbled off the bed.

'Christ, if you're going to be sick at least go be sick in the toilet.'

She looked at him with dazed eyes, and he pushed her in the direction of his ensuite. Flicking on the light switch, he heard her retch and slammed the door shut. His own stomach contracted into a tight ball; he never was any good with vomit. He placed her clothes on the end of the bed and left her to it, while he went into the open-plan kitchen to make himself some breakfast. By the time he'd grilled a full packet of bacon and fried a couple of eggs she'd emerged from the bedroom looking a lot less glamorous than she had last night. He smiled at her and pointed to the food, but she shook her head, putting one hand up. Her eyeliner had smudged; her mascara left dark trails across her pale face.

'I have to go, so sorry.'

'Should I call you a taxi?'

She shook her head. 'No, the walk will help.'

And with that she walked out of his door without giving him, or his penthouse apartment, a second glance. James crossed over to the large window that looked down onto the busy street and smiled. Her head was held high as she walked briskly away. He liked her more because she'd given him the brush-off. Now he would have to make it his business to see her again. It wasn't very often he didn't impress a woman, and his bruised ego needed to know if she was playing it cool or really didn't care. Grabbing his jacket, he ran out of the apartment after her.

Catching up with her at the bottom of a steep hill, he noticed her answer her phone and he heard her begin an animated conversation in French. She turned off by the corner of The Angel Inn on Helm Road which, if he wasn't mistaken, meant she was heading for the Hydro Hotel. Maybe he'd drag Ethan along tonight. They could accidentally bump into her at the bar and try to find out more about her, although Ethan was a bit of a lightweight when it came to drinking two nights on the run. He suddenly remembered he'd better ring him back, so turned and walked down the hill to the estate agency his family owned.

Marshall Estates had been a successful business from the day his father had opened it; there were branches in almost every town in Cumbria. Even though he no longer needed to work, his father still turned up three days a week at the head office in Bowness to oversee everything, and he was adamant that James should do the same. James hated it, but had a grudging respect for his parents and did as he was told most of the time. It filled his days, but he disliked the mundane office work. He usually only dealt with the wealthiest clients, but if James had his way, they would leave it all in the very capable hands of the branch manager.

What he much preferred to do was to charter out his boat for private parties. It was far more fun sailing around the lake with groups of drunken, single women celebrating birthdays, hen nights or even divorces. How many times had he screwed the prettiest girl in the room? Smiling to himself, he realised he couldn't even keep count. He was all about pleasure and he was pretty sure he could turn the private parties into a lucrative business of his own. He didn't see the point in working for a living when you could make money having so much fun. It was unfortunate his dad didn't agree with this line of business, but once he began to make a serious profit, he'd have to acknowledge that James was on to a winner.

CHAPTER EIGHT

When Beth walked into the mortuary she was surprised to find Abe wasn't there. She stared at the bank of fridges against the back wall. Her stomach churning, she wondered which one contained Robert. Telling herself it didn't matter, and that it was none of her business, was all very well, but it didn't stop her from striding across the room, her white rubber boots squeaking against the tiled ceramic floor as if announcing her intention to the entire hospital. Casting her eyes over the fridges, she looked for the one with his name written on the door plate but couldn't see it. No time to waste, she began frantically sliding open each drawer to read the tag on the body bag inside. The door slammed behind her and she knew Abe was there, watching but too respectful to ask her if she'd gone crazy.

There were three separate sliding shelves for bodies within each compartment. Sliding out the first, she read 'Alan Warner' on the label and pushed him back inside. Next she pulled out the one beneath and hit the jackpot. The body bag looked so small, but it was long enough. Robert had been tall, but so thin now he must have been a shell of his former self by the time he died. She read his name on the yellow tag which sealed the zip on the bag.

'Beth, I don't think…'

She turned to face him. 'I'm not. I wouldn't. I just had to see for myself, to check it was the right name, to see it was his name.'

He crossed the room towards her, and she stepped away so he could push the drawer shut. 'It's over.'

She nodded. 'I suppose it is. I need to see his post-mortem to really believe it though.'

'No, you don't. Why would you want to put yourself through that?'

'Yes, I do. I don't expect you to understand, it's just something I need to do. When's it scheduled?'

'Later this week. They requested Doctor Wilson to do it.'

Beth had only been on shift to work this morning; she had booked the afternoon off weeks ago. Had some sixth sense kicked in or was it all a convenient coincidence?

The loud buzz of the doorbell on the back door where the bodies were brought in broke the silence. Abe went to open up and the spell was broken; Robert was pushed to the back of her mind as the young woman who had been pulled from the lake was brought in. She saw Abe glance at her, as if he was checking she was back in the room and had stopped freaking out. Smiling at him, she gave a gentle nod and mouthed, 'I'm good.'

His shoulders dropped and she felt bad she'd caused him to worry. She would make it up to him; he was a blessing and she didn't like that she'd made him uncomfortable. She directed the undertakers to the table where the body was transferred to, and the accompanying police officer spoke.

'We've managed to get someone to ID her. Her supervisor from the hotel she is working at is on her way down here. The victim is possibly a Leah Burton from Devon. According to her supervisor, she has family still living there. They're trying to get the contact details for her next of kin, though they won't speak to them until it's confirmed it's her.'

'That was fast.'

'Yeah, sometimes these things are straightforward. Other times they're a complete disaster.'

Beth couldn't disagree, but at least that meant as soon as the identification had been completed, she could begin the post-mortem. She hoped for the sake of her family that the results would show the death as accidental, but the fact that the girl was naked still bothered Beth. Who in their right mind would strip naked and jump in the lake at this time of year? It seemed crazy, but she'd seen a lot more crazy than this in her many years of experience.

Normally once a body was brought into the mortuary any jewellery, personal belongings and even the clothes they were wearing were bagged up by the accompanying officer and booked into the property store at the police station until it could be returned to grieving relatives. She had checked at the marina; the girl hadn't been wearing any jewellery when she'd been pulled out of the lake. Everything had been left on the deck of the boat, which kind of suggested to Beth that if the girl had taken the time to remove her earrings and the chunky necklace before going into the water then she'd thought about it and hadn't been that drunk. Then again, alcohol was a great aid for freeing up your inhibitions. She knew that from personal experience. Wasn't that the reason she'd relied so heavily on a large glass of wine every night to help her sleep for the last seven years? A few gulps would relax her enough to keep her anxiety at bay. She drank quite a lot, but not once had she decided to get naked and run into the lake at the bottom of her garden. She shuddered at the thought; after being thrown in and almost drowning not that long ago she didn't foresee herself ever setting foot into the icy depths of Lake Windermere ever again.

CHAPTER NINE

Josh passed the statement over to Ethan to read and sign. He pointed to the different places on the form for signature and watched as Ethan scribbled his name next to them. Passing it back to Josh, Ethan looked up at him.

'What now?'

'Now, my friend, we get you home. Paton will drop you off; you need a hot bath and some sleep. You did a good thing, thank you.'

Ethan began to blink rapidly, and Josh could tell he was trying not to cry. 'Yeah, thanks. It would have been even better if I'd managed to save her. I really liked her. She was fun.'

Josh leant across and shook his hand. 'You did the next best thing, that takes some courage. None of this is your fault; like you said it's not as if anyone even saw her jump in. The only person to blame is the victim and her poor judgement.'

Paton held the door open for Ethan, and Josh watched as they walked out. How would he feel if the roles were reversed, if he had found the girl? He knew he'd feel awful; humans were very good at blaming themselves when things went wrong, even when it was out of their control. Hopefully after a few hours' sleep Ethan would realise he'd done what he could, but it had already been too late. Even an experienced swimmer in a wetsuit and no alcohol in their system would have struggled to stay alive. What chance did a naked slip of a girl like that have? He shuddered; it didn't bear thinking about. He would be there for her family when they arrived from Devon, to try and answer the many questions they would have, and the post-mortem. He needed to go to the hospital and speak to Beth; he wondered how she was and if the arrival of Hartshorn's body in the mortuary had sent her into a spin, or if she had taken it in her stride.

Walking back to the office, he retrieved his phone, which was charging on his desk, to find he had no missed calls from Beth, and decided it was more than likely a good thing. He did have a missed call from his ex, Jodie, though, which wasn't. He sighed; could he face speaking to her now? He'd had very little contact with his wife since the day he'd caught her in bed with another man and had walked out of their home with his most treasured belongings in a cabin-sized suitcase. Deciding to ring her back later, he pushed the phone into his pocket; whatever Jodie wanted could wait a few more hours. Leah Burton was his main priority now, closely followed by Beth.

At a desk nearby, Detective Constable Sam Thomas was on the phone, her voice low but the look on her face told him she was mid-argument with a petulant teenager. He smiled at her as she jabbed her finger against the screen, ending the call.

'Do you want to come out, get a bit of fresh air? Maybe grab a coffee?'

He smiled as her eyes narrowed, showing she was trying to decide if a coffee was worth the guaranteed work that went with it.

'Does this fresh air involve a car ride with you to Barrow?'

He shrugged. 'Possibly.'

'Does it involve a visit to a certain doctor's place of work?'

He laughed. 'If you're busy I'll get Sykes to come with me. Where is she?'

Sam shrugged. 'If she's got any sense, she's already gone out to buy her own coffee.'

Josh turned away, hiding the grin that had spread across his face. He liked Sam and her sense of humour. He liked all of his team, but after the last case he felt as if they'd made pretty good partners.

She grabbed her coat and they both strode towards the exit at the far end of the office that led to the back stairs and out into the car park. Pausing, Josh took a set of keys off the whiteboard and scribbled 1195, his collar number, next to the vehicle registration. Turning, he passed Sam the keys. 'You drive and I'll even run in to buy the coffee.'

She shook her head. 'I need to learn to leave this office before you go looking for unsuspecting victims to drag into your weekly disasters. I'll have a large latte, please, with an extra shot.'

They walked out to the car park, the sky a blanket of thick, black clouds; any moment it was going to throw it down. Hurrying to get into the car as the first splotches of water began to fall against the windscreen, no sooner had they shut the doors and Sam turned the key in the ignition, than the heavens opened and the sound of the rain hammering against the car was almost deafening.

Sam smiled at Josh. 'Shame you volunteered to go in for the coffee, you're going to get wet. That, Sarge, is karma.'

CHAPTER TEN

Beth had told Abe to notify her when the person who was going to do the ID on Leah Burton arrived. Realising she was staring into space, she moved her focus to the now-cold liquid inside her chipped mug and wished it was a large glass of wine. Although she'd never dream of drinking while at work, some days the thought of it made it all seem better. She would definitely be pouring herself a generous measure or two when she finally made it home tonight.

'Beth, Leah's supervisor is in the viewing room along with a police officer. Should I do the ID?'

She looked up and he smiled at her, and for the first time she acknowledged just what a good-looking man he was. She'd never really looked at him in that way before and knew she would never look at him in that way again. It was as if her mind was waking up from hibernation: things she'd taken for granted in the past were taking on new meanings. Standing up, she tipped the mug back, swallowing the cold coffee with a grimace.

'Is the body ready for viewing?'

He nodded.

'I'll go and speak to them. I want to get an idea of what she was like.'

Walking out of her office, she pushed the double doors open which led to the small corridor where the viewing room was situated. She stepped inside to see the police officer who'd brought the body to get booked in. Beth nodded at her and then at the woman standing next to her in a steel grey suit with a white shirt embroidered with the logo of a hotel. They shook hands.

'I'm Doctor Adams. Thank you for coming here at such short notice. The quicker we can establish her identity, the sooner I can begin her post-mortem and we can learn more of what happened. I'm so sorry for your loss.'

The words hung in the air of the small room for a moment before the woman nodded, then let out a loud sob which startled both Beth and the officer who had brought her in. Together, they guided her to one of the small, two-seater beige leather sofas. Beth looked around; grabbing the box of tissues off the coffee table, she passed them to the woman, who was having a hard time pulling herself together. She took a seat opposite her. 'I'm sorry, were you close to Leah?'

The woman blew her nose, then shook her head. Beth frowned, she looked over at the officer, who shrugged. Composing herself, the woman looked at Beth.

'Sorry, I'm Suzanne Morgan. I'm one of the duty managers at the hotel. I'm no good with anything like this. I get upset over commercials on the television. Especially if they have dogs in them. I told them I shouldn't come, that I wouldn't be much use nor ornament to anyone.'

Beth was confused now. 'Told who?'

'Hotel management, but they wouldn't listen. They said I'd know better than they would, which technically I suppose I should. I mean, I interviewed her and gave her the job.'

'Did you know her very well?'

'Not really, she's only been here a couple of months.'

'I have to ask, what was her mood like? Did she seem happy? Was she upset to have left her family? Is there any chance she may have been feeling suicidal?'

Suzanne shook her head.

'I don't think so. She was always smiling and chattering, but her friend Chloe Dubois would be better placed to tell you what she was really like. They seemed very close; they started working at the same time together.'

'Where is Chloe?'

'I don't know. We couldn't find her when the police turned up to ask for someone to come here. She wasn't in the room they share. Oh God, what if she drowned as well? How did it happen?'

Beth felt fingers of fear run down the full length of her spine. Could there be another body in the lake? It was a possibility. She wished Josh was here.

'Were they together last night?'

There was a knock on the door and the officer opened it. As if in answer to her prayer, standing on the other side was Josh and his colleague Sam. Beth felt a wave of relief wash over her. He would know the right things to say and do.

'Suzanne, this is Detective Sergeant Josh Walker and Detective Constable Sam Thomas. Josh, Suzanne is a duty manager at the hotel where the victim, who we think is a Leah Burton, worked. She's a bit concerned because Leah's friend is also missing.'

Josh's face drained of all colour, and Beth knew he was thinking, just like she was, that it couldn't happen again so soon after they had caught a serial killer who had been terrorising Windermere.

Josh composed himself and shook the woman's hand gently. 'Please could you explain to me what you were telling Dr Adams?'

She nodded. 'I looked for Chloe to come with me to do the identification, but I couldn't find her anywhere. Which is strange because the pair of them are usually inseparable. Do you think it's possible something's happened to her as well?'

Josh stole a glance at Beth.

'Where did you find Leah?' the woman asked, obviously not willing to hear the reply.

'She was discovered in the lake by the marina this morning, by a passenger on a boat who jumped in and pulled her out.'

'Which boat?'

It was Sam who answered. '*The Tequila Sunrise.*'

Suzanne shook her head. 'That boat. I warn the girls to keep away. It always ends in trouble whenever they go on there.'

Josh leant forward. 'Why?'

'It's a party boat owned by some rich kid. Everyone knows it's all sex, drugs, rock and roll and free-flowing alcohol. I'm surprised it's taken this long for someone to fall off it to be honest.'

So many questions were running through Beth's mind. Who owned the boat? Was it licensed? Had there been any other accidents on it? Before she could ask, Josh began to ask Suzanne exactly the same questions.

He turned to the officer. 'Please can you tell Control we need a search team to the marina? I want the boat checked and the waters surrounding it. I also want two officers to go to the hotel and do their best to locate Chloe.'

The officer nodded at Josh and stepped outside. Beth felt the strings on the tight knot that had begun to form inside her stomach pull even harder. It couldn't happen again, could it?

CHAPTER ELEVEN

Beth stood up. 'Should we carry on with the identification while we're waiting for news on Chloe?'

Suzanne's eyes widened as she nodded, opened her mouth to speak and a small squeak came out. Beth felt bad for the woman; when she'd arrived at work this morning, identifying a dead body would not have been on her to-do list – it probably wasn't even on her lifetime to-do list. Beth dealt with death on a daily basis and still found some cases upsetting. She had emotions just like everyone else, she'd just learnt to put them to one side while she worked. It was her job to figure out how and why the person who had once been full of life was now an empty shell lying in a mortuary refrigerator. It was a job she took very seriously; she was the voice for the victims who never got to tell their stories.

Beth left Suzanne standing next to Josh and Sam as she went into the viewing room to tell Abe they were ready. He had the body laid out on a steel gurney and covered with a white sheet so only her face showed.

'Everything okay, Doc?'

'I'll tell you when we're on our own.'

'That good?'

She shook her head and went back into the small room, which was now unbearably stuffy with the number of people crammed into it. Abe pulled the cord that opened the curtains on a window between the rooms and stood to the side. A gasp escaped from Suzanne's lips and she stepped closer to the glass, her nose almost pressed against it. She stared at the discoloured face of the girl, whose lips were tinged blue.

Josh broke the silence. 'Can you confirm this is the body of Leah Burton?'

He looked at the woman, who couldn't take her eyes away. 'I think so.'

'I'm afraid I need a yes or a no; if you're not sure it can wait until her next of kin arrive.'

She tilted her head, stared a little longer then nodded. 'Yes, sorry. I've never seen a dead person before. It's her, it's Leah.'

With that she let out a sob and sank down onto the sofa, burying her face in her hands. Sam sat down next to her.

'I'm sorry, it's not a nice thing to do. But we need to be one hundred per cent sure.'

She peered through her fingers. 'Yes, it is her. I'm positive. She has a small tattoo on the back of her neck of a cross embedded in a rose; it's pretty. She wore her hair in a topknot and you could just see it peeking out from under the collar of her uniform.'

With a nod at Abe to draw the curtains closed, Beth left the room to go and check the tattoo.

Minutes later, she came back and showed Suzanne a photograph of the tattoo on her phone. Suzanne's uncontrollable sobs at the sight of the small cross inside the petals of a rose was all the confirmation she needed.

There was a knock and the door opened and the accompanying officer walked in. 'Sarge, we've found Chloe, safe and well. Apparently, she arrived at the hotel an hour ago a little bit worse for wear.'

Beth exhaled the breath she didn't even realise she'd been holding, thankful that this girl who had left her country to see what life in the UK was like was safe and well. Bad enough that Leah hadn't found the happy ending she'd come in search of; for the two of them to have died in vain would have been unthinkable.

'Thank God; does she know about Leah?' Suzanne stared at the officer.

'I don't think so. I get the impression they're waiting for official confirmation from you. I think you may be the one to have to break the news.'

Suzanne shook her head. 'Could this day get any worse?' she asked out loud.

Josh shook his head too. 'We need to speak to Chloe and get an account of exactly what happened last night on the boat. Why don't we meet you at the hotel in an hour and then we can break the news to her together?'

'Really, would you do that?'

'Yes, I think it would be better. You can be there to support her and pick up the pieces when we leave.'

Beth thought the woman looked a lot paler now than when she'd arrived. 'Are you okay to drive back to Bowness? Would you rather someone came to collect you?'

She laughed. 'You must be joking, there's never enough staff on a good day. Now we're down two already because I doubt Chloe is in a fit state to work her shift. I can't spare anyone else, it will be mayhem.'

She looked around the room. 'Sorry, that sounds heartless. I'll be fine, it's just a bit of a shock.' She stood up, grabbed her handbag off the compact coffee table and walked out.

Beth let out a sigh. 'At least we have our ID.'

She felt Josh's eyes lingering on her and turned to look at him. 'Can I have a word with you, Josh?' She walked out of the room into the corridor, and he followed close behind, shutting the door so it was just the two of them.

'He's dead.'

'I know, I tried to ring and tell you. Are you okay?'

Beth hesitated . Was she okay? She should be bloody ecstatic, but she just felt totally shell-shocked. Unable to answer him, she shrugged and before she knew it, he'd pulled her into his arms and was holding her close. Shocked at his public display of affection, despite the fact it was only the two of them in the corridor, she squeezed him back as hard as she could then stepped away. His lips brushed the side of her face, kissing the scar she hid behind her hair, and her fingers reached up to touch the spot.

'I am now, thank you for asking. I guess I'm a little surprised and relieved at the same time.' The double doors leading to the corridor were rammed open by a porter pushing a trolley full of brown paper envelopes and they stepped apart from each other.

'Are you staying for the post-mortem?'

'Do you think I should? I wanted to come and check you were okay.'

'I don't think you need to. It all looks straightforward. If I find anything you need to know about, I'll call.'

'Thank you. You're sure you're okay?'

Beth laughed. 'With you and Abe fussing over me like mother hens I'm pretty sure I am. But I like it, and I'm very glad that you are.'

Josh smiled at her then opened the door. 'Come on, Samantha, we'd better get a move on and get to the hotel.'

'We don't need to stay for the examination?'

'Doctor Adams doesn't think so.'

Sam, who had been chatting to the officer, smiled and pressed her palms together in a silent prayer then followed Josh. She turned and waved at Beth, who was disappearing into the mortuary.

Beth lifted her hand and waved back. It was time to get dressed into her blue scrubs, clip the sides of her chin-length hair back under her cap, snap on a pair of nitrile gloves, and cover herself with a plastic apron to catch any spills.

CHAPTER TWELVE

Sam looked across at Josh. 'I suppose that trip down here was worth the drive then? I almost had a heart attack when she said Leah's friend was missing as well.'

He didn't want to tell her the reason he'd really driven her down to Barrow was to check on Beth. He had a sneaking suspicion that she already knew about the pair of them, but was being discreet until he decided to talk about it.

'I know, all I could think was: not again. At least we have more information than we started with. I had no idea about *The Tequila Sunrise* being a party boat, did you?'

She shook her head. 'Not really my thing if I'm honest. I know it's popular with the teenagers. I've heard my daughter mention it, but hadn't really paid a lot of attention.'

'Me neither; when I turned eighteen it was a night at the pub with my mates. I once ended up so drunk the lads had to carry me and my bag of chips home. They opened the front door and threw me in then left me semi-comatose at the bottom of the stairs. My dad found me and dragged me upstairs to bed. I consumed enough alcohol that night to put me off drinking for the next couple of years. There were no fancy party boats back then; a working men's club was as good as it got.'

She began to laugh. 'When I was a lad…' she mimicked.

Josh laughed with her. 'Cheeky, I'm not that old.'

'I never said you were.'

'Still, I'd like to have a look around it, and we need to speak to the owner. If he's supplied Leah with so much alcohol that she died, then things could take a different turn. We also need to speak to the other people present last night. I'll task that out when we get back.

They drove most of the way back in silence. Sam was furiously angry-texting on her phone, so he guessed the argument she'd been having earlier was still in full flow. He wanted to ask if everything was okay, but didn't want her to think he was being nosy. Eventually, she threw her phone in her bag and sighed. Josh took it as a signal to speak.

'Everything okay?'

'Kids, they're a nuisance. You do right not having any, Josh.'

He smiled. 'That bad?'

'Only twenty-three out of twenty-four hours. Grace wants to go to a party on Saturday night.'

'That's not too bad, is it?'

He had no idea how to handle teenagers, so didn't want to jump in and upset her.

'It wasn't bad at all until she told me it was on a private charter boat called *The Tequila Sunrise*, and I've just put two and two together.'

'Shit.'

'My thoughts exactly. I can't tell her why I don't want her to go either, although she'll read it on the Internet no doubt.'

'Yes, but in all fairness at this moment in time all we have is a woman who appears to have drowned through no fault but her own.'

'Yes, Josh. If my daughter gets drunk – which she will because she sinks shots of vodka like there's no tomorrow – she could fall in and drown as well.'

'I suppose you have to look at the chances of it happening again. I mean this is the first time we've had an incident related to that particular boat or party boats in general. People do drown in the lake, a lot. It's a huge expanse of water. I think she'll probably be okay.'

'Great, I'll send her to live with you then.'

Josh knew it was time to shut up. He was out of his depth. He would get Sykes to do some digging and see if there was any intelligence about the boat and its owner before he tracked him down. He still couldn't see that this was anyone's fault. How one stupid, reckless moment could result in death or serious injury never failed to amaze him.

His phone began to vibrate in his pocket and he passed it to Sam. She looked down at the display.

'Jodie. Should I answer it?'

'No, I'll ring her back later. Whatever she wants can't be that important.'

He hadn't spoken to her much since the day he'd left. He'd been home once to get the stuff he'd forgotten to pack when he'd left in a hurry. He owed her nothing. She wasn't his priority any more. He didn't even feel angry about their marriage break-up. It had been a blessing in disguise.

CHAPTER THIRTEEN

Beth walked into the mortuary feeling the cold in every part of her being. Abe looked over at her.

'Hope you're not coming down with something,' he said as she rubbed her hands and arms to warm them up.

She shook her head. 'No, I'm good. Or at least I think I am. It just feels even colder in here today than usual. Are we ready?'

'Yep, it's you, me and a cadaver makes three.'

Beth laughed. 'Have you considered taking up poetry in your spare time? With words like that it's bound to be a huge hit.'

'Never thought about it. Pretty sure it would though. Who's to say that poems from the mortuary wouldn't make a great book? Pretty lame though, Doc, if all it consisted of was one-liners of that nature.'

He'd already wheeled the body from the viewing room and had it on the stainless steel dissection table ready to begin. The Roberts digital radio, a gift from Josh a couple of years ago, was turned on and playing Smooth FM. Not loud enough to be disrespectful to the person whose body was about to be cut open, but enough to break the silence and cover the loud humming from the fridges. Occasionally she'd let Abe choose the station, but she had to have a clear head to deal with the loud thumping and heavy bass of the drum and bass he favoured. Today her head wasn't as clear as she liked; the early morning call out made it a little fuzzier than she preferred. It wouldn't stop her from doing her job, though; she would be as meticulous as always.

Walking across the room, she watched as Abe unzipped the black body bag then unwrapped the evidence sheet wrapped around Leah's naked body. Beth didn't even flinch at the smell that filled the air around her as she joined him and checked the tags, one on Leah's right hand, the other on the left big toe. Pausing for a moment, she silently made her introduction: *Leah, my name is Doctor Adams and I'm sorry that you're here, but it's my job to find out what happened to you. I hope you can forgive me.* Both tags read 'Leah Burton', her date of birth, the police log number, the place of death, sex, height and weight.

Taking the digital camera from Abe, she began to document the body before she began her internal examination. Abe wheeled over the portable X-ray machine and took images of the body in situ. Then they removed the sodden sheet and bag, checked them for evidence and put them to one side.

Beth talked into a Dictaphone as she worked. 'The body is that of a well-developed and nourished Caucasian female who appears to be the stated age of eighteen years old. Weight fifty-six kilograms.' She waited while Abe took the height, tilting her head to read the numbers on the tape. 'Measuring one hundred and seventy-seven centimetres in length. The body shows moderate, generalised rigor. The hair is blonde in colour and shoulder length.' Reaching out a gloved finger, she lifted the eyelids. 'Eyes are blue; there are no petechiae in the conjunctivae or sclera. The nostrils and mouth show a white froth consistent with drowning, and the ears are not remarkable. The neck, chest and abdomen show no abnormality and no surgical scars. On the right side of the shoulder and upper arm there are a number of superficial abrasions. Measuring approximately one to two centimetres in diameter. A slight superficial bruise is also noted in the same area measuring three centimetres in diameter.'

A rubber block was placed under the girl's diaphragm and Beth pressed one hand down on the abdomen, watching as a trickle of water was released from Leah's mouth. All signs were consistent with drowning, and the abrasions and bruise a result of the body being brought into contact with the side of the boat she was found floating next to. Examining the scalp and hair, she noted that there was an area of slight redness where a small patch of hair was missing. This too matched what the witness had told them; her hair had been caught in the boat's anchor chain and the poor sod had had to rip it out to get her away from there and out of the water. Beth shuddered. She knew first-hand just how awful it would have been to have choked down mouthfuls of the icy, foul-tasting liquid until she could no longer breathe.

'Doc?'

She looked up at Abe. His eyebrow arched: his way of asking if everything was okay. She nodded. Reaching out for the large syringe he was holding towards her, she took it from him, sinking the fine needle into the corner of Leah's right eye to withdraw the vitreous humour. She repeated the process again with the girl's left eye. The samples of the clear gel would be tested for the potassium levels in the body, which could help to narrow down Leah's time of death. Beth moved around to where the victim's small white hands lay. Picking them up, she closely examined first one then the other. There were no signs of defence wounds on them, no cuts, broken nails. Leaning closer, she noticed the tiniest fragment of something underneath the nail of the little finger on her right hand. She removed it with a pair of tweezers, placed it gently on a slide and carried it over to one of the microscopes to take a look. She instantly recognised the multiple layers which formed a flake of paint. Leah must have caught her hand against the side of the boat as she went into the water. She needed to ask Josh what colour the boats were in the area surrounding where she was found in the marina.

Working methodically, she clipped the rest of the nails and bagged them ready to be sent for analysis. Between them, she and Abe checked the rest of the body and rolled her to the side to check there were no injuries on her back. There was nothing to note. Beth also took the nasal, oral, rectal and vaginal swabs. There were no signs of a sexual assault but she would much rather rule it out than not take them and miss some vital evidence.

As if he could read her mind, Abe passed her the scalpel then placed a rubber body block underneath Leah's back, making her chest protrude and her arms and neck fall backwards. It was time to begin the internal examination.

CHAPTER FOURTEEN

Someone hammered on the door to Ethan's cramped cabin at the Freshwater Marine Biology site. His first thought was the police were back and he debated ignoring it: there was nothing more he could do for the girl. He'd spent all morning drifting between tears and guilt, feeling bad for her. His eyes were red and puffy; he didn't want to face them as he'd already told them everything. What more could they want? The banging continued and he forced himself to get off the bed. Blotting his damp cheeks with the corner of his sleeve, he opened the door.

'What the hell, James.'

James pushed the door open and marched inside. 'Jesus, it smells like someone died in here. Open some windows.'

Ethan only had one small window, and it didn't open very far. He gave it a nudge between the rusted blinds to crack it open as far as it would go.

'I'd open the front door as well if I was you, mate, it proper reeks.'

'Yeah, well we all don't have cleaners and floor-to-ceiling windows – mate,' he emphasised, to send the point home.

'What were all the missed calls about? Who died?'

His smile dropped the moment he saw Ethan's eyes begin to water and his face drop.

'You haven't heard? Someone… someone did die. Have the police not been in touch? I'd have thought they'd want to take a statement from you.'

'What? What the fuck has it got to do with me?'

'Seriously? Jesus, I woke up to find one of those girls that were on the boat with us last night floating face down in the water. It was horrific. I've never felt so scared. She was so cold and still. It was like a bad dream. Where were you anyway?'

James's whole body sagged as he flopped down onto the two-seater sofa. He ran his fingers through his hair, which Ethan knew was a sign he was nervous, although James would never admit it.

'You're not shitting me, this is for real?'

'I swear it's all real. Christ, I wish it wasn't. You didn't see her floating in the water. It was awful. I thought that she might still be alive so I jumped in to pull her out. I tried to drag her to the jetty, but her hair was stuck in the anchor chain. I had to tear her hair from her head to get her free.' Ethan shivered as the ripping noise filled his mind; he didn't think it would ever leave him.

'I'm so sorry, I had no idea. How the hell did she get into the water?'

'How would I know, I haven't got a clue how or why she was in there. Except that she was and now she's dead. Where did you all go?'

James lifted his face to look at Ethan. 'I took her friend back to my apartment. I thought I'd give you some privacy.'

'For what? We didn't sleep together, if that's what you mean. I was too drunk for one thing and I don't think she was that into me. I'm surprised you didn't take them both back with you.'

'I wish I had.'

'Yeah, so do I. Every time I close my eyes all I can see is her pale face turning blue. She was so small, but felt so heavy. The police made me go to the hospital to get checked out and then I had to go to the station to give a statement.'

James was shaking his head. 'I can't believe it. Do the police want to speak to me? I didn't see any of it.'

'Probably, she was on your boat after all . She left all of her clothes on the deck when she went into the water. They'll need a statement from you as well. You should go there and speak to someone. The detective I spoke to was called Josh Walker.'

James shook his head. 'Nah, if they want me, they can come find me. Like I said, I know nothing about it. Why should I waste my time going there?'

Ethan couldn't believe what he was hearing, but it didn't totally surprise him. James had regained his composure and could be so arrogant at times. Why should he be any different now? He found himself clenching his fists in anger. What was he hiding? Surely his conscience would kick in, should kick in.

'I know what we can do to cheer you up.'

Ethan eyed him suspiciously. 'What?'

'We'll go to the Hydro, grab a bite to eat maybe have a couple of drinks in the bar. Take your mind off everything. My treat.'

'I don't know, I'm not really in the mood.'

'Come on, you can't sit here feeling sorry for yourself all day. Yes, it's terrible what's happened, but it's already happened. It's too late and there's nothing you can do to change it. We can grab some food and if you want to talk, we can. It's got to be better than staying here in this shithole that smells like you have a carcass in the cupboard.'

'Bugger off, James.'

'You don't have anything rotting in here, do you, Ethan?'

'What are you trying to say?'

James began to laugh. 'Nothing, you know. I've read the stories about those weird serial killers, that's all. Who was it that liked to kill his victims and eat their brains? He kept their bodies chopped up in bits all over his flat?'

'Jeffrey Dahmer.'

'Yeah, that's the one. How do you know his name, Ethan? You always know the weird shit.'

'Everyone knows his name, and you don't complain about me knowing weird shit when we win at pub quizzes.'

'That's true. Have a shower and get changed. I'll give you ten minutes then we're out of here. You can sleep at mine tonight.'

Ethan wanted to tell him to get stuffed, but he didn't want to be alone and this was a better option even if it meant having to listen to James and his overinflated ego all night.

*

Ethan got out of James's Porsche 911 and put his hands in his pockets. He looked up at the hotel. He really didn't want to be here, but he didn't know what he wanted to do instead. He followed his friend into the recently refurbished reception area, which was dominated by two huge purple sofas, and through into the bar. Ethan tugged James's arm and pointed to an empty table on the patio area in front of the bar which overlooked the lake and headed in that direction. He'd had enough of the water for today and sat with his back to the view, staring inside at the empty tables. It was a nice place, much nicer than the last time he'd been here.

James headed towards the bar and came back with a Coke and a beer.

'I wasn't sure what you fancied.'

Ethan didn't have to think twice; he took the Coke. James sat opposite him, passing a menu his way.

'You need some food inside you. You'll feel better when you've eaten.'

'Is that it? Steak and chips and the horrific images of the girl whose life I didn't save will float away forever. You should take up counselling, James.'

'Bugger off, I'm trying to help. So why don't you stop acting all weird and feeling sorry for yourself. It wasn't your fault, it wasn't my fault. It was an accident. If it was anyone's fault then it was hers. What was she doing stripping off and jumping into the lake in this weather?'

'I don't know, you tell me. Did you give her any drugs? They'll do a tox screen at the post-mortem.'

'No, I bloody didn't,' James hissed, realising they were talking a little too loudly and the other customers sitting not too far away who had come out for a smoke were watching them. 'I'm just as shocked about it as you are. Okay, maybe not as much as you because you were there. You tried to save her; not many people would have. I know it's all been a bit of a shock for you, but you did what you could. Don't take it so hard.' James reached out his hand and grabbed Ethan's shoulder, gently patting it. 'Let it go, pal. Sometimes life can be totally shit, then sometimes it can be wonderful. Don't let the bad stuff get you down.'

Ethan let out a sigh; his fists, which had clenched into tight balls under the table, released and he felt his shoulders drop as all the tension left his body. James nodded.

'Sorry, you're right. It's a stupid accident; it wasn't our fault.'

'See, that's better.'

James took a long swig of the beer, so long he drank half of the bottle in one mouthful. Ethan sipped his Coke. His stomach let out a loud growl; he was hungry. In fact, he was bloody starving. Picking up the menu, he scanned it for the most expensive meal on there; if James was paying there was no point holding back. His friend might have many faults but being mean wasn't one of them.

'Can we go inside to eat, Ethan? It's freezing out here.'

Ethan stood up and they both made their way inside.

CHAPTER FIFTEEN

Beth watched as Abe gently inserted the biodegradable bag containing all of Leah Burton's internal organs back into her stomach cavity and left him to begin the painstaking job of sewing her body back together. She needed to type up the post-mortem report while it was still fresh in her mind. Toxicology, bile, heart blood, liver tissue, stomach contents, spleen and brain samples had all been taken and submitted to the lab for a full, comprehensive screen. Beth could find no evidence of major trauma.

She typed 'accident' under the manner of death on the report, but when she read it back to herself something made her pause before pressing save. A feeling of unease settled over her. There wasn't anything specific she could put her finger on, no evidence, apart from the tiny paint chip under her fingernail, to suggest anything other than death by accidental drowning. But it bothered her that a girl would voluntarily strip naked on a bitterly cold night and decide to go for a swim, alone. She was well aware of the statistics that state it is very rare for women to die by suicide in the nude. So why did Leah Burton decide to jump into the lake in nothing but the skin she was born in? Picking up the phone, she selected Josh's number and waited for him to answer.

'Hey, how are you?'

'I'm good, I've finished the PM. I thought you'd want to know how it went.' She didn't wait for him to answer. 'There was nothing remarkable about it. Everything substantiates Leah drowning; the only trace evidence I found was a tiny paint chip under her little fingernail. She must have caught the boat as she went into the water. I've sent all the relevant samples off, and we should hear back in a couple of weeks. Have you spoken to all the witnesses yet? Is there anything I need to know about?'

'Just the one that pulled her out of the water: an Ethan Scales. I'm on with that now. We're trying to locate them to get statements. I'll let you know what they say. What did you put down as her manner of death?'

'Accidental; I don't foresee it changing once the test results come back.' She paused.

'But something is bothering you?'

'It's probably nothing, but can you check the colour of paint on *The Tequila Sunrise*? I didn't really pay it any attention, I was too focused on the body.'

'It's blue, I'm pretty sure it is but I'll double-check and let you know.'

'I know this is stupid, Josh, but something doesn't feel right. Even though there's nothing to suggest that it isn't. Do I sound paranoid?'

'No, not at all. What do you mean, though, Beth? You've said yourself there is nothing to suggest anything other than an accident.'

She let out a sigh. 'I don't know, I don't understand why she removed her clothes for one thing.'

'Us humans are a strange species. We often do things for no reason. The only person who knows why she took her clothes off is the victim. Don't let it get to you. I've seen some tragic deaths over the years because of poor judgement on the victim's part, deaths that could have been avoided. I'm sure you have too. Thank you for letting me know. I have to go and track down the owner of the boat. I'll see you later, yeah?'

'I suppose so, yes. I'll speak to you later. Bye, Josh.'

'Bye.'

The line went dead.

The door opened and in walked her colleague Doctor Charles Wilson. The look of surprise etched across his face told her that he hadn't expected to see her sitting behind the desk.

'Beth, how are you? I thought you were off this afternoon. Why are you wasting your time here when you could be home enjoying that lovely house of yours?'

She sighed. There was no use pretending. 'I know about Robert and I know you've come in specially to cover. I appreciate it, I do. But I'd still like to be present, just to observe, once you get around to the PM.'

His eyes widened and she knew he was weighing up his options. After a pause he said, 'I know it must be hard for you, but you know that's not something I can allow. It would be a breach of guidelines and it's not really ethical, is it?'

'I don't want to touch him or have anything to do with the examination, that's your role and I know that. I just want closure, an end to the dark cloud that's been hanging over my head for the last seven years. Please, Charles, I need to do this more than you could ever imagine. Maybe watching his post-mortem will make me realise that it's finally over, that I'm done with him and he has no hold on my life any more.'

She watched as his mind frantically grasped at the right words to say to her, but his head was shaking gently even though he hadn't yet formed a reply. Cringing, Beth didn't recognise the whining, desperate voice that had just begged him to let her watch the PM. It didn't sound like her and she hated that Robert, even though he was dead, could still make her revert back to the scared shell of a woman she was trying to move on from.

'Look, Beth, I know you've had a terrible time and I admire your strength and determination, but this is…' He paused, searching for the right words. 'This is out of both our control and you know it. What will you gain from watching? Won't you be putting yourself through unnecessary heartache?'

Beth held up her left hand. 'Forget it, you're right. I know it's wrong. Forgive me for asking.' She spoke slowly; the knuckles of her right hand were bunched into a tight, white fist under the desk. She stood up, and he stepped back, almost tripping over the briefcase he'd placed on the floor as he'd walked in. Did he think she was going to slap him? As carefully as she could, she pulled her coat off the hook, picked up her handbag and walked out of the door. She needed to get out of here, out of this stuffy hospital and into the fresh air. She would apologise to him later.

Maybe she should ring the counsellor she'd been seeing. Despite her initial reservations and years of avoidance, Josh had finally talked her into it. She needed to offload today's events onto someone. She was too tired to keep bearing the weight of everything that had happened to her on her shoulders. Even though she had Josh, there was still a whole lot of stuff going on in her head that she wouldn't burden him with. If she did that, he'd run a mile, and who could blame him.

CHAPTER SIXTEEN

Josh walked into the busy CID office in Kendal police station and looked around at his small but hard-working team. DCs Paton, Sykes and Bell were busy on the computers. Sam followed him inside and went to sit at her desk next to Sykes. He walked to the front of the room.

'You'll be pleased to know the pathologist has confirmed Leah Burton's death was accidental drowning, unless further investigation gives us a cause for concern.'

A collective cheer went around the room: relief it wasn't going to turn into a full-blown murder investigation so soon after the last one. Josh knew that every one of them felt a sense of loss for Leah and her family, but the strain of a murder investigation took its toll on even the most seasoned of them. Paton definitely had a few more grey hairs than he'd had last month.

'It's just a simple enquiry she's requested. She found a paint chip under one of the victim's nails and wants the colour of *The Tequila Sunrise* and surrounding boats confirmed, to find a match. Paton and Sykes, can you two drive to the marina and get that ticked off the list? Let me know your findings, and I'll ring Beth.' He realised his mistake and felt heat begin to slowly burn along his jawline. 'I'll let Dr Adams know the score. Myself and Sam will chase down the elusive James Marshall to get an account from him.' He looked at them; no one seemed to have picked up on his slip, but he was relieved all the same when his phone began to vibrate once more in his pocket, giving him a reason to escape. He took it out and saw Jodie's name again flashing across the screen.

Walking out into the corridor, he answered the call.

'Yeah.'

'Josh, it's me.' Her voice sounded different, much quieter than the last few times they'd spoken on the phone. He'd almost forgotten what it sounded like because for the last few months of their marriage she'd done nothing but shout at him. 'Is this a good time to talk?'

He wanted to tell her no, there would never be a good time to talk between them ever again, but something stopped him.

'I'm at work, but yes I can talk.'

'I'm in the hospital, ward nine. I wondered if you could come and see me, but only if you can and you're not too busy.'

'Is something wrong?' He winced as the words left his mouth. *Of course something's wrong, you moron.*

'Yes, but I'm okay. I just really need to speak to you. It's easier to explain in person than on the phone.'

'What time's visiting?' He could think of nothing worse, but this sounded important.

'I don't think they'll mind, just tell them you're a copper and they'll let you in.'

'I'm not sure what time, but I'll be there soon.'

'Thank you.' The line went dead.

That was the first civil conversation they'd had in some time, and it left him wondering what on earth was going on. He went back into the office.

'I have to go out; I'll be back though. If you need me for anything, I'll have my mobile on.'

No one took much notice of him, so he left them to it. He debated about telling Beth where he was going, then changed his mind. It was better to find out what was going on first. He didn't think she'd mind, though he didn't want to upset her for no good reason.

CHAPTER SEVENTEEN

Archie Palmer waved goodbye to his mum, hoisted his fishing rods over his shoulder and began the walk down the footpath to Miller Ground which led to Lake Windermere. It was already getting dark, but it didn't matter to him. He liked being on his own, and he'd been brought up fishing for carp on the lake since he was a child. His dad and grandad were both keen anglers and he'd inherited their love of the sport. At seventeen most of his friends preferred to spend their time in the pub playing pool and trying to get served alcohol with their fake IDs, but he would much rather set up his rods in his favourite place, then sit and watch the world go by or read a book. A fine mist on the far side of the lake was heading his way, but he wouldn't let himself be scared. He'd cast his rods then sit in his compact tent and wait.

He walked along the shore picking up a couple of discarded chocolate bar wrappers and stuffing them deep into his pocket. He hated when people dropped litter, though it was even worse when they threw it off their boats into the lake; locals would never dream of doing such a thing. It was so bad for the environment. There was no one around; it was late and this time of year the lake was never overly busy. Only the diehard used it and most of them wouldn't venture out when the visibility was this poor. Eventually, he reached the secluded spot his dad had shown to him years ago; the North Basin of the lake was much better for catching carp, especially at this time of year. Last October he'd caught a couple of monsters.

He unpacked his pop-up tent, then began to set his pair of carp rods up. Satisfied everything was good to go, he suddenly realised the mist had almost reached the shoreline and cursed. He was going to have to wait this one out for a while; it was dangerous to be too close to the water when the visibility was this poor. He may be experienced, but he wasn't stupid.

Tucked up inside his tent he opened the plastic box of tuna mayo sandwiches his mum had packed for him, sat on his folding chair, turned his headlamp on and flipped open his current book: *The Ghosts of Sleath*, by James Herbert. He was thankful he'd finished *The Fog* last week. As brave as he was, the Lakes were still an eerie place to be when there was zero visibility.

An hour later he'd eaten all of his sandwiches and almost finished his book. He unzipped the tent and looked out. The mist had cleared enough that he could see where he was going and to safely check his rods. Reaching the shoreline, he stopped in his tracks when he saw something large and bulky not too far from where he stood. It was hard to make out so he shuffled as close to the water's edge as he could. The water lapped at his feet as he squinted and took a step into the lake.

'What the...?' he said aloud. He didn't have his waders on, but took another step, gasping as cold water soon began to fill his rubber boots. It seemed too lumpy to be a log and, as it drifted past, he wondered if he should leave it in the water. But it looked like a sleeping bag or someone's discarded tent and his conscience wouldn't let him just leave it there polluting the beautiful Lakes. The water slapped against his legs. He reached out; a couple more feet and he'd be able to grab the offending article and drag it back to shore. His fingers snagged the dark, sodden material and he tugged, surprised at how heavy it was. Changing his grip, he pulled it towards him.

As if in slow motion, the thing bobbed in the water and turned to face him. A bloated, discoloured face stared back at him, eyes unblinking. Archie screamed. Splashing so much he almost lost his footing, he tried to run back towards the shore, terror ripping through him. Grabbing a fistful of reeds, he pulled himself onto land and fell to his knees, shingle digging into the flesh of his bare knees like tiny needles. Fumbling for his phone, he did the only thing he could think of and dialled 999.

CHAPTER EIGHTEEN

The hospital car park was relatively quiet, so Josh left the car without bothering to buy a ticket. He didn't intend to stop long enough to justify it. Inside and waiting for the lift doors to open, a woman with a sweet little boy came and stood next to him. The boy had a wild Afro framing a pair of huge brown eyes and the cheekiest grin Josh had ever seen. Josh smiled back at him and let them in first when the lift arrived. For a fleeting second, he wondered what it would be like to have a child of his own. He and Jodie had never really talked about it when they were together. They'd argued so much that he knew it had been a wise choice not to have any. But Beth was different; they rarely disagreed and when they did it was for good reason and never for long. She'd been through so much in her life already, perhaps she just had a better grasp of what was worth fighting over. It was still early days for them, but he didn't foresee that Beth would ever want to have children. It didn't bother him, though, as he'd rather have her in his life, but he also didn't want to leave the conversation until it was too late and neither of them could. The lift door opened and he stepped out, the smell of school dinners filling his nostrils as the heavy steel food cart was pushed around the corner towards them.

'What's on the menu?'

'Beef stew with chocolate pudding and chocolate custard.'

He nodded. 'Smells good.'

The tiny woman, who didn't look heavy enough to push the big cart even a few inches, threw her head back and laughed.

'Bless you, it always smells a lot better than it tastes. But whatever you do don't tell the cook I said that.' She winked at him, making him laugh.

'I won't, your secret's safe with me.'

He helped her guide the cart and then made his way towards the entrance of ward nine. His stomach began to tie itself into knots with every step. He had no idea why he was here or what he should expect. But he knew in hospital it was unlikely to be good news. The nurses' station was deserted, so he ran his eyes over the whiteboard nearby searching for Jodie's name. He couldn't find it and wondered for a moment if she'd been discharged, or maybe even playing a trick on him.

'Can I help you?'

The voice behind him made him jump and he spun around to face the nurse.

'Yes, I'm looking for Jodie Walker. I can't make visiting time, but I'm with the police so I hope you can make an exception.'

'We haven't got a Jodie Walker on this ward. Are you sure you have the right one?'

He nodded.

'The only Jodie we have is Jodie Phillips, in room six.'

He felt his cheeks flush; she'd reverted to using her maiden name.

'Sorry, yes, Jodie Phillips. Walker was her married name.'

The nurse opened her mouth to say something then thought better of it. Instead she smiled at him with kind eyes. He thanked her and walked down the long corridor towards the side room with a number six above the door. He hesitated outside, wondering suddenly if he should have brought her some chocolates, or maybe a get-well card, but it was too late and he knew deep down that he was just stalling. The door swung open in front of him before he had a chance to knock, and a nurse gasped to see him standing there. Then she started laughing.

'Blimey, you gave me a heart attack.'

'Sorry, I'm really sorry. Is Jodie in?'

He heard the words echo in his brain and cringed. His already pink cheeks turned pinker.

The nurse nodded. 'She certainly is.' She stepped to the side and he had no choice but to walk into the room.

A woman he didn't recognise was perched on the bed, short brown tufts of hair sprouting limply from her head in patches. He had the wrong room, he thought, and was about to turn and leave when she looked up.

'Thanks for coming, Josh.'

'Jodie?' he replied, squinting at her in the dim room. Something was very wrong. 'Is that you?'

The words hung in the air for a moment before she pointed to the chair next to the bed.

'Have a seat.'

Shocked, he forced his feet to walk towards the chair and sat down, taking in the dark shadows under her eyes, her pinched cheeks and the lines on her forehead that hadn't been there a couple of months ago.

'What's happened?'

'Leukaemia,' she said quietly.

He felt his head shake. 'How?'

'Christ knows, but look at the state of my fucking hair.'

'I always said you would suit short hair.' He smiled, limply.

She laughed and for a moment she looked like the feisty girl he'd married all those years ago.

'You always did know the right thing to say.'

He shrugged. 'Got to try, haven't you.'

This made her laugh again, and he joined in. The nurse popped her head around the door at the commotion and nodded in approval at the scene. Jodie waved at her, and she winked and left them to catch up.

'I told her you might still be mad at me for being such a complete bitch to you.'

'It wasn't all your fault. I worked too much and didn't give you enough attention. You remember; not enough staff and too much crime.'

'You care too much about people, Josh. That's not a bad thing, it really isn't. I just used to get jealous that you spent more time with your victims than you did me. I was stupid.'

He realised she was being sincere and reached out for her hand. 'We both were.'

She nodded, squeezing back.

'I'm sorry. I know you're busy and I don't expect you to say yes, but I have a favour to ask. You can say no. Please don't agree to it because I look a state and you feel sorry for me. I mean, I do look a state, but I'm not trying to guilt trip you in any way.'

She paused.

'Go on.'

'I want to go home. I hate it in here. Don't get me wrong, the staff are lovely, but like Dorothy said in *The Wizard of Oz*, "There's no place like home". Only I can't because I have no one to check in on me. Last time I messed my meds up and ended up taking too many. They said I can only leave when they've sorted out someone who can come and check on me a couple of times a week and help with my meds. Can I tell them you'll do it? I don't expect you to; I'll be fine on my own and I'll be careful, but you just need to make them believe.'

'What about Carl? Will he not help?'

She shook her head. 'Carl was a mistake; as soon as I told him I might be ill it was over. He wanted a good time, not the baggage that went with it.'

Josh felt even more anger towards the man than he already did. He'd caused such a huge mess and hadn't even had the decency to stick around.

'He's an idiot. So you want me to lie and say that I'm helping you when I'm not?'

'Yes, please.'

'I can't do that, Jodie. What if something happens to you?'

Tears filled her eyes. 'Sorry, I shouldn't have asked.'

'No, I don't mean that I won't do it. I'm just not going to say I'm helping you, and not help you. I'll only say it if you let me do it. I can pop in, sort your tablets out, pick up some shopping, whatever you need. We might not live together any more, and I know it all went horribly wrong, but I still care about you.'

She bent her head, her shoulders heaving up and down and Josh realised she was crying. He sat on the bed next to her and pulled her now tiny frame into his arms. All the anger he'd felt towards her dissipated. They were adults; they could still be friends. He didn't even think about how Beth might feel about the situation because he knew she would want him to do the right thing.

They sat that way for a few minutes until his phone began to ring loudly in his pocket. Jodie pulled away from him as he fumbled to find it, berating himself for not turning it off when he arrived. He saw Sam's name on the screen and silenced it. No sooner had he done that than it began to ring again, vibrating and flashing in his hand. Jodie smiled.

'Go on, you'd better answer that. You're in demand, Josh, you always have been. Thank you. I'll let you go and I'll message you when they say I can leave.'

'I'll pick you up; make sure you ring me.'

She nodded and stared down at his phone, knowing it must be important or Sam wouldn't keep ringing. Standing up, he bent down and brushed his lips against the side of her cheek, left her and walked into the corridor, sliding his finger across the screen.

'Yeah?'

'Boss, where are you? We have another body.'

Josh felt his heart sink. 'Where?'

'A teenager fishing at Miller Ground pulled it ashore thinking it was a sleeping bag in the lake. Apparently, it's in a bad way.'

'Christ.'

'I'm on my way; do you want picking up? Oh, and Sykes said *The Tequila Sunrise* wasn't painted. It's white, probably made of fibreglass or whatever they make modern boats from.'

'No, I'll meet you there and tell her thanks.' He hung up.

Was it a coincidence? Who could it be this time?

If they were in a state, they'd been in the water a while.

CHAPTER NINETEEN

Beth arrived home, relieved to be able to finally strip off and bathe away the memories of the day. As she let herself in, she noticed Josh's car wasn't on the drive, which was unusual when he'd been on a day shift. Kicking off her boots, she hung her coat in the closet and went to the kitchen, where she opened the fridge and took out a bottle of wine. She wasn't on call this evening so the plan was to drink a couple of glasses of wine and curl up on the sofa with a book. There was leftover pizza in the fridge she could warm up if she got hungry. Josh would sort something for himself. She liked that about him; he was independent and didn't rely on her to look after his every need. This was just as well because she didn't look after her own needs well at the best of times, not since before Robert. How different life had been before the night of her attack. Robert had been her colleague, lover and friend before he'd tried to kill her. Maybe not so much leading up to that night: he'd started to distance himself from her and act a little strange, but she had put it down to stress at work. Never would she have guessed that it was his twisted desire to murder her weighing heavy on his mind, and not his caseload at the hospital. He was on *her* mind now and she didn't like that; he didn't deserve a single segment of her head space. Yet there he was. She was annoyed with herself, and with Charles for shutting her out. It wouldn't have hurt him to let her observe.

She took her wine glass up to the bathroom, a blissful haven with floor-to-ceiling windows and a clear view of the lake. It was almost dark out and the lake looked majestically foreboding and unforgiving. A cold scene of real natural beauty. Until the summer just past she'd spent every spare minute by the lakeside staring into its inky waters, but ever since she had been nearly killed there it didn't hold the same appeal; she twisted the pole to close the blinds as soon as she entered the room. The lake brought up many raw memories and tonight they were too much; she could still taste the water in the back of her throat when Phil, Robert's accomplice, had thrown her overboard, plunging her straight into the murky depths.

Turning on the taps, she took a large gulp of wine, grateful she had something legal and easily accessible to take her mind away from that dark day. The house phone began to ring and she decided not to answer it; whoever it was could ring her mobile if it was important. It stopped, but a few seconds later the ringtone of her mobile filled the air.

'Hello.'

'Doctor Adams, I'm sorry to bother you. It's Jo from call handling. A body has been recovered from Lake Windermere and we wondered if you could attend?'

'I'm sorry, it's not my turn to be on call. Have you phoned my colleague, Charles Wilson?'

'He's had to attend a family emergency and can't attend the scene.'

She rolled her eyes and longingly swilled the almost full glass of wine in her other hand.

'Right, I suppose it's down to me then?' She knew it wasn't the woman on the other end of the phone's fault and adjusted the tone of her voice. 'Sorry, long day.'

'I'm sorry, Doctor Adams, but the DS insisted you were called with it being the second one today.'

'Don't be, Jo, it's not your fault. Where is it?'

'Miller Ground; are you familiar with the area?'

'I am.' Beth used to enjoy a walk along the front of the lake down there, but it had been a while since she'd been.

'You won't be able to miss the circus; police cars and an ambulance are already there. Apparently, they are near to the public footpath, if that means anything to you? I'm not familiar with the area.'

'Yes, it does. Thank you.'

She ended the call, turned off the bath taps and poured the wine down the sink, leaving the glass on the shelf above it. Staring at her reflection in the mirror, she sighed. She looked tired. Splashing cold water on her face, she blotted it dry and wondered what she might find. Bodies found on the shoreline had usually sunk first and then resurfaced once the gases from putrefaction had caused the body to float and rise up, usually minus a lot of soft tissue thanks to the marine life that liked to feast on the ripe flesh. This one was going to be messy. She was more than a little concerned that two bodies had been pulled from the lake in the space of twenty-four hours. Not unheard of, but it was certainly unsettling.

CHAPTER TWENTY

Josh parked behind the ambulance, and as he climbed out of the car another pulled up beside him. But there were no other cars around, which was good. He smiled at Sam, who mouthed 'suits and boots?' He nodded. Until he was sure it was accidental death, he wasn't taking any chances. It wasn't unheard of to have two drowning cases so close together, but it was unusual. They would take all the precautions they needed.

Sam joined him at the boot of the car as he ripped open the plastic packaging for his paper suit.

'This is a bit strange, don't you think?'

'Yes, it is. It's not the first time we've had a spate of drowning in the lake though; it does happen. Apparently this one isn't so nice. Wonder how the lad is who found it?'

Sam was already dressed and fastening the shoe covers around her legs, and he did the same. Lastly, they tugged on the powder blue nitrile gloves that were standard issue throughout the constabulary.

'I was ready to go home, have a glass of wine, put my feet up and watch a couple of episodes of *Killing Eve*. Have you seen it?'

'No, I don't tend to watch thrillers. Not in front of Beth anyway.'

'God, no. I can see why, but if you ever did want to, I think you'd enjoy it.' They walked towards the wooden gate which led onto the public footpath and he pushed it open, holding it for her to walk through.

'What a gentleman.'

'Yeah, most of the time.'

Turning on torches to illuminate the slippery path, which was littered with fallen leaves, they walked the short distance to the shore at a brisk pace, the thundering sound of a nearby waterfall rushing down Wynlass Beck towards Lake Windermere getting louder as they approached.

'It's beautiful.' Sam nodded at the view. 'I always forget about this part of the lake. I used to bring the kids when they were younger to go canoeing and windsurfing.'

'Don't they canoe any more?'

She laughed. 'No, sinking shots of vodka is the current sport of choice.'

Josh smiled, remembering how easy his life had been as an eighteen-year-old. They rounded the bend and saw the assortment of officers, paramedics and a pale-faced teenager with a silver foil blanket wrapped around his shoulders. A sense of déjà vu washed over Josh, so overpowering that he blinked hard as an officer approached him.

'Sarge, the body has just been recovered by the lake wardens.' He looked towards the shore where a dishevelled, sodden black mass lay. 'The poor kid's pretty shook up.'

'Cheers, I'll go speak with them now.'

The smell of decomposition filled the air as he got nearer to the body, but the two wardens didn't look phased at all. Spotting his approach, they walked towards him, introducing themselves as they met in the middle.

The woman held out her hand. 'I'm Melanie, this is Fraser, we were on our final lap of the lake when we heard the screams. Poor kid looks traumatised.'

'Thanks, both of you. It's very much appreciated. It can't have been easy. If I could ask you to give your details to the officer standing over there we'll be in touch for a statement.'

'No problem. We weren't aware there were any missing persons alerts for the lake. This is a bit of a shock to be honest.'

Josh glanced over at the teenager, who was staring at the body in front of them. He whispered to Sam, 'Get one of those officers to put him in the back of a car and away from the corpse.' He then turned back to Melanie. 'Thanks again, good shout.'

They followed Sam towards the officer and the paramedics.

Alone now, Josh took a deep breath and prepared himself to face whoever it was that had been released from their watery grave.

CHAPTER TWENTY-ONE

Beth arrived at Miller Ground, parking on the grass verge as there was no room in the small lay-by. As she carried her heavy case down towards the shore, she couldn't help but admire the beauty of the area. It was dark and an officer had met her at the gate, leading the way and shining a dragon light to illuminate the steep path in front of them. She was thankful to have some company – it stopped her heart from racing too fast – and even more thankful she'd had the foresight to wear her walking boots. The ground underfoot was soft, slippery from the low mist which had settled over the area as the sun had set. The cool autumn air blew away the overwhelming exhaustion she had felt back at home; she was wide awake and in full professional mode now. It always amazed her how she could slip from one persona to the other in the blink of an eye: exhausted, anxious Beth left at home, while cool, confident, professional Beth attended the scene of a sudden death.

She wasn't usually called out to drownings – paramedics were more than capable of certifying that life was extinct – but she understood Josh's unease; everyone was still on high alert since they'd caught a serial killer burying his victims in other people's graves just over a month ago. They rounded the bend where the path opened up onto a small cottage; a bit further around and there was the lakeside. There were a couple of stone jetties jutting out into the water; steeped in darkness they looked as if they disappeared into the lake. A few police officers, two paramedics and a teenage boy wrapped up in a foil blanket were sitting on a low wall. She recognised Sam sitting next to him, her head bent near to his as she chatted to him.

She looked around for the body and her heart skipped a little beat when she saw Josh standing over it. Even though she couldn't make out his handsome features in the shadows, just knowing he was there was enough to make her pulse quicken. As if he sensed her staring at him, he looked up, lifting his hand to wave. She waved back and began to walk towards him. He came to meet her, shining his torch along the uneven shoreline so she didn't stumble.

'I thought you weren't on call tonight.'

'I'm not, but something came up with Charles so here I am.'

'Good, not good about Charles, but I'm glad you are here.'

'What have we got?'

'I'll let you see for yourself. That poor lad was fishing and thought he saw a discarded sleeping bag floating in the lake and did his civic duty by wading in to pull it out. Got the fright of his life when he saw two empty eye sockets staring back at him. Whoever it is has been in the water for some time.'

As they moved closer to the corpse, the stench overwhelmed them. Beth took the torch from Josh and shone it down onto the distorted, bloated face. It was hard to tell whether it was a man or a woman; any distinguishing features had gone. As she moved the torch down the torso she shuddered. It looked as if the body was still breathing although she knew it was impossible. Bending down, she lifted the black jumper to reveal a writhing mass of tiny crabs and fish that were feasting on the rotten flesh. Josh groaned, and she tugged the material back down, not needing to see any more.

'There's a lot of skin slippage. I'm sorry but you're going to have to wait until we get the body back to the mortuary before I can tell you what sex it is. I don't want to risk damaging any evidence out here. We're better off waiting until it can be properly undressed, hosed off and safely contained on the table.'

'It's horrific. I didn't think this sort of thing happened in real life. You know, maybe in a movie, but for the life of me…' Josh shuddered.

'We need to get them to the mortuary, Josh. There's really nothing I can do or tell you in these conditions. I'm sorry.'

He looked at her, concern etched across his face. 'You have nothing to be sorry for, Beth. I know you're a doctor but you're not a miracle worker. I just feel bad for whoever this is. When we do identify them, their family isn't going to be able to view them or to say goodbye. I can't think of anything worse.'

'I'll go straight there. I'm sure Abe will be happy to meet me. Until I know for sure what's happened, I want everything treated as evidence. Tell the undertakers I want full forensic removal. Have you had any missing persons reports for the area?'

'Paton is on the case with that. Thanks, I'll get the attending officers to meet you there. I have a couple of loose ends that need sorting out here. I'll see you later, OK?'

Picking up her case, she made her way back to the car alone. The body would be wrapped in a nylon sheet then bagged ready for her and Abe to do their best to find out who this was and how they had ended up in such a terrible state.

CHAPTER TWENTY-TWO

Beth sped through winding lanes to the hospital at Barrow to wait for the body. There was talk about moving all forensic post-mortems to the Royal Lancaster Infirmary, but she was holding out as long as she could. Lancaster was nearer than Barrow, but Abe worked in the Barrow mortuary and although she had no doubt the staff were as competent at Royal Lancaster as he was, she didn't want to risk losing him. He made her dark and disturbing job easier to bear, always pre-empting her needs and never questioning her painstaking attention to detail. Mortuary assistants like him were hard to find; she supposed it didn't matter what career he turned his hand to – he would be outstanding because that's the kind of person he was.

The drive to Barrow was pleasant, the roads almost deserted. Knowing she would arrive before the body, she decided to treat herself and Abe to a coffee from the drive-thru Costa on the way into town. Although it would take her past the hospital to get there and she'd have to double back on herself, it was worth the extra ten minutes. Her mind was getting tired again; she needed caffeine if she wanted to be alert.

Armed with two large lattes, both with an extra shot, and two lemon tarts, she drove back to the hospital. The only good thing about being called out at this time of night was she could park almost next to the entrance. For a moment she wondered if she should have offered to pick Abe up as it was late and he always cycled everywhere. But spotting his bike leaning against the wall she realised he was already here. Grabbing the coffees and bag of cakes, she approached the double doors and hesitated over how she was going to ring the bell with her hands full. As if by magic, one of them opened and she grinned at Abe.

'You're a mind-reader and a life-saver.'

'I think you might be the life-saver, Beth, I was almost asleep. That coffee smells good.'

'Bribery and a thank you.'

'For what? It's my job. If you need me, I'm always available. Don't tell Dr Wilson that, though, I'm not available for him out of hours unless I'm on call.' He winked.

'You are far too good to me, Abe, but I appreciate it.'

She followed him inside the spotless mortuary, and the smell of disinfectant hung in the air. Clean and sterile, but not for long. They went into the small staff room and sat either side of the table, and she passed over a coffee and the paper bag towards Abe. He looked inside and nodded enthusiastically at her choice of pastry. Sliding it back over, she took hers out and began to eat, not realising how hungry she was. Abe chatted happily about his new favourite crime novel by Angela Marsons until they both fell into an easy silence, preparing themselves for the horror of what they were about to face.

When the buzzer on the back doors echoed throughout the mortuary, the pair of them jumped, and Abe laughed; the infectious sound filled the air and she joined in. He stood up and saluted her, then went to open the double doors for whoever had escorted their body here. Beth wondered if the undertakers had bowed out, leaving it to the fire service. As she walked into the mortuary, she smiled at the two solemn-looking men both dressed in overalls, looking more like sheet metal workers than undertakers. The older of the two nodded at her.

'I thought our job was bad enough. You've got your work cut out for you with this one, Doctor.'

She nodded, thinking that this wasn't the worst body she'd ever seen by far. The guy who'd decided to climb a rickety wooden ladder one winter evening after six cans of cider to cut some branches for his woodburner was one of the top three. He'd carried the chainsaw up the ladder in the dark with only a head torch for light. Then he'd started the chainsaw, lost his balance and managed to almost decapitate himself. He hadn't been found for two days; by then his almost severed head had been frozen solid as his body dangled from the tree like a frozen, life-sized marionette. When they'd tried to get him down his head had come clean off, the few tendons that had held it together tearing apart, making a sound that she could still hear today if she closed her eyes. His head had bounced off a hedge and the nearest fireman who'd been assisting. It had landed on the floor, rolling until it came to a standstill almost at Beth's feet.

She smiled at the undertaker. 'It's bad, but not the worst. Although I'm not too keen on the marine life still nibbling at the intestines, but what can you do?'

He lost what little colour there was in his cheeks just as the officer who had led Beth to the lake walked in behind them. 'What are we going to do?'

Everyone turned to look at him. It was Beth who answered.

'We're going to put the body onto the table and open the bag, as we need to remove the outer clothing and see if there is anything that could give us a clue to the identity. We'll remove any personal possessions for you to bag up and take back with you to book into the property store. Abe will wash down and remove the creatures in the torso.'

There was silence as they all contemplated the task in hand. Then the undertakers began to back away. 'Yeah, well you don't need us for that, do you? We'll leave you to it.'

'Actually, we might need a hand to roll the body, if you can stay a little longer?'

The two men looked pained and she felt bad for asking, but the body was in a bad way. The more of them to handle it the less chance of causing even more damage than there already was.

CHAPTER TWENTY-THREE

Ethan sipped at his lager. His stomach wasn't really ready to consume more alcohol. He glanced at James, who had spent the last few hours watching everyone in the bar, occasionally focusing his attention if someone entered the reception area which was just visible from where they were sitting. They'd spoken very little. Ethan hadn't realised how hungry he was until the plates had been placed on the table in front of him. Then his stomach had let out a loud growl and he'd realised he was ravenous.

'When do you think you might go and see the police?'

When James didn't answer, he turned to see what he was staring at. He caught sight of the blonde-haired girl from last night, the one who James had left with early. She was whispering into the ear of another girl who was standing behind the reception desk.

'I don't believe you, oh my God. You're such a dick at times, James.'

James held up his hand to stop him talking and Ethan felt a hot, fiery ball of anger form in the pit of his stomach. He pushed his chair away from the table and stood up.

'I'm going home; you've been as much company as that statue of Buddha over there. Thanks for the food.'

Ethan walked off, not sure how he was getting home. It was a long walk, but he'd rather head back. At least it would clear away the last of his hangover. He wasn't waiting around for James to pick up the girl. Christ, he was obsessed with women and sex. *Do you think you're just a touch jealous, Ethan?* he heard the voice of his mother whisper in his ear and shook his head. He wasn't jealous; well, maybe he was a little. It would be nice to never have to worry about money or popularity and be able to live the lifestyle that James did. But not at the price of being a self-absorbed arsehole. He'd rather be skint and genuine.

*

As he reached the end of the steep hill, he heard the familiar sound of James's convertible Porsche coming down the road. He didn't turn around. He really couldn't be bothered with him. A horn blared behind him.

'Father, forgive me for I have sinned,' he heard James shout.

A group of Japanese tourists who turned the corner to head up to the hotel all stared. A couple of them lifted the expensive cameras from around their necks and began to snap pictures of them. Ethan felt the redness that had started at the base of his throat spread across his cheeks. He carried on walking, shaking his head. Behind him James shouted.

'Ethan, don't leave me this way. I love you, we can work it out.'

Ethan turned to face the grinning idiot, who, despite the biting cold wind, had put the roof down and was standing on the front seat of his car, his arms outstretched. Ethan crossed to the middle of the road where James was pretending to sob into his hands and tugged open the door. He got inside and James threw his arms around him. The group of tourists went wild, clapping and cheering.

Ethan whispered, 'I'll bloody kill you for this, you're an idiot.'

James sat back down, grinning. 'No, you won't. You'll forgive me because we're mates, and it was funny.'

Shaking his head, he tried to maintain an air of anger; instead, he began to laugh. The pair of them were laughing until the car behind them had had enough and beeped loudly at them to get moving. James stuck his arm up in the air, giving them the finger and sped off.

'Were you really going to walk all that way home?'

'Yes, I wasn't waiting around for you. Why didn't you say you wanted to go there to see her again?'

James shrugged. 'I didn't think it was such a big deal. No offence, mate, but the world doesn't revolve around you. I'm sorry that girl died; I'm even sorrier you had to drag her out of the water. On your own. It must have been horrid. But shit happens, it's done. She's dead, there was nothing you could do that you didn't already. No point in moping around feeling sorry for yourself, is there?'

'You should be a life coach; the no-nonsense approach goes down well with normal people who have feelings and a conscience.'

James clutched at his heart. 'I have feelings! Granted, most of them are in my boxer shorts, but I do have them.'

This set Ethan off laughing and he shook his head. 'Did you speak to her then? Don't tell me she didn't give you her number after your night of passion.'

James didn't answer.

'Oh my God, she didn't. She wasn't interested or impressed by your money. Wow. You know what you have to do then, don't you?'

'What?'

'Marry her.'

It was Ethan's turn to laugh. It wasn't often women weren't impressed by James.

'Very funny. I went to talk to her and she didn't give me a second glance. She walked away.'

'She's just found out her friend is dead. The world definitely doesn't revolve around you, believe it or not. Why don't you send her some flowers, not something ridiculous and over the top. Something classy and understated. Girls love that kind of thing.'

'Now you're the relationship expert? The guy who is so entertaining the woman he was with decided jumping overboard and drowning was the better option.'

Ethan shook his head. 'You're an arsehole, James.'

They didn't speak the rest of the way back to Ethan's crappy cabin. He got out of the car, thanked him for the ride, but never looked his way. He knew James was only trying to be witty, but still it hurt. He didn't have much luck with women, he never had. It was hard to get anyone to pay attention to you when your mates were all loaded, better looking and flashing cash around like confetti.

Letting himself in, he wrinkled his nose at the smell. It did stink in here, James had been right about that.

CHAPTER TWENTY-FOUR

Josh stopped the car outside the terraced house that he and Jodie had shared for the last ten years. It looked different all in darkness. Even when he'd worked late into the early hours of the morning there was always a light left on for him, sometimes several. Jodie had never liked the dark. He got out of the car and walked up the path, pushed the key into the lock, turning it and opening the door. Stepping inside, it felt strange to be back home; the faint smell of vanilla lingered in the air. He felt as if he was an intruder. The living room was messy, not dirty but untidy. There were magazines scattered all over the coffee table which had seen better days. A thick layer of dust had settled over the television and the black glass stand it stood on. Occasionally, back when they'd been happy, he'd draw a smiling face with a fingertip to wind Jodie up. She'd purposely leave it there to get him back. He smiled; it hadn't always been arguments and anger.

He went into the kitchen to check what shopping she might need. The cupboards were almost empty apart from a few tins of tuna and chopped tomatoes. Opening the fridge, he frowned; there was nothing in it except an almost empty bottle of vodka and an open packet of ham with the edges all curled up. He took out the ham and threw it into the bin which smelt almost as bad as the body that had washed up earlier. Removing his coat, he rolled up his shirt sleeves, retrieved the polish, cleaning spray and bleach and set about cleaning the house from top to bottom.

By the time he had finished he'd worked up more of a sweat than the last time he'd been to the gym. Lifting up his armpit, he sniffed, grimacing. He couldn't go home to Beth smelling like this. He realised how tired he was. Taking out his phone, he dialled the takeaway that he and Jodie had used a couple of times a week. He ordered enough food to feed him for the next few days.

While he was waiting, he went upstairs, stripped off his clothes and had the longest shower he'd ever had in this house. When the small bathroom was so steamy he couldn't see, he towel dried himself. Wrapping a towel around his waist, he went into the spare room to see if he'd left any of his clothes. He found a pair of clean boxers screwed up at the back of one of the drawers, but nothing else. It didn't matter, they would have to do. He grabbed his clothes and went into the kitchen and pushed them into the washing machine. Switching it on, he took the vodka from the fridge, the last few remaining chips of ice from the bag in the freezer and poured himself a large shot. He carried it into the living room and sat back on the sofa and closed his eyes. How easy it was to relax here. It had been his home for a long time; in fact, he'd spent more time in this house than any other. It was nothing fancy, a simple two-up, two-down terraced. It wasn't anything like the modern, light, airy, huge home that belonged to Beth. And he realised that was the problem; he may live at Beth's but it wasn't his. None of it belonged to him. He was nothing more than a live-in lover and lodger. The vodka burned his throat as he swallowed; what a mess. He didn't love Jodie, but they could still be friends and she needed a friend now more than ever. He couldn't stand the thought of her on her own, too ill to go shopping for food or run the hoover around. The thought of her not being well enough to even take the right medication made him feel crap. His eyes began to close and he felt himself drifting off.

A loud knock on the front door woke him. Stumbling to his feet as if he was drunk, he looked around for something to wear and grabbed a pink fluffy dressing gown off the banister.

'Long time no see, Mr Walker, how are you?'

He smiled at the man who was way past retirement age holding two large paper bags full of food.

'It's been a while, Bill, I'm good. Yourself?'

'Still delivering Thai food to the good people of Kendal.'

'There's worse things, Bill.'

'I suppose there is. How's Mrs Walker? My wife said she sees her in the oncology clinic.'

'Not too good, she's in hospital. How's your wife?'

'As good as she's going to get. Still nagging, so she's not that ill.'

Josh smiled. 'Good, I'm glad to hear that.' He pulled the twenty pound note from his pocket and passed it to Bill. 'You buy her a nice bunch of flowers on your way home, Bill.'

He offered the money back. 'I can't take that.'

'Yes, you can. Thank you.'

Josh shut the door before he could hand the money back, and smiled. The food smelt divine. Taking it into the kitchen, he piled a plate high and sat at the table. He was going to eat as much of it as he could then pass out on the bed in the spare room. He knew he should ring or message Beth so she didn't worry about him, but he had a feeling if he told her where he was she'd worry even more. Hopefully, she'd think he was still working. It was wrong, but it seemed like the easier of the two options.

CHAPTER TWENTY-FIVE

Beth scrubbed her hands and arms under the warm spray of water in the ladies' changing room, trying to block out the images. They had managed to get the body out of the bag in preparation for the post-mortem first thing tomorrow, and the only thing they could say for definite at this stage was that the victim was female. There had been nothing pertaining to any identification in any of the clothes pockets that Abe had gone through. She was waiting to hear from Josh, to see if there were any reported missing persons who this could be.

Satisfied she was scrubbed clean, she was ready to go home. She glanced at the clock. It was almost eleven. So much for her night off and bottle of wine. She checked her phone and was disappointed to see she had no missed calls from Josh. Hopefully, he'd already be home. She loved going home to see the house lit up and signs of life in it. Living on her own had long since lost all its appeal since he'd moved in. Abe had already left; she'd offered to drop him off and he'd refused. Tired and drained, she wished it wasn't such a long drive home. As she went out to her car she hoped to God no more bodies washed up.

*

As she drove through the electric gates twenty-seven minutes later, she sighed; the house wasn't in darkness because she'd left some lights on, but Josh's car wasn't there. She had needed to see him tonight more than she had ever before. It had been a few weeks since she'd come home this late to an empty house and it unsettled her.

Going inside, she knew she could take off where she'd started a couple of hours ago, run herself a hot bath and soak away the tensions of today. But after staring at the bloated corpse dredged from the lake it no longer had the same appeal. She poured herself an even larger glass of wine and this time had drunk half of it before she'd even made it up the stairs. Turning around, she looked at the bottle, so chilled there were rivulets of condensation running down the side. *You're an adult, Beth. Tonight has been tough, you've earned this drink.* The voice of reason inside her mind made perfect sense; who was she to argue with it? She'd had the shittiest of days. Robert was dead and she'd had to deal with two drownings in the same day.

She went upstairs to the bedroom where she'd left the original wine bottle on the bedside table. Topping her glass up, she went into the bathroom for the second time. This time turning on the shower, she caught sight of her reflection in the mirror. Tucking her hair behind her ears, she turned her head and stared at the scar on the side of her face. Force of habit sent her fingers reaching up to rub the puckered line of tissue as if trying to erase it. Robert had hurt her, scarred her. Robert, the man who had haunted her dreams for seven years. *Fuck you, Robert, I'm glad you're dead.* She raised her glass and took a huge mouthful. *It's finally over.*

Wearing soft flannel pyjamas which were covered in a Cath Kidston spray flowers print – a gift from Josh – she finished the wine and fell onto the bed. She wasn't drunk, but she'd certainly sleep well tonight. No more bad dreams, or at least so she hoped.

She checked her phone hoping to see a missed call, text or messenger alert from Josh, trying to ignore the tiny spark of unease inside her chest when the screen was empty. He was busy working; there was nothing more to it. Knowing him his phone had probably died – he never remembered his charger. Pulling the soft duvet back, she lay down, her head sinking into the pillows, and closed her eyes. Sleep came fast, taking her to a different world. One where she wasn't staring into rotting corpses that were being consumed by tiny creatures that feasted on flesh.

CHAPTER TWENTY-SIX

Josh blinked open his eyes, wondering where the hell he was. He was in a single bed. He stared up at the pastel pink, flowery light shade and remembered. Sitting up, his head felt too heavy for his shoulders. He remembered finishing off the rest of the neat vodka and grimaced. Why had he done that? He couldn't answer; it had felt like the right thing to do under the circumstances. *What circumstances?* his mind asked. Groaning, he stood up, catching sight of his reflection in the mirror. He asked himself aloud this time. 'Yeah, Josh, what circumstances?' *This whole mess of a situation, that's what.* His phone began to vibrate and for once he wished he'd left it in the car so he didn't have to answer it. Instead, he picked it up and heard Beth's voice, a touch of concern making it sound higher pitched than usual.

'Hi, just checking you're okay. I missed you last night.'

'I'm good thanks, well as good as I can be.' He didn't tell her he had a hangover.

'Do you want to be present for the PM of the body from the lake? Just thought I'd check.'

'I don't know, do you think I need to be?'

'There is absolutely no way to say one way or the other. At the moment, the only thing I can say is she's female. I'm assuming it's an accident, or maybe a suicide. But seriously it's a mess; it's going to be hard to tell you much at all apart from whether she drowned in the lake or died on land.'

She didn't ask him where he was, but he could feel the weight of the unasked question hanging in the silence. He couldn't do it.

He couldn't tell her that he'd gone to his old home, had cleaned the house from top to bottom while finishing off a bottle of neat vodka. Even though there was nothing in it: he had no feelings towards Jodie except maybe the weight of responsibility and the feelings of guilt that she was ill and alone.

'I'll pass then if it's okay with you. I need to locate the owner of *The Tequila Sunrise* and take a statement from him.'

'Has he not been to the station? I'd have thought he'd have come to see you and get it over with. How strange.'

'I'm assuming he's a very busy man, or that he might not even be aware of what's happened.'

'Or he's simply avoiding talking to the police. Why would he not want to speak to you? Unless he has something to hide.'

'Like what?'

'He knows what happened; he pushed her in, although there are no marks or bruising to evidence this.'

'Or maybe as Ethan put it: the man who found her gave the impression when I took his statement that he's an arrogant arsehole who is full of his own self-importance.'

Beth laughed. 'Yes, I suppose there's always that. I'll let you know what I find.' There was a slight pause and then she added, 'I'll see you later.'

'Yes, you will. I missed you too. Bye.'

She hung up the phone and he felt like the world's biggest arsehole. Why didn't he just tell her about Jodie? He didn't know. It felt uncomfortable; maybe he was scared Beth would freak out and tell him he wasn't to help her. He could understand her feeling that way, but it wasn't in his nature. He spent his life being there to help people in their greatest hours of need. Jodie wasn't any different; the fact that they were separated didn't mean he couldn't support her. His conscience would no longer let him ignore her than it would a cat stranded up a tree. Sometimes it sucked being a good guy.

He went downstairs to retrieve his clothes from the dryer, pulling out his shirt then trousers. They were creased, but not too bad. They'd have to do. He needed to get to work. He'd do a shop on his way home, stock up the fridge a bit with the stuff he knew Jodie ate. He wondered if she still had an appetite. It didn't matter, at least there'd be something in to eat if she fancied it. Even though Jodie had told him it was over with Carl, the betrayal had hurt, despite the fact that they'd already drifted apart. Although he couldn't be sure whether it was his ego or his feelings that had taken the brunt of that one.

He left the house for the short drive to work. It wasn't the scenic route like when he drove in from Beth's. It was a lot faster though and he reached the station in record time. Today his mission was to track down the owner of the boat and hope that Beth could get him an ID for the body from last night.

CHAPTER TWENTY-SEVEN

Josh directed Sam to park in the loading bay outside the shops near to the marina.

'We need to find the guy who owns the boat. Why do you think he hasn't come to the station?'

'Busy, feels bad, hates coppers.'

Josh frowned at Sam. 'Everyone hates coppers, even coppers hate coppers.'

She laughed. 'That's true. Not as much as parking wardens though. I think they hate them more than us. Just.'

They got out of the car and walked down to where the boat was moored, passing a man, wrapped in layers of dirty clothes, his long straggly ginger beard peppered with grey and a dirty white baseball cap pulled over his unkempt hair. He sat on his own staring at the boats. Sam nudged Josh.

'I can't believe he's still here.'

'Who?'

'Pete. He's been hanging around here since I joined the force, probably longer.'

'Why? Does he have a boat?'

'Does it look like he owns a boat, Josh? I mean, look at the state of him. But he may have seen something or know something.'

She headed in his direction. 'Hello, Pete, how are you? It's been a while.'

He stared at her and nodded.

'I didn't realise you were still around.'

'Hmph.'

'Do you know anything about the girl who was found in the water yesterday? Were you here? Did you see what happened?'

'No,' he barked. 'Wasn't here. I don't sleep here, you know. I do have a home to go to when I get tired or too cold. I don't like it much but it's safe and warm. Well it is when I remember to top up the smart meter. I just like to watch the boats. I like the water, it's nice. Especially this time of year when…' He paused. 'Well, you know what I mean.'

Sam shrugged. 'Not really, Pete.'

'When it's not full of tourists, coachloads of them messing the place up.'

'If we didn't have those tourists this place would be a ghost town. It's okay, I just wondered if you'd been around. You usually see everything. Sorry to have bothered you. See you later.'

She turned back to Josh, who whispered, 'Lovely guy.'

She laughed. 'Worth asking, you never know.'

They walked towards *The Tequila Sunrise*, which didn't look as if it had moved since the day before. Josh spotted someone going below deck and whispered, 'Bingo.'

'Might not be him, don't get your hopes up.'

'If it isn't, at least whoever it is can ring James Marshall and tell him to get his backside here and pronto.'

The jetty bounced and thumped under their brisk footsteps. When they reached the boat, Josh shouted, 'Hey mate, anyone home?'

Sam looked at him, shaking her head and stifling a laugh.

'What?'

'Hey mate? What about, ahoy there sailor?'

'Bugger off.'

There was no answer. Josh was about to call out again when Sam walked to the ladder and began to climb up it. 'It's too bloody cold to hang around on a jetty that keeps moving every time you lean too far forwards.'

Rolling his eyes at Sam's impatience, Josh followed her up the ladder. He hadn't even reached the top when a voice came from below the deck of the boat.

'This is a private boat. If you want to hire one there's an office a bit further down.'

'We don't want to hire a boat, we're from the police.'

The man's head popped up through a hatch.

'What do you want?'

Josh shrugged. 'I'd have thought it was pretty obvious what we wanted.' He turned to Sam. 'Do you think you'd be able to hazard a good guess as to why we're here if you were Mr Marshall?'

'I'd like to think so, especially when a dead girl was drinking on my boat just hours before she died. It can't be good for business. It would certainly make me think twice about stepping on board for a good time.'

The young lad looked at them. 'Show me your ID. You could be anyone; might be reporters for all I know.'

They both pulled out their warrant cards and held them up.

Pulling himself through the hatch, he moved closer to study them, then nodded and stepped back.

'Sorry, officers, you can't be too sure.'

Josh found his attitude more annoying than he let on.

'Very wise, you can't be too careful at all. Let's start again. I'm Detective Sergeant Josh Walker and this is my colleague Detective Constable Sam Thomas. We'd like to talk to you about Leah Burton.'

'What do you want to know?'

'How well did you know her? How much alcohol did you all consume? Where were you when she went into the water? How about that for starters?'

'Come down below, it's cold up here.'

As they followed him downstairs and out of the biting wind, Josh looked around. It was a very nicely fitted out boat with a surprisingly big galley kitchen, a plush seating area and a couple of doors which he assumed led to bedrooms.

'Nice boat.'

'Thanks, have a seat.'

Sam and Josh slid into the seated booth behind the table; James sat on a chair opposite them.

'Do you have parties on here much?'

'I hire it out for private parties, and occasionally use it myself.'

'I take it you have all the legal documents and licences for that side of the business?'

James glared at him. 'Of course. I wouldn't be able to conduct business without them. The insurance alone probably costs more than your yearly wage.'

Josh didn't bite. 'So, where were you when Leah went overboard?'

'I don't know when she went into the water. I left around eleven with her friend. We went back to my apartment. Everyone was drunk and I didn't want to sleep with her on the boat. I wanted some privacy, so we left.' James ran his fingers through his fringe unnecessarily for the third time in as many minutes.

Josh wondered if it was a nervous twitch, or if he was just that vain – perhaps it was both.

'Did you sleep with her at your apartment?'

'What has that got to do with anything? Yes, we did. She was with me until the next morning.'

'Who was left on the boat?'

'Ethan and Leah, though I didn't even know her name until today. They were just a couple of girls we picked up, took for a sail on the lake then slept with.'

'Ethan said he didn't sleep with Leah, and the post-mortem confirms there was no sexual activity prior to her death.'

'Well that's his loss; he was probably too drunk. He really can't handle his drink.'

'Are you in the habit of letting drunk people sleep on your boat – your very expensive boat – unsupervised?'

'Ethan is my best friend, of course I would. Look, I don't understand what all of this is about. I'm sorry that girl was found dead, but it's no one's fault except her own. Who in their right mind wants to jump into the water at this time of year?'

'I'm just doing my job. Why are you so upset?'

'I'm not, I just don't like your questions. I have nothing further to say to you. If you want to speak to me again please make an appointment. I'll have a solicitor with me.'

James stood up, signalling the interview was over. Josh and Sam did the same, and James led them back up onto the deck and watched them disembark with his hands folded across his chest.

Turning back, Sam said, 'Thank you for your time, Mr Marshall. I'm sure you understand how difficult it is trying to find out the answers to questions we don't know in order to help Leah's family cope with their grief.'

James's shoulders relaxed and he uncrossed his arms. 'Yes, I do. I'm sorry about this whole mess, but all we did was have a good time. I never meant for anyone to come to any harm. I hope you can understand that.'

Josh nodded. 'We do, that's why we do this difficult, underpaid job. To help grieving families come to terms with the loss of their loved ones. We also make sure that if anyone is to blame for their deaths that we take the appropriate course of action.'

They left him standing there. It had started to drizzle while they'd been below deck but James didn't turn back inside until they were off the jetty and back on dry land. Josh could feel his eyes on them all the way to the shoreline.

CHAPTER TWENTY-EIGHT

'What did you think of him?' Josh asked once they were inside the warmth of the car out of the rain which was coming down in sheets.

'I don't like him, he's a rich arsehole.'

Josh laughed. 'Me neither. I don't think he gives a shit about Leah.'

'I don't think he gives a shit about anyone. How many times did he have to run his hand through his quiff?'

'Yeah. It's odd that he clammed up and threatened us with a brief. If he wasn't there when it happened, what's he got to hide?'

'Maybe he's worried about bad publicity. It won't do his party boat any favours if it gets out someone died on his boat. There's no way I'm letting Grace go anywhere near that boat now, especially if he's on it. I bet he sleeps with all the punters.'

'You need to find a way to talk her out of it then.'

'That's great advice, Josh, really it is.'

'Sorry, I don't have kids. I don't know anything about them. I suppose the more you tell her to stay away, the more likely she is to go.'

'Absolutely right, Detective.'

Defeated, Josh took out his phone and rang Paton. 'Have you found me any missing persons that could be the body pulled from the lake yet?'

'Morning, boss. There are two possibilities. First is thirty-eight-year-old Melanie Thorp who was reported missing six days ago by her husband. There was activity on her bank account in Manchester three days ago, but nothing since.'

'Who's the other?'

'Twenty-four-year-old Julia Bach. She was reported missing by her roommate at The Hounds Inn on the eleventh of October. According to the report she'd been talking about going home to Poland or looking for another job before she disappeared.'

'Was she down as a high-risk mis per?'

'No, medium. There was no immediate concern and she already had most of her stuff packed in a case ready to leave. According to her file she disappeared after an argument with the supervisor. Her co-workers all assumed she'd left, all except for the one who reported her missing.'

'I'm in Bowness now. Sam and I will go and speak to the staff, see if her belongings are still there. We might be able to get some DNA from her toothbrush or hairbrush.'

'If they still have it. They might have binned it if they thought she wasn't coming back.'

'Hopefully not.' He ended the call. Paton was right, they might have got rid of it all, but fate might be on their side. It wasn't as if they could ask her roommate to do a formal identification, because right now whoever was lying in the mortuary no longer resembled a human. Still, a weak lead was better than no leads at all.

CHAPTER TWENTY-NINE

Beth studied the body of the unidentified female lying on the mortuary table. Bodies submerged under water for any length of time become bloated and unrecognisable. Maceration occurs when the skin changes due to water absorption. It first appears on the fingertips, then palms of the hands, same with toes and feet; the skin becomes whitened, sodden, thickened and wrinkly. Beth loved nothing more than a long soak in a hot bath to wash away the stresses of the day. How often had she got out of the tub with wrinkled hands and feet like an old washerwoman? But when skin is submerged for a long period, over time the surface becomes loose and peels off, followed by the hair and nails. Beth knew from her studies that maceration is accelerated in warm water, but the water in Windermere was only about six Celsius in October. At that temperature, it should take around eight to twenty-four hours for the changes to become apparent. In seven to ten days epidermal separation may have started, and in around three to four weeks skin and nails may be sufficiently loose to fall off. Of course, temperature was one of many environmental factors that could increase or decrease maceration, so looking at the loose skin in front of her, Beth estimated that this body had been in the water at least two weeks.

Stirring herself into action, she began to speak into the Dictaphone as Abe finished washing away the last of the tiny marine life that were clinging to the body. 'This is the unidentified body of an adult female in moderate decomposition. The body weighs one hundred and fifty-six pounds and measures 157.46 centimetres. The head appears to be normocephalic and is covered by blonde hair. There is no balding and the hair can be described as shoulder length, straight.' Bending over the head, she used a gloved finger to lift up each eyelid. 'Examination of the eyes reveals irides that appear to be blue in colour and sclera that are white. There are no petechial haemorrhages of the conjunctivae of the lids. Oronasal passages are unobstructed. Upper and lower teeth are present. Dentures are absent. The neck is unremarkable. There is bloating to the torso due to prolonged submersion in the water. The body, legs and feet all show greening with marbling on the upper thighs. The hair and scalp easily slough with slight pulling. The head and face are bloated with bulging eyes; the face shows skin slippage on the forehead. Skin slippage is also present on the chest, back, arms, hands and both lower legs. The skin on the palms, fingers, soles of the feet and toes all show marked wrinkling.'

Beth gently picked up an arm to look at the fingers. 'I'm going to have to try to get some prints from the fingers of the left hand. It looks in slightly better condition for some reason.' What Beth meant was she was going to remove the top layer of skin and lay it over her own gloved hand to fingerprint. Not her favourite part of the job, but thankfully a task she seldom had to perform. It was very efficient in getting results, however, and the sooner they could identify their Jane Doe the better. She heard Abe's teeth grind as she carefully slid the loose skin over her own fingers; he hated this part. Satisfied the skin was wrapped as tight as could be, she lifted her hand up to the light; all except two of the fingernails were attached. They were loose and holding on by a thin layer of skin, but still intact.

'There's something under two of these nails; Abe, can you get a pair of nail clippers and tweezers?'

Despite the grimace on his face he did as he was asked. He also spread some paper towels onto the other table to catch any trace evidence when she trimmed the nails above it. Abe sifted through the detritus as she worked. Grabbing a pair of tweezers, he prodded at some silt that has fallen from the sheet and pulled out two flakes of blue paint, holding it under the light so Beth could see. Beth's heart skipped a beat at the sudden realisation that, perhaps, both bodies retrieved from the lake could be connected.

'Put them on separate slides, please, I want to take a closer look once we've printed,' she said, trying to supress the anxiety in her voice. As much as she didn't want these two drownings to be connected, she knew instantly and instinctively that they were. It was too much to be a coincidence. If the samples were paint flakes and of similar property to the sample from Leah Burton's fingernail then it meant that both women had either crossed paths or been in the same vicinity before they went into the water.

CHAPTER THIRTY

Josh parked in the almost empty car park of The Hounds Inn. The only other car was a rusted old Mondeo. It had been years since he'd seen one of those. He'd driven one himself not long after he first passed his test.

'Earth to Josh.' Sam's voice startled him. He turned to look at her. She waved a hand in front of his eyes and he blinked.

'I'm reminiscing about my misspent youth.'

She looked from the car to him. 'I don't want to know! The car park is empty, business can't be good; even at this time of year there's normally some tourists still knocking about.'

'Or the food is crap.'

'Maybe.'

They walked to the front door and Josh pushed it hard, only to find it locked. There was a sign on the wall next to it with the opening times. It didn't open until six thirty on a Friday. He frowned; what a peculiar day to close. Lifting his hand, he rapped loudly on the peeling black painted door with his knuckles. The sound echoed inside. They waited, but no one came.

'Surely there's someone in? Is this the only pub that doesn't open on a weekend? It can't be right.'

He knocked again, and they were about to give up when they heard footsteps dragging from inside.

Sam whispered, 'I'm scared; who do you think is going to open that door, Bela Lugosi?'

Josh chuckled as the door was unbolted from the inside and drawn back. A pair of eyes peered out of the gloom at them.

'Yes?'

'Police, we'd like a word about one of your members of staff. Can we come in?'

The woman on the other side tutted loudly. 'If you must.'

She opened the door wide enough for them to step through. Josh went first. The smell of stale beer lingered in the air, along with the aroma of fried onion rings and burgers, which made his stomach groan. His type of food: hot, greasy and fried. The woman, who wasn't as old as he'd first thought, sought shelter behind the bar, putting some distance between them. He looked around; it was actually much nicer inside than he'd imagined. It was modern and looked as if it had recently been refurbished.

'It's nice in here. I've never been in before.'

'It looks like a dump from the outside, but it won't when the lazy-arse painting contractor finally turns up to give it a coat of paint.'

'Are you not busy on a Friday? I would have thought it was a good day for trade.'

She shrugged. 'In the summer yes, not so much this time of year. The owner likes to go out with his mates on a Friday. He won't pay for extra staff when it's quiet, so he'd rather shut the pub and open up later.'

'Have you worked here long?'

'Long enough. What is this, twenty questions? What do you want?'

Sam spoke. 'I'm DC Thomas and he's DS Walker from Kendal CID. We need to speak to you about Julia Bach; when was the last time you saw her?'

The woman sighed. 'I'm Andrea Smile.' Josh supressed a smirk; Smile was quite the surname for someone with such a sour-looking face. She pointed at the bar stools, and they both sat down. 'I couldn't say for definite, but around a fortnight ago. Has she filed a complaint?'

Sam answered. 'About what?'

'About our idiot of an employer, that's what.' She looked around as if to make sure there was no one else with them then continued. 'He's okay, most of the time. But he's also an arrogant pig. He had a bit of a thing for Julia, but she wasn't interested in him at all. Men aren't her type, if you get my drift.'

Josh was a little bit slower on the uptake, so Sam stepped in with the next question.

'Do you know where she went? We're trying to locate her.'

Andrea shook her head. 'I thought she'd had enough and left. We spoke a little but she didn't speak very good English. Her roommate was better friends with her, she would know.'

'Is she here?'

'No, it's her day off. She disappears to her boyfriend's; he works at a hotel in Newby Bridge.'

Josh wondered if the person they'd pulled out of the lake was Julia and felt a chill run down his spine.

'Can you tell me your boss's name and phone number? We need to speak to him. Also, the name of the hotel in Newby Bridge so we can go and find Julia's roommate?'

'Stacey Jefferson is her roommate, and her boyfriend is called Jack. He works at The Swan. Our esteemed employer is Marcus Johnson.' She walked over to the cash register and opened a black book next to it. Picking up an orange sticky note, she wrote his mobile number down then passed it to Josh.

'One last thing: on the missing person's report Stacey submitted she said that Julia had been talking about going home to Poland; do you have her home address?'

'I don't. Marcus keeps all the employee files locked up in his office. You'll have to speak to him.'

'Stacey also said that Julia had packed her suitcase and has never come back for it; do you know where it is?'

'Yes, it's in the storeroom. I'll go and get it for you. Marcus said if Julia wasn't coming back to clean out her stuff from the room and put it all in storage… he said he'd give her a month and if she didn't collect it, he was chucking it into the skip out the back.'

She disappeared, and Josh asked Sam, 'What do you think?'

'All a bit suspicious really, isn't it? We need to speak to Marcus and find out what the situation was, how much he liked her and whether he believes she upped and left out of the blue.'

They heard Andrea before she came back into sight, the wheels on the suitcase clattering along the uneven slate flooring. She came into the bar area dragging the case behind and with a small box tucked under her arm.

'This is everything that Julia left behind; at least he can't moan her stuff is taking up valuable space. You might as well take it with you. It's a bit strange, I'm sure Stacey said her passport is in there. She can't leave the country without it, surely; she'd want to collect that and her purse. But there is nothing as funny as folk. You wouldn't believe what guests leave behind: brand-new walking boots because they have a bit of mud on them, North Face jackets galore, make-up, perfume. It never fails to amaze me.'

Josh took the box from her, Sam the case.

'Thank you, if we need anything else we'll be in touch.'

He was hoping that if she'd left behind her passport, she'd definitely have left a hairbrush or toothbrush, too, something they could extract DNA from to help identify her. He didn't think things were looking hopeful they would find Julia alive. They loaded the stuff into the back of the car and headed back to the station, where he would hand the box and case over to the duty CSI, who could then go through it and send off the relevant stuff to the forensic science service labs. Hopefully, they'd have a positive ID for their Jane Doe soon.

CHAPTER THIRTY-ONE

Beth had one more post-mortem to conduct before the end of the day. It wasn't a full forensic, thankfully, but the sudden death of a seventy-nine-year-old man with a known history of heart disease. She tried desperately to clear her head and concentrate, but every bone in her body was screaming to her it was no coincidence that the bodies of the two girls in the lake HAD showed up at the same time, and both with similar material found under their fingernails. But with no supporting evidence so far, it was impossible to say for sure, not unless the toxicology reports came back for both women showing high levels of drugs in their system, which could explain their sudden desire to go into the unforgiving, bitterly cold water of Lake Windermere. She opened up a new Word document and began to type.

Victims
Both female
Both blonde
Paint chips found under fingernails.

She needed a sample of the paint from *The Tequila Sunrise* and if Josh and his team couldn't get it to her soon, then she had no other option but to go herself. She'd be damned if she just sat back and let another woman turn up floating in the lake. She finished her cold mug of tea and decided to take an evidence kit home with her. If it wasn't too late by the time she was done with the old man on her table, she was going to do a detour to the marina. Standing up, she went back into the mortuary where Abe was in the process of setting up.

'I honestly don't know what I'd do without you, Abe. You spoil me.'

He laughed. 'The feeling is kind of mutual, Doc, you're pretty good to me too.'

'Why don't you and Rosie come around to mine next time we're both not on call? It would be lovely to spend some time with the pair of you, especially when we're not hovering over a dead body. I could cook you both a meal and you could stop over. A few glasses of wine and a night away, how does that sound?'

'Wonderful, we don't get out of Barrow very much. Rosie loves the Lake District and she'd adore your house. I've told her all about it.'

'That's settled then.'

He grinned at her and she grinned back. Beth couldn't remember the last time she'd invited anyone over for drinks and dinner. It felt good, it felt normal. She caught a glimpse of her life as it used to be before she turned into a recluse for seven years and became scared of her own shadow. Thank God she'd come out of the other side of that. Josh had a lot to do with it. He'd been there for her through everything, and she couldn't believe how lucky she was he felt the same way about her. Sometimes nightmares did have happy endings; despite her years of living in fear there was the chance to live a normal life and this time she was grasping it with both hands and never letting go. Now there was just the matter of the body in front of her to examine and then she would do some digging of her own.

*

Two hours later she snapped off the gloves, relieved it had been a straightforward post-mortem, because she couldn't push thoughts of the two drowned girls out of her mind.

She needed to know if there was any news or results. Even though everything of forensic value had been fast-tracked it could still take days, more likely weeks to be processed and the results to come back. Checking her phone, there were no messages or voicemails. She then checked her emails in case Josh had decided to send the information about the paint on the boat over that way. Nothing. At least, not since this morning. It was no good, she was going to have to go to the marina on her way home. There was no way she'd be able to settle at home without knowing the simplest of answers. The police did their best with limited resources and complicated processes, but sometimes it stopped them from being able to act fast or follow their noses the way she could.

Wondering how many drownings had occurred over the years, she brought up Google and typed 'Lake Windermere drowning' into the search bar and waited for it to load. As numerous pages of news articles fed through, one thing which struck her was the large number of male drownings compared to female. All of them were tragic, but it struck her as odd that it had been such a long time since a woman had been pulled out of the water. Reading through the articles, she made scant notes on a couple, not sure what she was expecting or looking for. After an hour or so of trawling, frustrated, she rang Josh hoping he'd have something for her, some piece of information to help put her troubled mind at rest.

CHAPTER THIRTY-TWO

Josh was mid-shop in Asda when his phone began to ring. He saw Beth's number and instantly felt a wave of guilt wash over him.

'What's up?'

'I finished the PM on the girl a couple of hours ago. I left you a message; I found a couple of interesting things. Where are you?'

The noise of the tannoy filled the air to announce that there was a Mini Cooper in the car park with its lights still on. He slapped his palm to his head when he realised it was his.

'Asda, just getting a few bits. Bugger, I've left my lights on; they've just announced it to the world. Do you need anything?'

'I'm good, thanks. There's plenty in, you didn't need to bother.'

Tell her, Josh, the voice whispered in his ear, but he couldn't. 'So what did you find?'

'I'd rather tell you in person, can you come down here?'

'Not really.' His voice came out much sharper than he intended. 'I've got a lot on.'

'Oh, okay. So, I managed to de-glove her left hand and take some fingerprints which I've sent to the identification bureau. Underneath two of them were traces of what look like paint chips.'

He stood still, staring at the ready meals and wondering if Jodie would eat them. 'What kind of paint chips?'

'Hard to say one hundred per cent until they've been analysed, but they weren't too dissimilar to the one I retrieved from underneath Leah Burton's nail. It could put them both in the same area when they went into the water, or mean they came off the same boat. We need a sample from the boat Leah was on before she went into the water to compare. Do you think the owner will give permission?'

Josh thought about his meeting with James Marshall that morning. 'Well, I wouldn't like to say no.'

'But?'

'He's a bit of an ass.'

Beth chuckled down the phone, the rare and lovely sound making Josh feel even worse about not being upfront about Jodie.

'Can't you get a search warrant or something?'

'On what grounds? As far as we're concerned there's nothing suspicious. Unless you found any injuries or the post-mortem showed neither of them died in the lake.'

'Nothing outstanding; the scrapes and bruises on both bodies are consistent with where they were found. Both post-mortems showed that the victims died from drowning and the transient hypervolemia – the amount of water absorbed into the bloodstream – confirms this. They both drowned in fresh water. I completed a full post-mortem which showed no evidence of trauma. Toxicology won't be back for some time but I have to say that the manner of death is classified as accidental.'

'But?'

'I don't know, Josh, I get the feeling something isn't right. I just don't have any evidence to prove otherwise.'

He let out a sigh. 'I hear you. I'm not that happy myself that two women have been pulled out of the lake. We think we have a possible ID for her, if it's who we think she is. She's a hotel worker who travelled from Poland to work here. That doesn't sit very well with me, but like you have said there is no evidence to support foul play.'

It was Beth's turn to sigh. 'It's a bit of a coincidence though, isn't it?'

Another call came through; he looked at the number and felt even worse. 'Beth, I have another caller on the line. Sorry, I'll have to go. See you later.'

Beth ended the call from her end, not even questioning who it was calling, and he knew she was pissed off with him. He'd make it up to her.

'Josh, sorry to bother you, it's Jodie. Do you think you could pick me up when you have the time? I've told them you're going to be checking in on me and they said I could come home.'

'Of course, I'll be there as soon as I can.'

He ended the call and finished his shop, piling all sorts of food into the trolley. If she didn't like it, she could always donate it to the food bank.

CHAPTER THIRTY-THREE

Beth parked her car. It was later than she'd hoped and much darker. The marina was lit up well though, which was some comfort on this rainy night. As droplets pounded the windscreen of her car, she wondered if she should shelve this crazy idea, wait until tomorrow or at least when it was daylight. *What would Scarpetta do?* she asked herself silently. Kay Scarpetta was a fictional forensic pathologist Beth loved to read about, and a bloody good one. Scarpetta wouldn't wimp out at a bit of rain.

Throwing open the car door, she got out and was immediately blown to one side by a strong gust of wind. She grabbed the evidence sample kit and pushed it deep into her coat pocket. Tugging on a woollen hat and zipping her coat up to her chin, she walked into the wind towards the water's edge hoping the boat was still there.

As she got onto the lakeside she saw *The Tequila Sunrise* bobbing in the water with a light on below deck. The lake was choppy and the moored boats were lurching with the force of the wind and the water. Behind her, even the pub was closed – not much cause for business in weather like this. She felt a chill just looking into the inky waters of the lake. Hurrying to get to the boat, her head bent against the driving rain, she almost ran straight into the sodden, bedraggled man. A small scream escaped her lips. 'Oh, gosh. I'm sorry, I didn't see you.'

He grunted a reply at her, then pushed past her walking away from the marina towards the car park. The pungent smell of damp clothes that haven't been washed in forever assaulted her nostrils. She turned to look at him once more, catching the sight of the back of him as he disappeared. He didn't look as if he owned a boat. Christ, he didn't look as if he owned a tent. She couldn't help wondering who he was and what he was doing down here. She'd mention it to Josh, see if he knew who he was and why he'd be down here in this weather. For a moment she felt awful, judgemental. Would she have questioned him being down here if he'd been smelling of expensive aftershave and wearing a Berghaus jacket? She knew that she wouldn't, nobody would. She turned back towards the boats, her racing heart beginning to slow down. Whoever he was he'd given her a fright.

The metal jetties that ran between the rows of boats were slick with rain. She was going to have to tread carefully or she could slip and end up in the water. The very thought gave her palpitations, her nightmares and memories of the last time she'd ended up in it fighting their way to break out of the box she'd hidden them in. She shook her head – this was different; she was here to do a job, someone had to find out what had happened to those two women. She knew that Josh was only doing his job as well by playing it safe, waiting for sufficient evidence and not taking it any further. There wasn't enough evidence to suggest any foul play, but it didn't mean that there wasn't.

Carefully she stepped down onto the jetty and walked towards the boat. It rocked under the weight of her, but she forced herself to carry on. It would only take a moment to get a sample and she could be back in the car with the heating on. When she reached the boat she realised it was a little further away from the jetty than she'd realised. Taking out a torch, she shone it at the side of the boat, to see if there was anywhere she could reach to scrape a good sample. And then it struck her: the boat wasn't wood, it was fibreglass. The paint chip couldn't have come from it. Her heart sank; she had been so sure she was onto something. She stood on the edge of the jetty, her arms folded across her chest, feet apart trying to keep herself from being blown into the water as she looked around at the other boats nearby. They were all fibreglass, varnish or sleek white plastic. She felt all determination drain away from her. Where did those flakes of paint come from?

As she turned to walk back to the safety of the lakeside, she saw movement from behind *The Tequila Sunrise*. She peered round the boat to see a small wooden rowing boat tethered to a buoy not too far away from it. It was a dark colour; the paint flakes had been dark. Shining her torch around, she couldn't see any others that were similar in this part of the marina.

Walking to the very end of the jetty she wondered how she was going to get to it and realised there was a ladder on the side of the bigger boat in front of her. If she got onto that one, she could climb down the ladder to reach the rowing boat, get her sample and then go home for a hot shower and huge glass of wine. All she had to do was to get onto the boat. It was simple, but she was so cold now it was hard to feel her fingers. She knew she should come back tomorrow when the sun was up and the rain had passed, but what if the rowboat had gone? Before she could talk herself out of it, she was leaning over and climbing up the ladder on the side of the large boat closest to it. Safely on deck, she breathed out a sigh of relief that she hadn't slipped and gone into the water. Now all she had to do was to climb down the other side of the boat, lean over and scrape a bit of paint off and get the hell back to her car. It was reckless and dangerous, she knew, yet here she was about to ignore all her own advice and carry on.

She took the small, plastic pot out of her pocket and unscrewed the lid. If she climbed down and leant across all she had to do was to scrape it along the side of the boat. Hopefully, she'd get a big enough sample of the paint to send off to the lab for a comparison. Hanging onto the metal ladder with one hand in an iron grip, she reached out as far as she could and ran the small pot against the dinghy.

'What the fuck are you doing?'

The voice was loud and angry, distorted in the wind. Cold fear filled her insides.

'Get up here now, you're going to kill yourself.'

Beth pulled herself up, trying to push the sample pot into her pocket. 'Sorry, I'm coming up now.'

A strong gust of wind blew her off balance and she felt her grip loosen on the slippery metal rung she'd been clinging on to. A scream escaped her lips as she fell, clawing to get a hold of the ladder, but her fingers were too cold and the metal was too wet. She fell towards the water and was plunged into the black depths of the lake. It was beyond freezing. So cold it took her breath away and choked her scream. Her arms and legs splashed wildly, propelling herself back to the surface, but her heavy coat dragged her back down.

For a moment she wondered if she was going to die. Then a strong hand gripped the back of her coat and she felt herself being pulled up above the water. One more heave and she was by the ladder again.

'You have to hold on, I can't lift you any higher,' the voice bellowed at her. She did as she was told, her teeth chattering. The man rearranged his grip and dragged her up as far as he could. She did her best to climb back up but her limbs were numb and useless. When she was almost near the top, he put his arms under her armpits and pulled her onto the deck. She stared up in shock at the face staring down at her.

'You bloody idiot, you could have drowned. Do you know how dangerous it is? If I hadn't come out on deck…' He ran his hands through his dripping hair.

Beth was panting for every breath, the cold air stinging her lungs. Her whole body began to shake with the cold as she coughed up mouthfuls of the water. The man held out his hand for the second time, and she took it, knowing it wouldn't be long before hypothermia set in if she didn't get out of the cold. Tugging her to her feet, he pointed to the step that led below deck.

'It's warm down there and you can get those sodden clothes off, have a warm shower; I'll make you a cup of tea. You need to warm your body temperature up.'

'Thank you,' she managed.

He smiled at her. 'Lady, I don't know who you are or what the hell you were doing, but I've already had one guest on my boat die this week, I'm not having another. After you've had a shower I want to know who you are and what the hell you were doing, deal?'

She nodded then followed him downstairs.

'The shower cools down after a few minutes, but it should be enough to warm you up. I have some spare clean clothes that I'll leave outside the door for you.'

She stepped inside, closing the door behind her. Quickly she stripped off her soaking wet clothes and left them in a pile in front of the door so it would be difficult to open. A part of her was glad she'd left her phone in the car. She turned on the shower and stepped under the spray, relieved to be able to warm herself up. He was right, no sooner had she began to thaw out than the water turned cold. She stepped out, and began to dry herself with a luxurious, soft towel. Wrapping another around her head, she kicked her sodden clothes to one side and opened the door to find a set of brand-new Nike joggers and a matching sweatshirt neatly folded on the floor. Grabbing them she dressed quickly, putting the wet clothes into the shower tray and mopping the floor with a hand towel. She looked in the small mirror and shook her head. *You're a bloody idiot. You could have died and no one would have known where you were until your body washed up.*

She walked into the galley kitchen to find the man who had rescued her pouring boiling water into a teapot. He turned to her, pointing at the bench underneath the table.

'Take a seat. You look a bit more human.'

'Thank you.' She sat down as he carried a tray over with a china teapot, two mugs, sugar, milk and some chocolate biscuits. Pouring out two mugs of tea, he passed her one and she added milk as well as a heaped teaspoon of sugar. Her hands were still shaking and she knew it was a combination of the cold, and the realisation that she'd had a very close call.

'So, what do I call you?'

'I'm James, this is my boat. You are very lucky. I'd come to make sure she was battened down and secure for the night. Would you care to tell me what you were doing?'

Beth wondered if she should lie, and then decided she couldn't. He deserved the truth; he'd risked his own life to save hers. A killer wouldn't do that, would they?

'I'm Beth Adams, Forensic Pathologist. I'm investigating the drowning of Leah Burton and an unknown female that washed up yesterday evening.'

'Right. But that doesn't explain what you were doing hanging off the side of my boat in a storm.' He smiled at her.

'I found trace evidence on both bodies and thought maybe it had come off this boat, but when I got here I realised it couldn't have. I saw the rowing boat attached to the back and thought maybe it had come from that. Thank you for saving me. I was very stupid. I really appreciate what you've done for me.'

She picked up the mug, blew the hot tea and began to sip it.

He nodded, and then seemed to realise what she'd said. 'There's another body? I didn't know. I mean, how could I? I haven't had anything to do with either of them, if that's what you're wondering. I already had two coppers here this afternoon questioning me.'

Josh would be furious with her when she told him what she'd done. Maybe she wouldn't tell him. He didn't need to know how reckless she'd been, did he? Robert's face flashed into her mind. Was she being so careless because, deep down, his death was affecting her more than she cared to admit? He'd messed with her head all these years; was she crazy to think it would stop now he was dead?

CHAPTER THIRTY-FOUR

Jodie had smiled so brightly at the sight of Josh walking onto the ward that a pang of guilt flashed through him. He felt sorry for her. He would do right by her, help her, stand by her; but he didn't love her. He hadn't loved her for a long time, and he desperately hoped she wasn't thinking they could carry on where they'd left off, because they couldn't. He didn't have the heart to upset her right now though, not when she was this frail and the sight of him made her look this happy.

He'd pushed her in a wheelchair all the way down to the main entrance, then went to get the car. Then he'd helped her in and driven her home, where they were now in the middle of putting the shopping away. In the past, he'd leave her to do this, but she looked exhausted, almost crushed under the weight of a large paper bag full of her medications on her lap. It would take a pharmacist to work all of them out – no wonder she'd almost overdosed herself.

It was late, and he hadn't heard from Beth. He'd rung several times to speak to her and tell her where he was, but she hadn't answered and he figured she was either working late or had fallen asleep. She didn't go out much, but she was better than she had been in the past. He didn't leave a message: what could he say? *Sorry, I'll be late, I'm just helping my wife put the shopping away.* He pushed away the thought and zoned back into what Jodie was saying to him.

'—So, anyway, I told them unless they could actually find me a wig that looks natural it didn't matter. I mean it's winter, I'd rather wear a hat.'

He stared at her, not having a clue what she was talking about and nodded.

'Does Beth know where you are?' she said suddenly.

'No, I didn't tell her.'

'Why? It's not as if you're doing anything wrong, is it? You're just helping me out. I don't think she'll mind.'

Josh couldn't answer because he didn't know if she would or not. He knew he didn't want to hurt her and this – he looked down at the frozen lasagne he was holding – this might hurt her a lot. She didn't deserve that after everything she'd been through. 'I haven't had chance; we've both been very busy at work. I didn't even see her last night. I'll tell her when I go home.'

Jodie nodded and began to walk towards the stairs. 'I need the toilet and then I need to lie down. Those tablets wipe me out. I have no energy. Can you manage to finish off?'

Once upon a time he would have taken that as her being sarcastic, but he looked at her and realised it was a genuine question.

'Yeah, I can.'

She began to climb the stairs in a slow shuffle, and he turned away. She reminded him more of her elderly gran than the thirty-five-year-old who had been his wife. Life was shit at times…

There was a loud thump and a muffled cry from upstairs. Josh dropped the jar of mayonnaise he was putting away, shattering it into a thousand pieces all over the tiled floor as he ran to find Jodie collapsed on the floor at the top of the stairs. He took them two at a time, and when he reached her, she was curled up in a ball, sobbing.

'Are you hurt, what happened?'

She shook her head. 'My stupid knee gave way, I'm fine.'

'You don't sound fine.'

She smiled. 'I'm crying because I'm pissed off, Josh. I'm sick of feeling like this.'

He helped her to her feet. Gently taking hold of her elbow, he guided her into the bathroom, where he left her and waited outside on the landing for her. What was he supposed to do? He knew this wasn't right. It wasn't his responsibility; they weren't a married couple any more. Yet, he could no longer leave her like this than he could any other friend. Despite their differences, she deserved more. He felt a stab of guilt as his mind whispered: *what about Beth? She deserves more too.*

CHAPTER THIRTY-FIVE

James passed Beth a pair of rubber boots. 'Thank you, I'll return these, and your clothes. I really am very grateful.' She slipped them on and stood up; her frozen hands and toes had finally thawed out. The magnitude of how stupid she'd been was weighing heavy on her shoulders.

'Like I told those detectives earlier, if you have anything you need to speak to me about I'd appreciate it if you made an appointment with me. Next time I might not be around if you decide to do your own stunts. I don't mean to rub it in or anything, but that really was a crazy thing to do. Aren't you supposed to work on the bodies in the mortuary? Are the police that hard up for cash they have you out doing their job as well?'

She smiled. 'I was investigating to satisfy my own questions. I don't think I have anything further to ask you.'

He nodded, passed her a black bin liner containing her sodden clothing and followed her as she made her way back up onto the deck. Beth didn't know if he was making sure she got off his boat, or whether he was ensuring she didn't fall overboard. The wind was still blowing, but the rain had eased off to a steady drizzle. She moved cautiously – one dip into the lake was enough for one evening. He took the bag from her to allow her to climb off the boat using two hands, and once she was safely on the jetty he passed it back to her, then climbed over himself to walk with her along the jetty and back to where her car was parked. He left her to go to the private car park for boat owners, and she turned away, mortified that her mediocre investigating had almost cost her her life.

Inside the car she turned the heaters on full and recoiled at the initial blast of cold air that was expelled through them. She drove in silence, not in the mood for anything, except maybe a glass of wine and for Josh to wrap his arms around her.

*

As she drove in through the automatic gates her heart sank once more; Josh was late home again. When she'd spoken with him he was in the supermarket. Surely he hadn't gone back to work with a car full of shopping? Letting herself in to the house, she went straight into her open-plan kitchen, took a bottle of wine from the fridge and poured herself a large glass which she drank almost in one go. Then she refilled it.

Realising she'd left her phone in the car, she went outside to retrieve it and the bag of clothing. She went inside and wondered if she'd managed to lose the sample that had almost cost her her life. Ripping open the sack, she found her waterlogged coat and pushed her hand into the pocket. A small gasp of joy escaped her lips as her fingers curled around the small plastic evidence jar. For the first time since she'd fallen into the water, she smiled. Taking it to one side, she lifted it to the light. There wasn't much inside it, the smallest curl of paint, but hopefully it would be enough for a comparison. She would send it off to the lab first thing tomorrow, fast-tracked.

Taking it into the kitchen, she put the jar into her handbag which she'd left on one of the bar stools. Now if only Josh would come home soon everything would be better. She wanted to lie next to him and absorb every ounce of his body heat. She looked at her phone to see there were three missed calls from him. She rang him back, but it went to voicemail. They were like passing ships in the night and it was driving her mad. Taking her wine and a family-sized bag of salt and vinegar crisps, she went up to bed, to watch television until he came home.

As she sat cross-legged on the bed in her fleecy pyjamas watching *Bridesmaids* for the tenth time, she tried not to think about James Marshall. He didn't seem like a killer to her; he had saved her life, there was no doubt about it. Maybe those women had really drowned because of their own stupidity; hadn't she just proved to herself how easily it could happen – and she'd been sober. They knew from eyewitness reports that Leah Burton had consumed a large amount of alcohol while on the boat. Was she being overly cautious and finding suspicious motives when there were none? It was possible. She didn't know what to think.

Finishing the last of the wine, she stood up and brushed the crisp crumbs off herself and the bed. Leaving the television on because she couldn't bear to lie in the dark, in silence, she lay down and closed her eyes. The room began to swim slightly and she threw the duvet back and put one foot onto the floor as if to anchor herself. A packet of crisps and a full bottle of wine was probably not the best choice for her evening meal, although she could count the grapes in the wine as part of her five a day. Her stomach lurched and she just made it to the bathroom before she threw up all over the side of the toilet, giving off the smell of wine and the crisps mixed with the underlying earthy smell of the water from the lake she'd swallowed. She retched again, memories of swallowing a huge mouthful of the water when she'd plunged into the water making her stomach churn. When she could only dry-heave she stood up, washed her face then cupped her hands and drank as much water as she could stomach. Her head was now pounding and all she wanted to do was lie down and go to sleep, black out and forget about what had happened.

Back in bed, this time the room stayed still. She closed her eyes and began to count. Before she'd managed to get to thirty, she let out a gentle snore and the world went blank.

CHAPTER THIRTY-SIX

When Beth opened her eyes she realised the house was suddenly quiet and still. It was still dark but the howling wind and lashing rain had died down. The bed was empty beside her and she felt an overwhelming sense of loneliness engulf her. She climbed out of bed in search of ice cold water and some painkillers to numb the throbbing inside her head. As she made her way downstairs, she hoped to find Josh sprawled out on the sofa; occasionally if he was home too late he'd sleep there, not wanting to disturb her. She peered into the lounge. It was empty. Maybe she should get a dog; at least it could keep her company on the nights Josh wasn't around. She hated how needy she was getting. She never used to be this way. How things change.

After swallowing two paracetamol along with a large glass of water, she went back to bed. It niggled her that he was working all night even though both the girls' deaths were filed as 'accidental'. She lay down in bed, checked her phone again then decided to ring him back. About to end the call, his voice suddenly whispered down the line.

'Hi.'

This completely threw her.

'Morning, just checking you're okay?'

'I'm good thanks, are you?'

'Where are you, Josh?'

There was a slight pause. 'I'm still at work, helping with a case in Barrow.'

For the first time since they'd been together, she didn't believe him. For one thing, he usually told her exactly what he was working on, no names, but they'd discuss cases over dinner most nights. He was being secretive; this wasn't like him and she didn't like it. It also didn't sound as if he was in a police station. It was far too quiet.

'I'll be home soon, you get some sleep.'

'Okay, bye.' About to end the call, she heard a woman coughing in the background and a sharp, shooting pain shot through her heart. Dropping the phone on the bedside table, she felt hot tears sting her eyes as her mind ran through a list of names of the women he worked with. Josh and Sam worked together a lot, but she was married with kids and Beth got the impression from her she was happy with her home life. No, she didn't think it would be her. There were plenty of young female officers for him to choose from though. If Josh was cheating on her she knew it would destroy every ounce of her faith in humanity; she had come so far and knew that it would send her reeling back into her shell and that existence of never being able to trust another human being again.

She didn't know she was properly crying until she realised her pillow was wet. Her fingers reached up to wipe the tears from her eyes, then moved up to the side of her forehead where the scar was: her personal reminder that life was precious and could be taken away in the blink of an eye. The tips of her fingers rubbed against it, tracing the puckered pink line. A voice whispered inside her head: *you're wrong about this, Beth, completely wrong. There's no way he would cheat on you. He would tell you to your face if he wasn't in love with you.* She wanted to agree with it one hundred per cent, but something was telling her it was wrong. Something was going on, and she needed to find out what.

CHAPTER THIRTY-SEVEN

Beth lay in bed; it was Saturday, her day off and technically she wasn't on call. She stretched out thinking she would love nothing more than to stay in bed. If Josh were here then she definitely would have. It was a rare treat for them both to be off on the same day. She tried hard to push the fluttering feeling inside her chest away, to stop those tiny wings of fear from taking over. She was being irrational. If he had worked all night at the station then it was likely Sam or other colleagues would be there with him. Maybe that was why he was whispering. Where else could he be? As long as she'd known him, and despite being unhappily married to Jodie, he'd never strayed. Occasionally he'd stopped over at hers when things got bad at home, but it was rare, and he'd always slept on the sofa or the guest room depending upon how drunk he was and if he'd been able to navigate the stairs. The thought hit her hard: Jodie. What if he'd decided to go back to her, give her another chance? She sat up and swung her legs out of the bed. The only way she would know was if she drove past their house.

Ten minutes later, wearing no make-up and her hair in a short ponytail, she left her house, unable to eat anything because of the sense of dread she was feeling. On the drive to Josh's old house she told herself over and over again she was being ridiculous. Reaching the outskirts of the town, she realised she would be passing the police station. It was better to check the car park which surrounded it out first; he was more likely to be there, or his car was. If she saw it parked up, she'd drive past and go to McDonald's to buy them both breakfast, dropping it off for him on the way back.

As she drove down the small road which opened onto the station and surrounding car parks, she couldn't spot his Mini. Just to be sure she did a loop of the whole area, checking out all the nooks and crannies where a car could be parked to double-check. Her heart was beating double time and she questioned why she was doing this to herself; why was she being so suspicious? She didn't know, never pegging herself as needy, but perhaps a little insecure. Okay, a lot insecure, but only because of her past. Who wouldn't be after having almost died twice at the hands of the same killer? Then last night she had foolishly put herself in the most dangerous situation possible and could have died again. *How many lives do you have, Beth Adams?* she whispered to herself.

Driving along the one-way system to get to the street where Josh used to live with Jodie was slow as morning traffic was starting to build, and she wished she'd thought of this earlier. All she wanted to do was to get this over with. *What are you going to do if his car is there?* she asked herself. She couldn't answer because, truthfully, she had no idea.

Finally, the turning for the street of terraced houses loomed in the distance; a part of her wanted to drive past and not even turn her head in that direction. Ignorance was sometimes bliss; it had served her well for the last seven years of her life. With trembling hands, she indicated and turned into the street, not quite sure what number his house was. She knew it was three quarters of the way down, but before she was even halfway down her heart lurched at the sight of Josh's familiar racing green Mini. Bile rose up her throat, the bitter taste lingering there.

Having no option but to continue, she drove towards it. She didn't want to look at the house, but her eyes glanced sideways, and she saw everything she needed to confirm her worst fear: Josh was standing with his back to the window, his tousled hair sticking up like it did every morning when he woke up beside her. Her vision blurred as tears filled her eyes and she had to blink several times to dispel them – she wouldn't cry over him. She'd be damned if she let herself cry over any man. Slamming her foot down, she drove to a small café she knew nearby and used to favour when she was on her own – before Josh came into her life as more than her good friend. Parking nearby, she dabbed her eyes with a tissue, grabbed her purse and crossed the road.

Riverbank Coffee's industrial décor and clean white walls were exactly to her taste. The food was good, the coffee even better. It was empty inside; she placed her order then went and sat at a table that faced out onto the fast-flowing water of the River Kent. She was glad the owner wasn't in yet; she didn't feel up to polite conversation. As she stared at the swollen banks of the river, she felt her eyes begin to well up.

'Here you go.'

The voice startled her. She smiled at the girl, who didn't look much older than sixteen. 'Thank you, that smells divine.'

Blushing, the girl nodded then disappeared out the back leaving her alone. She stirred the foam and licked the spoon, then picking up the large cup, she blew and sipped. It tasted as good as it smelled: liquid heaven. She shivered as the block of ice which had begun to thaw from around her heart frosted over again. She'd spent seven years protecting herself from people, not trusting anyone. She didn't know what she was going to do about Josh, but she wouldn't be taken for a fool; she'd survived on her own long enough without him. She could do it again. Pain shot through her heart and silent tears began to fall. She didn't blink them away this time; she let them flow. The girl came out from the back room, took one look at her and hurried back inside leaving her to sip her coffee and cry.

CHAPTER THIRTY-EIGHT

Josh walked into the station, knowing he should really go to see Beth. He owed her an explanation. Her voice had been strained when he'd spoken to her, but Paton had phoned to say they'd had a definite match from the prints that Beth had taken from the body. It didn't matter that it was Saturday; the station was still full of officers, PCSOs and staff.

He didn't blame the PCSOs for hanging around: the weather was dire, the sky was full of big, grey rainclouds; he wouldn't want to be out on foot patrol either. He took the steps up to the first-floor office two at a time, eager to get the second girl's identity confirmed. Then he would phone the mortuary and let whoever was on call know so they could release her body for burial. He thought about what Beth had said, that she wasn't happy but couldn't find anything that looked suspicious apart from the trace evidence under both victims' nails.

Paton and Sykes were already in the office when he entered.

'Morning, you two. Good news on the ID; at least we can inform her family.'

Sykes nodded. 'Yeah, it is. Though it's not the knock on the door you expect. It must be worrying enough that your daughter is leaving to go and live in another country. It's every parent's worst fear.'

'What is?'

'That they'll never come home.'

He stared at her; she was right. He didn't have kids, so he never really thought about the other side of it. To him it was a job that needed to be done. He very rarely let himself get emotional. The last murders he'd dealt with had definitely got to him, but he wouldn't let that happen again. He turned the kettle on and spooned coffee into three mugs. Carrying the drinks over, he sat opposite Paton and Sykes. 'Dr Adams isn't happy with the circumstances.'

Paton sipped his coffee. 'I can understand that, it does seem a bit odd.'

'Odd, but not uncommon. I guess the fact that neither of them is local is a bit strange.'

Sykes shrugged. 'Then investigate some more. We're not exactly rushed off our feet here.'

He thought about it; on the surface it should be straightforward, but the fact that it was ringing alarm bells with almost everyone he talked to unsettled him.

'You're right, I think we should. We can inform the next of kin, but I don't want the bodies released until I'm completely satisfied both deaths were accidental.'

Sykes clapped her hands. 'See, that wasn't hard.'

'I would have made that decision anyway.'

'You just needed a shove in the right direction.'

Josh decided that yes, it was his duty to follow through and make sure that every line of enquiry had been followed up.

'Paton, can you do me some intelligence checks? I want to know if there are any previous reports by either Burton or Bach. One of Bach's co-workers said she knew the girl was fed up of her employer making advances towards her.' He looked down as he flipped through his pocket notebook. 'Marcus Johnson. Can you also do some background checks on him, please?'

Paton was scribbling a list of the names Josh had given him on a scrap of paper, his head nodding. Sam slipped in through the rear office door, taking a seat at the desk she favoured. She didn't take her coat off, just logged onto the computer and waited for it to load.

'I need to know if there is any history of complaints from the local Polish community about any incidents concerning females; let's cover all bases. We will also chase up the roommate who reported Julia missing.'

He looked at Sam; since working so closely together on the last investigation he automatically chose her to pair up with. He didn't think it was favouritism, not really. If Sykes or Paton had drawn the short straw that fateful day not that long ago it would have been one of them. He liked how they worked together; it was easy. No having to make polite, strained conversation and she wasn't afraid to tell him when he was wrong. He wasn't sure if the others would be so forthcoming, and besides, he knew he could trust her and valued her opinion. If she disliked being pulled out of the office to accompany him, she never complained. He thought they made a pretty good team, although maybe he should check with her that she didn't mind. Somehow, he didn't think she'd put up with him if she didn't have to.

'Is that okay with you? Do you have anything else on that's more pressing?'

'Not really, it's fine by me.'

He drained the last of his coffee, pushing down his guilt about Beth and Jodie so he could concentrate on work. At least he was helping Beth by following up on these enquiries. He was hopeful it might go some way to making up for the mess he was in.

Sam was quiet in the car, which suited him fine. He wasn't really in the chatting mood either, but he thought maybe he should check she was okay.

'Is everything all right?'

She didn't even look at him. 'Yes, thanks. Well apart from another huge argument with my daughter about this stupid bloody party tonight.'

'It's tonight? I didn't realise it was that soon. She's still adamant she's going then?'

'More than ever since I told her I'd rather she didn't.'

He shook his head. 'Kids, eh, who'd have them?'

This made her laugh.

'Why don't you go as well? Gatecrash the party and hide in the toilet all night, or something.'

'Josh, it's on *The Tequila*. It's big, but not that big. She'd see me or wonder who was hogging the toilet all night. It would cause a riot. I suppose we could hire a boat and follow it, you know, just to make sure nothing bad happens. Are you busy later?'

He looked at her in wide-eyed horror, and she laughed so loud it made him jump.

'You're so gullible, I'm joking.'

'You had me there, very funny.'

But she'd planted an idea in his mind. It might not be a bad call. Maybe they could see if anyone was on duty who used the police boat, or at least ask the lake wardens to keep a close eye on *The Tequila* to make sure there were no more accidents. He had no idea who to contact, but decided to swing by the office at Ferry Nab on their way back. It would make Sam feel better, and Beth would appreciate the fact that he was taking her concerns seriously.

Satisfied with his plan, he dialled the number from the sticky note with Stacey Jefferson's phone number on, relieved when she answered, because they were almost at The Swan Hotel in Newby Bridge. She agreed to meet them in the car park, and that suited him fine; at least he wouldn't have to go inside another bar. Lately all his job seemed to entail was speaking to hotel workers and bar staff.

He parked the car, but left the engine running.

A tap on the window surprised him; he hadn't noticed anyone here. He pressed the button.

'Stacey?'

She nodded.

'I'm Detective Sergeant Josh Walker and this is Detective Constable Sam Thomas; can we have a word with you about Julia Bach?'

Her arms were crossed over her body, and he realised she was shivering. She wasn't wearing a coat.

'Do you want to get in and out of the cold?'

She hesitated, eyed them both up, taking in their suits and Josh's police radio in the cup holder, then opened the rear door and scrambled inside.

'Have you found her?'

'We might have located her, yes.'

'Oh, thank God for that. I've been so worried; she's so lovely but very quiet. Did she tell you why she left all her stuff? I bet it was because of that pig Marcus.'

Josh turned around. 'Why do you say that? About him being a pig, I mean.'

'He's a creep; he's always standing too close to you when he speaks. His eyes never look at your face, always your cleavage. Thank God it's cold and we all wear roll-neck jumpers in this weather. He brought in a uniform of tight, white shirts with low necks that we had to wear in the summer. They were bloody awful. I've never been so glad to see the back of the warm weather, and I hate the cold.'

'We spoke to Andrea; she said something similar. Have you not thought about reporting him?'

'For staring? He doesn't do anything you could report him for, at least I don't think so. Plus, we need the money. He pays pretty good wages and most of the time he's okay. Staff accommodation is pretty cheap as well; he only takes a tenner a week out of your wages. Some places take up to eighty. Did Julia tell you why she left?'

'There's no easy way to tell you this, Stacey, but we've found a body floating in the lake and it's highly possible that it's Julia.' He watched her face, feeling cruel. He didn't want to tell her it was a definite until the family had been notified. Her jaw slackened as her mouth fell open; her eyes opened wide as they brimmed with tears. Sam glared at him as she reached over and patted Stacey's arm.

'We don't know for definite yet; it's a possibility though. Do you think you could talk us through the last time you saw her before she left?'

Stacey moved her head up and down. 'She told me she was going to see a friend about a job she'd heard might be available, working on one of the boats in the marina. I can't believe it. I mean, how did she get into the lake? No one in their right mind would go into the water this time of year. It's flipping freezing.'

Josh rubbed the side of his head, the dull throb inside his brain signalling he was in for a real killer of a headache. This seemed to be the consensus: why would two healthy young women go into water so cold it would kill you in minutes? There had to be more to this than they'd figured out.

CHAPTER THIRTY-NINE

The setting sun set the sky aglow; hues of red, orange and pink spread across it and *The Tequila Sunrise* looked like a fairy tale all lit up with thousands of tiny white lights. Banners and balloons were hanging from the side and the mast. It looked amazing even if he said so himself. He and James had worked hard on it all afternoon. Thankfully, the driving rain and wind had subsided over the course of the morning and it was a perfect autumn evening.

Ethan hadn't wanted to help; he hadn't been back on the boat since the morning he'd found the girl in the lake. He was tired and hadn't slept much either. He'd finally dozed off to be woken by James continually phoning him this morning. He'd ignored him for the first hour until after the tenth call, when he'd given in and James had practically begged him. He'd also asked another of their old school friends, Marcus, to pitch in. This was a big charter, and there were to be lots of teenagers on board the boat tonight. It crossed Ethan's mind to wonder why their parents would be letting them anywhere near *The Tequila* if they knew the girl found dead had last been seen on here drinking before she died. James was so matter of fact about it all; he didn't seem to care one bit. Marcus was no better most of the time. What was it with these rich kids? Maybe they needed to live like a normal working class person for a while, to see what life was like when mummy and daddy couldn't afford to pay for everything. He wasn't jealous, or bitter, it was just a fact. He would have loved it if his parents had been able to afford to buy him nice things, but they didn't even buy each other stuff.

They'd both worked hard all their lives, and Ethan had the same work ethic, although he wasn't so prudish about being working class when James offered to buy the beers. Besides, they were friends and friends didn't care whether you were rich or had acne. The whole point of being friends was because you liked each other the way you were, no strings attached.

'Christ, if I had a pound for every time you were daydreaming or skiving, I'd be rich. What fantasy land are you in now?'

He turned to look at James, shaking his head. 'You're an idiot, you already have enough money. I don't even know why you bother doing this. It's not as if you need the cash, and is it really worth the hassle?'

Marcus stopped what he was doing, turning to watch them both.

'I do this because it's easy money and you're almost guaranteed an easy lay. All those gorgeous, young women drunk on champagne and desperate to lose their virginity. It's only right to oblige. Who am I to say no? I see it as my civic duty. Who wouldn't want to sleep with me?'

Marcus laughed. 'You might as well just advertise a shagfest and be done with it.'

James joined in. The only one who didn't think they were funny was Ethan, who scowled at the pair of them.

'Wankers, both of you. I'm amazed you can even fit below deck with the size of your heads.'

'How would you know how big it is?' More raucous laughter, then James continued. 'No, you're the wanker. All alone in your smelly cabin filled with ancient issues of *Playboy* with the pages stuck together.'

Now Ethan was really annoyed with him; how dare he? He turned to leave, and James shouted after him. 'Sorry, don't take any notice. I'm being an idiot. Blame Marcus, he's a bad influence.'

Ethan hesitated. He could leave and go back home to his damp little room, or he could stay, put on the tuxedo James had loaned to him, smile at people all night, hand out glasses of cheap champagne and pretend to be nice. It was better than being on his own, and James always paid him a hundred quid cash in hand. Better than a kick in the teeth, as his dad used to say. For a hundred quid he could put up with these two idiots for another couple of hours.

CHAPTER FORTY

After talking to Stacey, Josh nipped back to the station with Sam to check in with everyone and do a team briefing before jumping in the car again and heading to Ferry Nab car park. If this was summer, they'd be hard-pressed to find a space on a grass verge somewhere miles away to squeeze into, but the lake warden's office was only a short stroll away from their space.

Josh pushed the door handle of the office; it didn't move.

'Shit.'

Sam peered through the window. 'I think there's someone in. It's dark inside but I can see movement at the back.'

Josh rapped his knuckles against the glass. They waited as hurried footsteps crossed towards the door. It opened and he was surprised to see Sergeant Karen Taylor, out of uniform, on the other side.

'Well of all the people to open this door, I didn't expect to see you here.'

She grinned at him. 'What do you want? I'm helping out; they're short-staffed. My son works here.'

'A huge favour. I don't know if you can help or not, but thought it was worth asking.'

'You'd better come inside; he's just out the back. Is it a personal favour or police business?'

Sam answered, 'Both.'

Karen led them through to the staff room at the back of the building. A young man turned to see who she was bringing in. He had two mugs of coffee in his hands.

Sam smiled. 'Looks as if we timed this right for a change; mine's not too strong with two sweeteners and he'll have a strong coffee with a heaped spoonful of sugar.' She added, 'please,' as an afterthought.

Karen introduced them. 'Cal, this is Josh and the cheeky one is Sam.'

He grinned at them both. 'What brings you here? Are you that desperate for a brew you've had to come find her?' He pointed at his mum.

Josh began to explain. 'No, not at all. I need a favour if you can do it. I don't know if you do this sort of stuff. I'm sure you're aware of the two bodies that have been found in the lake recently.'

Cal nodded. 'Yes, I wasn't on duty for either of them. It's so sad.'

'The thing is, although both post-mortems haven't found anything suspicious around their deaths, both the pathologist and I are suitably concerned that they could be. This is between us. I don't want to start a panic, but both victims are blonde women from out of town. It's either a tragic coincidence, or they were targeted. One of them was last seen on a boat called *The Tequila Sunrise* the other was on her way to the marina to enquire about a job on a boat, which could have been the same one. Are you familiar with it?'

'Yes, very. The owner is a bit of an idiot. He seems to host a lot of parties on there.'

Josh glanced at Sam, who looked miserable. 'Is he flouting the conditions of his licence?'

Cal shook his head. 'Oh, no, not from a business side of things. Everything is all above board when it comes to the private charters he takes out sailing. We've never been able to fault him for that. It's more his, er… personal entertaining that is the issue.'

'That's very interesting. Can you not revoke his licence or whatever you do?'

'It's being looked into; safety on the lake is paramount. If two deaths are being linked to the boat, I'm pretty sure it will speed things up.'

Sam's eyes lit up. 'Can you tell him not to take the boat out tonight?'

Cal turned to her. 'I'm afraid not. I don't have that sort of authority. Can't the police do that?'

Josh shrugged. 'Mate, I'm at a loss about what we can and can't do regarding James Marshall. I have someone looking into it all now. If I can, I will. But in case we don't have the authority to do that either, which I don't think we do, I have a plan B.'

Karen eyed him suspiciously. 'What might that plan involve?'

'I was wondering if the lake wardens could take their boat out and keep an eye on *The Tequila* to make sure no more young women decide to go for late-night swims. Then if they do, someone will be there to help them before they get into serious trouble.'

Cal didn't even pause to think about it. 'Yes, I will. I don't know if I'm supposed to or if it's even in my remit, but I'd be horrified if someone else died. I need someone to help me though, I'm the only one on shift. That's why Mum's here; she's been manning the office for me on her afternoon off.'

'I'll come out with you, but I don't know anything about boats.' Josh smiled at Sam. 'You go home, get your daughter to the boat and you won't have to worry about a thing because Cal and I will be out on the lake keeping a close eye on it.'

Karen butted in. 'You're not a babysitting service, Cal, you might get in trouble. I mean is this sort of stuff even in the job description?' She looked at Sam.

'Mum, we're responsible for the safety of the lake users. If there's a party on a boat and the possibility someone else could come to some harm then, yes, I think it would be part of my job description. Leave it with me; I'll speak to my supervisor and get the okay.'

She tutted as she glared at Josh. Cal left them to go into the office and use the phone.

She whispered, 'What the hell are you playing at, Josh, this is ridiculous.'

'Is it though? Something fishy is going on. Two women have drowned and I want to make sure there isn't a third. You're not at work now; Cal is the one in charge.'

He wondered for a moment if she was going to run at him and smack him in the mouth; her eyes were sparkling with what he knew was fury. They stared at each other in some kind of stand-off until Sam interjected.

'Should I take the car and come back for you once I've dropped Grace off?'

Josh threw her the keys. 'You might as well.' Judging by the disgusted look Karen was giving him, he wondered if she might push him into the water and drown him. Sam left them to it, obviously not wanting to get into a pissing contest with the pair of them. She had other concerns.

Cal came out of the office, a huge smile on his face. 'Sorted, my supervisor said it's definitely okay to do what Josh has asked. You can get off home, Mum, thanks for your help this afternoon, I really appreciate it.'

'Sod off. If you two idiots are going out in the dark following that party boat then I'm coming too. Why should you get to have all the fun?'

She walked towards the toilet and left them both.

Josh stepped closer to Cal and whispered, 'Did you really speak to your supervisor?'

'No, but don't tell her. She'd go mental with me. I want to help you, Josh.'

Josh didn't know whether to laugh, cry or pray to God to help them. He hoped that he wasn't going to get all three of them into trouble. He was in enough of that already without adding to the problem.

CHAPTER FORTY-ONE

Beth couldn't settle; she was desperate to know if anything had come back from the paint samples that she'd fast-tracked. Leaving the café, she drove home, made herself a mug of tea then went into her office to do some more digging into drownings in the lake. She'd only looked at a couple of pages so far, so she typed 'drownings Lake Windermere 2000 to 2019' to see if any better results came up. Surely not only men had drowned in the lake? Scrolling through, she paused on a photograph of a group of laughing teenage boys. She looked at the date on the article: 5th July 2011.

SCHOOLBOY DROWNS ON FIELD TRIP

Tragedy struck a group of teenage boys from Lake Fell School on a field trip to Fell Foot Park yesterday. They were having fun before they went into the water, laughing and enjoying the warm weather, racing each other and playing games.

It wasn't until the others reached the safety of the shore that they realised fifteen-year-old Tyler Johnson was missing. A frantic search was then undertaken by the lake wardens, police and boat users in the area. Tyler's lifeless body was found an hour later. A spokesman for the school said they were devasted at the loss of Tyler's life. 'He was a wonderful, bright boy with a fabulous future in front of him,' one teacher said. Tyler's twin, Marcus, who was also on the school trip had been taken home to his family, who are being comforted by family liaison officers. Tyler's parents have declined to comment.

A full investigation into the accident is being carried out, and the teacher supervising the trip, Miss Foster, has been suspended pending further enquiries.

Beth leant closer to the computer. Poor Miss Foster probably lost her job over that, and she doubted the woman would ever recover from the shock and the guilt. She studied the boys' faces: young, grinning, handsome. One boy in particular had floppy hair and a brilliant white smile. He looked perfect. He looked popular. Could that be James Marshall? Sipping at her tea, she couldn't say whether it was, but the more she stared the more she thought there was a slight chance that it could be. She sat back. It was probably nothing, her tired mind playing tricks on her, but it wouldn't hurt to do some digging, would it? Sending the page to the printer so she had a hard copy for her records, she typed 'Lake Fell School' into the search bar which brought up the website for the prestigious private school, and then rang the number on the screen.

'Good afternoon, Lake Fell School. Diane speaking.' The voice that answered sounded like an older woman, which Beth hoped meant she'd worked at the school a long time.

'Hello, my name is Doctor Beth Adams. I'm looking to speak to any member of staff who worked at the school in July 2011.'

There was a pause on the other end of the phone.

'Oh dear, now you're asking. I don't think I can tell you off the top of my head; I'd have to make some enquiries. The staff are all off today, you just caught me. I popped in to pick something up. Can I ask what this is regarding, Doctor Adams?'

'I'm a forensic pathologist and I'm investigating some recent drownings in the lake. I was wondering if you knew of anyone who may still work there who was at the school when Tyler Johnson drowned on a field trip.'

The woman inhaled sharply. 'Terrible tragedy, he was such a nice boy.'

'Did you work there then?'

The voice laughed. 'I've worked here forever, but thankfully I'm retiring in ten weeks, three days and one hour, give or take a few minutes.'

Beth laughed. 'You're not counting down the minutes then?'

'Now you've mentioned that terrible day my memory has been jogged. Mr Carruthers, the head, retired last year; Miss Foster, who is now Mrs Williams, is still here. Can I make you an appointment to come in for a chat? I think that would be the best thing to do.'

'That would be fabulous. Thank you.'

'Let me speak to Mrs Williams. Give me your phone number and I'll ring you back.'

Beth reeled off her number. 'Thank you, Diane. I really appreciate your help.'

She ended the call and sat back wondering if she should be doing this and decided that, yes, she should. The police were busy enough. If she came up with a tangible lead she could pass it on to Josh and his team. If it turned out to be nothing, well the only thing she'd wasted was an hour of her own time.

No wonder she couldn't settle; so much in her life was uncertain: she didn't know what was going on with Josh; there was a chance the drownings weren't as innocent as they seemed, and she couldn't stop thinking about Robert's post-mortem, which Charles would have performed this morning. Was he still in her mortuary taking up precious room? Or had he been released to the funeral directors? Even though she wasn't supposed to be in work she knew she'd go mad if she didn't find out. She needed to see his body, and now the post-mortem had been completed, technically, she wouldn't be doing anything wrong. If Robert's body wasn't there she could at least nip in to check her emails. At least going to work would give her something to take her mind off the situation with Josh and Jodie. A part of her wanted to go find Josh and demand an explanation, another wanted to shut herself off from the world entirely – and she knew how to do that better than anyone. Ignoring the voices in her head, she finally decided, and pushed herself to go to the hospital.

Getting out of the car, she kept her head bent low so she didn't have to speak to anyone as she passed; she didn't have a good reason to be here. She bumped into a woman who had her head bent as she was texting on her phone.

'Oh, I'm so sorry. Are you okay? I wasn't looking where I was going.'

Lifting her head, Beth was horrified to see a familiar face smiling at her. 'That's okay, I wasn't looking either. My knee is giving me a bit of bother and keeps giving way on me. I might have fallen into you. Beth, how are you?'

Beth felt her heart skip a beat. How cruel and unfair was this? If the universe was working its magic it was in the most peculiar way.

'I'm okay thanks, Jodie. How are you?'

Jodie shrugged. 'I've been better…'

'Good, I'm sorry. Look, I have to go, I'm in a rush. I have to get to the mortuary. Take care, okay.'

Inside, Beth felt her knees give way and she lurched forward, the palm of her hand resting against the wall to hold her up. What was going on? She felt even more confused than ever. She tried to ring Josh and he didn't answer. She felt a scream well up inside her chest. All she wanted was an explanation. If she wasn't such a coward she would go and ask Jodie what was going on. She couldn't though; she was too scared of what the truth might be. A voice behind her made her jump.

'Are you okay?'

She turned to see a junior doctor in a white coat, her pink stethoscope wrapped around her neck. Beth nodded.

'Yes, thank you. I've been feeling a bit dizzy; I'm okay now.' The white lie ran off her tongue so easily.

'Well you know, you're in the right place if you need a check-up, Dr Adams.'

Beth stared at the doctor's name badge. It seemed the whole world knew who Beth Adams was, yet she didn't even know herself who she was.

'Thank you, I guess I am. I'm okay; a couple of betahistine and I'll be good to go.'

'Good, I'm down in A & E if you need anything for the next eight hours. Although I'm on my way to find a decent cup of coffee first.'

Beth smiled. She was a mess and she knew it, and by the look on the face of the doctor smiling at her she knew it too, but was far too polite to say anything else.

'Good luck finding the coffee, have a good one.'

Beth hurried along the corridor, eager to be alone in her office once more.

She needed to see with her own eyes that Robert Hartshorn was truly dead if she was ever going to get a grip on her life again. And she needed closure with the demon from her past if she was ever going to successfully confront Josh and the nightmare of her present. Together, it was too much to bear.

Beth pushed the heavy door that led into the mortuary. It was empty and a sigh of relief escaped her lips as she took in the familiar hum of the bank of cold storage fridges lined against the back wall. She slipped inside, flicking on a couple of light switches. Before she knew it, her feet had carried her over to the back wall and she stared at the unnamed drawer which had contained Robert's body.

Ignoring the voice of reason inside her head, her fingers reached out, wrapping themselves around the cold handle. She tugged it open and dragged the middle shelf towards her. The body bag looked the same as it had on Thursday, but the yellow tag had been cut off, signalling the post-mortem had been completed. She didn't realise her hands were shaking until she tried to pull down the zipper. Stopping, she took a deep breath to steady her hands, then it was open and she was staring at the man who had haunted her for seven years and consumed her life completely, dominating her worst nightmares. The dreadful memories she harboured had built him into a terrifying, scary monster. When she dreamt about him, he was huge, with black eyes, powerful arms and a grin that made her knees quake. Only he didn't look so scary now; he looked frail, old and very dead. She stared at his grey stubbled face – once he'd never have been anything but clean-shaven – and whispered, 'I hope you rot in hell, Robert, it's what you deserve. Despite everything you put me through I'm not the one who's decomposing in a mortuary fridge. I won. I bet you hate that, don't you. I've wasted seven years of my life because of you. Not any more. Today it ends. I'm alive, which is more than can be said for your sorry arse.' Before she'd finished speaking, she was pulling the zipper back together, then shoving the shelf back, she slammed the door and walked out of the mortuary.

She held her head high; this part of her life was over for good.

CHAPTER FORTY-TWO

Marcus, James and Ethan stood below deck dressed in tuxedos. Even if Ethan said it himself, they did look mighty fine. Marcus and James both had long, heavy fringes which the pair of them were continually running their fingers through to push out of their eyes. Ethan, who normally lived in a bobble hat, caught a glimpse of himself in the mirror; those two looked like they'd come fresh off the set for *Made in Chelsea*, and he looked more like a young, skinny Jason Statham. He liked the difference. It would be nice if the girls appreciated it as well, but he could almost guarantee they would focus on those two, as if they could smell the money exuding from them.

Opening the small fridge in the kitchen, James took out three bottles of Budweiser and passed them around. Ethan took his, hoping it would calm his nerves a little. He always got a bit hot under the collar being dressed up like this; mixing with wealthy people always made him acutely aware of just how working class he was. They clinked bottles together. James and Marcus simultaneously said 'cheers' and he muttered it a couple of seconds later. James shook his head.

'What's wrong with you today? You've been a right grump. I hope you're going to smile when my customers arrive. I'm not paying you to scare them away. You'll have to put on a brave show if you want to get laid. I'm telling you now, these girls want a good time. Don't go making them all feel as miserable as you look.'

'Are you not even bothered about that girl whose body I found?'

'No, not really. Christ, Ethan, you can't keep feeling sorry for yourself because of that. Yes, it was sad, but it was an accident. How

many times do you need telling? I don't get it. We had nothing to
do with what happened to her.'

'How can you say that? She was on this fucking boat, James.
Drinking your crappy champagne and vodka. Don't you at least
feel a bit responsible?'

Marcus rolled his eyes. 'Why should he? Accidents happen and
we know that more than anyone. You can't spend the rest of your
life blaming yourself for her stupidity. James is right, Ethan, you
need to snap out of it.'

Ethan shook his head. 'I can't believe what I'm hearing; do
neither of you have a conscience?'

They both replied 'no' at the same time then began to laugh.
Ethan wanted to leave them to it, rip off this stupid suit and go
home. It might be small, cramped, damp and smell like shit, but
it was better than spending time with these two heartless pricks.
He wondered if he'd finally outgrown their friendship, if it had
ever been more than a way to have a good time without costing
him anything. Only now it had cost them something; someone
had died. Whether or not it was their fault, it had happened, and
he didn't feel very good about it.

Taking his beer, he went up on the deck, leaving them to their
laughter. He should walk away now; this wasn't his lifestyle, it never
was. He'd been playing at it for the last eight years. He began to
walk slowly along the ramp onto the jetty wondering if he really
had the balls to leave.

'Hi, I'm a bit early; is anyone else here yet?'

He jumped, so lost in his own thoughts he hadn't noticed the
girl standing around on the side of the marina.

'I didn't see you there.'

'Sorry, my mum dropped me off and I couldn't stand her moaning
at me in the car. I thought I'd rather hang around down here.'

She smiled at him, and he felt his frozen insides begin to thaw.
She was pretty; her shoulder-length dark blonde hair was a lovely

colour. It looked natural, not bleached within an inch of its life like most of the girls who James associated with. Her nose had a tiny bump on it, and she definitely hadn't had her lips done. She was naturally beautiful, which in James's circle of friends was a rarity.

'You're the first but come on board. It's too cold to be waiting around on the side of the marina.'

The desire to leave had been replaced by the desire to get to know her better, although he didn't doubt for one moment that the minute she laid her eyes on James or Marcus he would be instantly forgotten.

'I'd better not. I don't want to go on before the birthday girl arrives.' The echo of slamming doors and loud, screeching laughter filled the still autumn air. Ethan laughed.

'I think you might be safe; it sounds as if the circus has arrived.' He held his hand out. 'Ethan Scales, at your service.'

She grinned and held hers out and, instead of shaking it, he lifted it to his lips and softly brushed them against the skin of her hand. She giggled, and he was pretty sure her cheeks had turned pink although it was difficult to see in the rapidly fading light.

'Grace Thomas; it's lovely to meet you, Ethan.'

'Likewise; come on, let's get you on the boat. You can tell them I dragged you on if they ask why you're here before them.'

Taking her elbow, he led her onto the deck.

She whispered, 'It's so pretty. I love fairy lights.'

'I'm glad you like it; this took all afternoon.'

He led her to the bar area, popped the cork on a bottle of champagne, filled a glass and handed it to her. He then began to fill the glasses on a tray ready to offer the noisy party that were making their way down to the marina. His anger at James and Marcus had subsided as fast as it had arrived. He liked Grace. She seemed very down-to-earth, on his level, and he was hoping he could spend a bit of time with her between hovering around with a tray passing out glasses of champagne.

CHAPTER FORTY-THREE

Cal handed out waterproof jackets, trousers and life vests to Josh and Karen. Then he disappeared into the staff room and came back with three woollen hats. 'It gets cold on the lake this time of evening, better to be warm.'

He handed one to Josh, who tugged it on his head; Karen took one look at hers and grimaced.

'I'm not wearing that. I don't know whose sweaty head it's been on. I've got my own in the car.' She left them to go and get it.

Josh smiled at Cal. 'Thanks, I really appreciate this.'

'No problem, fingers crossed we aren't actually needed.'

Josh hoped they wouldn't be; there would be a lot of explaining to do if they were and rocked up unannounced. James might accuse him of harassment and get him in a lot of trouble. Then again, if nothing happened, he would never know that he was being watched, would he? Josh would rather take the chance.

He wondered if Beth was okay. It was getting dark and he should have finished his shift and gone home by now. He hadn't seen her for two days, only spoken with her on the phone and the last conversation had been strained. Jodie had said she was going to the hospital for treatment and, depending on how it went, she might be there some time. He'd had no missed calls from her, but at least he knew she was in the best place for her while there was no one at home to look after her.

'So, anyway, what are we having for tea? I'm hungry, I thought I was going to be in my pyjamas watching television now. I reckon it's your treat, Walker, seeing as how we're risking life and limb on some stupid whim of yours. You can buy the pizzas or a Chinese.'

He realised she was talking to him. 'I'm easy, pizza would be better. Chinese is too messy. We can eat slices of pizza. You order and I'll pay.' He dug in his trouser pocket and pulled out a bent, misshapen debit card. She rolled her eyes.

'Does that actually work?'

'Yes, well the contactless does. It won't go into the card machines, it gets stuck.'

She went into the office to use the phone.

'What time is the party?'

He looked at his watch. 'About now; I suppose they're not going to be moving away from the jetty until all the guests have arrived. We probably have a bit of time before they sail.'

Cal nodded. 'I think so. What happened to birthday parties in the room at the back of the pub?'

Josh shrugged. 'That's exactly what I said. There was nothing like this when I was younger.'

'Money talks, I suppose, the rest of us mortals just celebrate in crappy pubs.'

Karen walked back in. 'You didn't want the eighteenth or twenty-first I offered, so I hope you're not being ungrateful.'

'He wasn't, we were just kind of saying how the other half live; spending thousands on lavish parties when you could get pissed down the pub and a takeaway for less than twenty quid.'

She began to laugh. 'When I was a boy…'

They sat around playing cards until the pizza arrived. It was dark now. Josh didn't know if he was being overly cautious or plain ridiculous about the whole situation. He hadn't managed to speak to either Marcus Johnson or James Marshall about the second body; he'd been so tied up with Jodie. It was too late now, but he would visit them at home first thing in the morning and catch them off guard. It wouldn't hurt to speak to Ethan Scales again either. Brushing pizza crumbs from his jacket, he stood up.

'Should we go? They've had an hour to get into the swing of things.'

Cal nodded. 'I guess we should. Mum, are you sure you want to come? It's probably going to be freezing cold and boring.'

'What's my other option? Stay here on my own in this creepy building that creaks and groans all the time? No thank you. I'd rather freeze my arse off on the boat with you two.'

Josh smiled at her. 'Or you could just go home and watch television; honestly, I don't think anything is going to happen. There's no point in all three of us being stuck on a boat so late.'

'If I didn't know better, I'd say you two were trying to get rid of me. What are you playing at, Walker?'

'Nothing, I feel bad you're having to spend your day off doing this.'

'I'll be the judge of that; anyway, I've got nothing better to do. Why should I let you two have all the fun?'

What Josh was thinking was that if it all went wrong then she wouldn't get into trouble with them. Cal could blame being pressured by Josh to take the boat out, but it would be harder to do that if his mum was along for the ride. He was trying to protect them both, but he knew it was futile. She wouldn't be talked out of it.

CHAPTER FORTY-FOUR

The party was in full swing, and despite his reservations, Ethan found himself enjoying it. Claudia, whose birthday it was, had unsurprisingly made a beeline for James. He wondered if there was some kind of unspoken code among women for these kinds of occasions. Did the hostess get first pick of all the single men? The rest of them seemed to be hanging around Marcus like dogs on heat. Grace was different though, not like any of them. He'd spotted her standing alone a couple of times and she reminded him a lot of himself. He wondered if she was on the outside of this friendship circle, just like him.

James signalled he was about to take the boat out, so he untied it from its mooring and jumped aboard.

'I guess you like sailing?'

Grace was beside him.

He nodded. 'I do, I've always loved the water. Especially this lake, it's beautiful and the views are incredible.'

'Yes, I suppose they are.' They both looked across the water, the hills, mountains and trees forming a shadowy backdrop. The moon was full, its bright light illuminating the middle of the lake in a sparkling path to nowhere. Grace sighed. 'It is beautiful. I don't think you appreciate it when you're brought up around here. I was always dragged on family days out to the Lakes; sailing, rowing, kayaking and fell walking are just not that appealing to a teenager. I'd spend the whole afternoon in a right sulk because I'd rather be in bed watching reruns of *Friends* on my MacBook.'

'How old are you? Sorry, that's rude, I know men should never ask women their age.'

She threw back her head and laughed. It was the most beautiful sound he'd ever heard. The moonlight glinted off her blonde hair and he realised that Grace Thomas was not just pretty, she was stunning. He had butterflies in his stomach, but maybe it was just lust. What would James do in this situation? Flirt with her until she was eating out of the palm of his hand and then take her below and sleep with her, but Ethan knew he couldn't do that. He wanted more than a quick leg over with this beautiful creature.

Leaning in close to him, she whispered, 'I'm old enough.'

He felt a torrent of heat rush through his veins.

'Ethan, what am I paying you for? Can you refill glasses, please.'

And just like that the moment shattered and Grace pulled away. If he didn't know better, he would say that James had purposely embarrassed him. Hot rage replaced the excitement that had been fizzing through his veins. He mumbled a reply. 'Excuse me, Grace, my boss is calling.'

She smiled at him, dismay in her eyes. He wanted to punch James he was so angry with him. This was the last time he was ever doing this, a hundred quid or not; he could be his own skivvy.

He stormed below deck only to find Marcus with the girl he'd been fawning over all night wedged against the wall. Before he could open his mouth to speak, the girl screamed and a loud crack filled the air. The girl had slapped Marcus hard across the face, and Ethan couldn't hide the grin that filled his face as the girl rushed past him to go back to her friends. Marcus shrugged, rubbing his cheek and making to follow the girl upstairs.

'You win some, you lose some. Onwards and upwards,' he joked as he squeezed past Ethan.

Rolling his eyes, Ethan grabbed as many bottles of champagne as he could fit under his arms and took them above deck to the makeshift bar. He could see the top of Grace's head in the crowd.

Marcus had closed in on her, leaning in close so she could hear him above the noise, so he could touch her arm. Ethan looked down, colour filling his face, concentrating on opening bottles and filling glasses until he was brave enough to look up again. Relief washed over him; Grace had rebuked Marcus and was now chatting to two girls as far away from him as she could get. An argument began between another two girls, one of them the girl who had slapped Marcus. She was loud, much louder than the other. James rushed across to try and separate them, Marcus and Ethan too. Claudia, who had been wailing down the microphone to some god-awful karaoke version of 'Don't Stop Believin', stopped singing and began imploring everyone to calm down. The boat lurched to one side as everyone crowded around to watch the fight unfold. There was a high-pitched scream as the loud girl fell towards the railings, slipped and toppled over into the icy cold waters of the lake.

James bellowed, 'Stop.' Ethan rushed to the side of the boat. He couldn't see the girl in the water. He needed help, but where was Marcus? Grabbing the spotlight, he shone it down into the lake and saw the girl had resurfaced a few feet away and was struggling to keep her head above water. He kicked off his shoes, readying himself to jump into the lake for the second time that week, when the sound of a powerboat revving its engine broke through the darkness. Ethan saw a bright light zooming towards them and before he could even remove his jacket, two men were grabbing hold of the girl and dragging her out of the water and into another boat. Marcus, who had now appeared beside him with James, stared, horrified. Everyone on the boat fell silent as they watched the men throw a blanket around the shivering girl and speed off back towards the shore.

'Jesus, she could have drowned,' James whispered to Ethan, finally acknowledging just how dangerous this whole thing could be. Alcohol, teenage girls and a huge lake were definitely not a good mix; for once Ethan actually felt sorry for James and the huge mess this would put him in.

'Take the boat back, James, we need to make sure she's okay and get these girls home.'

'But—'

Ethan hissed, 'Take the fucking boat in, enough is enough.'

James nodded as he was dragged away by Claudia, who was seething over how that silly bitch had ruined her night and she wasn't paying James a penny. Marcus grabbed her arm and said something in her ear. Ethan had no idea what he'd said but it shut Claudia up. The boat was eerily quiet now; everyone had sobered up in an instant.

From nowhere, Grace approached Ethan, took hold of his arm, took an eyeliner from her bag and wrote her phone number on the inside of his arm. He nodded at her, and she walked back to the girl who had been arguing and was now sobbing into her hands. Wrapping an arm around her shoulders, she began to console her, and Ethan watched in awe. This had turned into a complete disaster, yet it was still the best night of his life up to now.

CHAPTER FORTY-FIVE

Josh and Cal had watched in horror as they'd heard the loud scream followed by a splash. Cal slammed on the throttle and sped the boat over to drag her to safety. She was now sitting shivering wrapped in a foil blanket. Karen was trying to coax her out of her wet clothes.

'I'm a police sergeant, this is my colleague who is also a policeman, and this is Cal, one of the lake wardens. We're going to get you to safety now, but you need to get those wet clothes off. They'll turn the other way. Do you want me to help you?' She shook her head from side to side. 'I'll shield you with the blanket and we'll wrap you in several layers of foil blankets so you don't get hypothermia.'

The girl conceded and once she was done Karen sat next to her, wrapping her arms around her to share what body heat she could. Josh and Cal had been rendered speechless. Josh had wondered if he was being ridiculous by asking Cal to take the boat out; now, he was relieved. There was one thing for sure: he would shut down that bloody party boat for good after this. He turned to the girl.

'What's your name?'

'Tamara.'

Josh felt a pang of relief; he was pretty sure Sam's kid was called Grace.

'I'm Josh. Can you tell me what happened on the boat?'

She shook her head once more. He didn't know if she was embarrassed, shocked or scared.

'Do you feel okay? We'll call an ambulance and get you checked over.'

'No, please.'

'We have to, you went into the water. We need to make sure you're okay.'

'I'm fine, apart from my new shoes being ruined and my dress is a wreck,' she said through chattering teeth.

Karen squeezed her shoulder. 'I know you are, petal, but it won't hurt to give you a once-over. If you want, we can drive you to the hospital if you don't want the fuss of an ambulance. How old are you?'

'Eighteen. I just want to go home. Please, just get me away from here.'

Minutes later, they were moored to the jetty in the marina. Cal helped Tamara off the boat, and then Karen took her arm and walked her towards the car park.

Cal asked Josh, 'Now what?'

'Well I'll be filing an incident report and letting the licensing committee know what's happened.'

'I'll see if we can get his licence suspended; between the pair of us we should be able to keep that boat from sailing for the foreseeable future.'

'Good.' He looked over at the sound of Karen mid-argument with Tamara.

'You really need to get checked out,' she pleaded.

'No, I just want someone to take me home.'

Karen offered. 'Fine. But we need to know what happened?'

Tamara stayed silent.

Cal looked at his mum. 'I need to take the boat back and write up an incident report. My car is at the Ferry Nab car park.' He lowered his voice and spoke to Josh. 'Please can you get her details for my incident report?'

'Of course, thank you so much, Cal. It was a good job we were there.'

He nodded. 'It was, glad to have been of some use even if she doesn't seem that grateful.'

Josh laughed.

Karen turned towards them, shock in her eyes. Then said, 'She thinks she was pushed overboard.'

Josh's smile faltered as alarm bells begin to ring inside his mind; he turned to look at Tamara and realised that although wet and bedraggled, she had long, blonde hair just like the other two victims.

Out on the water, the party boat was docking, the music had been turned down and the decorative lights switched off.

He pulled out his phone and rang the control room.

'This is DS Walker, I need a couple of available patrols to Bowness Bay Marina as soon as possible.' He wanted the boat locked down and every single person onboard interviewed.

CHAPTER FORTY-SIX

Sitting at the computer in her office, Beth sighed; there was only one new email, and it wasn't from the Forensic Science Service in Chorley with the results of the fast-tracked samples she'd sent for the paint chips. The only new email she had was a long-winded one from Charles, informing her that he'd completed Robert's post-mortem. His closing words were: *I hope there's no hard feelings between us, Beth, I was only doing my job. You would have done the same.* She pushed her chair back, the realisation she would have done the same hitting hard. What had come over her? She should apologise to him for putting him in a difficult position, in person. She would much rather deal with situations, especially ones she'd caused, face to face and not hide behind a keyboard.

She stared out of the small office window which looked out onto a staff car park and nearby memorial garden area lit up by the dull orange glow of street lights. It was time to lock up and go home.

Her phone was where she'd left it, tucked into the driver's side pocket of the car and she checked to see if Josh had rung. Nothing, not even a text message. She didn't understand what was going on with him. Deciding to stop being so needy, she pushed it into her trouser pocket. Two could play that game. If he wasn't going to bother with her, she damn well wasn't going to bother with him.

*

Back at home, she poured herself a generous glass of wine, while asking herself, *Is wine the answer to your problems?* She knew that it wasn't, but it made them a whole lot more bearable. She collapsed, exhausted, onto the sofa. She didn't watch television very often, preferring to lose herself in a book, but tonight she needed a distraction. She brought Netflix up and settled on *Stranger Things*; Abe had been telling her to watch it for months. Before she knew it, she was absorbed and rooting for the kid who had been brought up as a scientific experiment. It had been months since she'd had a Netflix binge and she was enjoying every minute.

Her phone vibrated on the kitchen side and she paused the TV; she'd almost forgotten about everything she'd been so sucked into the 1980s. Crossing the room, she picked up her phone to read a message from Josh.

Sorry, work is crazy. There was nearly another drowning, but we saved her. Will tell you about it later, but it might be late. Don't wait up xxx.

A sigh escaped her lips. All she wanted was to see his face and have a conversation with him about what was going on. Part of her wished she'd gone to find Jodie; at least then she'd have known one way or the other instead of waiting around trying to pretend everything was okay when it clearly wasn't. What did he mean there was nearly another drowning? Did that mean he thought the other two were more than just tragic accidents? For the first time in a while she had no idea what was happening, or why. She hated the feeling of being out of control. Instead of texting back, she pressed the call button, not expecting him to pick up. She was so relieved to hear his voice whisper, 'Hi, you.'

'Josh, is everything okay?'

There were muffled voices in the background, which sounded as if they were getting agitated and louder.

'Not at the moment. You were right to be concerned, I…
Tamara, where are you going?' He yelled so loud she pulled the
phone away from her ear.

'Oh shit, she's a bloody nuisance. Got to go!'

He ended the call and Beth smiled, feeling a little better. She
knew something was suspicious about a pair of bodies turning up
on the same day, in the same lake. She'd felt it in her bones and
was suddenly glad she'd pushed to question it. Charles wouldn't
have. Maybe it was fate that she'd been called to deal with them. It
didn't matter; the main thing was Josh believed her and they had
averted another drowning, a third victim. She wanted more than
anything to drive to the marina to help, but she'd been drinking.
Instead, she refilled her glass and returned to her show, confident
that Josh and his team would be doing everything they could to
get to the bottom of this.

CHAPTER FORTY-SEVEN

Josh ran after the girl, who was heading back towards the boat. He caught up with her and gently took hold of her arm.

'What are you doing? We need to get you home and dry if you won't go to the hospital to be checked over.'

'I don't want to go just yet and I don't want to go with her.' She pointed at Karen.

'Should I ring someone to pick you up?'

'No, bloody hell. As if my night hasn't been ruined enough. Why can't you take me?'

He didn't have a car, that was why; he'd left it at the station. He looked around to see a couple of officers getting out of an unmarked car.

'Come with me then.' He gently led the girl to where they were.

'Evening, can I take this car and you get a lift back? I need to get her home sooner rather than later and she won't go with Sergeant Taylor.'

'If you want, Josh. Unless you want us to take you home, love?'

The response officer looked at Tamara, but she shook her head.

Josh sighed. For some reason she had taken a liking to him which might make her more talkative in the car. He needed to find out what had happened. The officer handed him the keys.

'Thank you.' He turned to Tamara. 'Let's go.'

She did as she was told.

He heard a voice behind him whisper, 'Good luck,' followed by laughter and he shook his head. 'I need all of those people on the boat spoken to about what happened. I need to find out how she ended up in the water; if anyone saw anything; if it was an accident and someone maybe stumbled into her. I also want everyone's names and addresses for follow-up interviews tomorrow. Get them to leave the boat two at a time and take their details as they disembark. There's more officers on the way.'

All three of them looked over to the boat. On board, someone, presumably the birthday girl could be heard sobbing and wailing about her party being ruined; the two officers looked back at Josh, who shrugged.

'Sorry, but it's nothing to do with me. I didn't ruin her night. As soon as I've taken Tamara home I'll come back. If anyone points any fingers at a pusher, arrest the person in question and get a full witness statement.'

He ducked into the car before the officers could complain too much.

Inside, Tamara managed a little smile with her still-blue lips. 'Claudia is going to be so pissed with you for ruining her party.'

'Actually, I think you were the one who ruined it. I'm not taking all the blame.'

'I guess that's me off her guest list for future events. You're not even in the running.' She laughed.

Josh joined in, turning the dial on the heater all the way up and looking to check she wasn't still shaking. A small trickle of blood ran from her right nostril.

'Oh – your nose is bleeding. Are you sure you're okay? How old are you really, Tamara?'

She pulled the sun visor down to check her nose. Using the sleeve of the jumper Josh had given her from the back of the car, she blotted it away.

'What's that got to do with anything? I'm eighteen.'

'I just want to make sure you're above the age of consent.'

She reached out and slapped his arm. 'Why? Not you as well.'

'To be questioned without an adult present.' His cheeks burned as he realised how bad that question might have sounded.

'Oh, yes, I'm definitely old enough for that as well as voting, drinking alcohol and having sex, although I've had sex more times than I've voted.'

Josh felt his cheeks turn redder. What was it with this younger generation? They talked about the stuff most people kept private as if it was nothing. He wished Karen had come with them, or that Sam had arrived a bit earlier, because he felt awkward.

For a few minutes they drove in silence, then it was Tamara who broke it.

'I can be a bit of a nightmare, sorry. I went below deck to use the bathroom and one of the guys serving drinks was down there. I sort of know him through going in the pub he owns. I don't know what he was doing on the boat.'

'Marcus Johnson?' Josh felt his heart begin to race; this was too much of a coincidence to be ignored.

'Yeah, Marcus. I don't know his second name. Anyway, he sort of backed me into a corner. His hands were all over me.'

'What did you do?'

'Slapped him. Then another guy came down, the one with a shaved head. He looked horrified at what he'd seen. I pushed my way out and went back on top. Next thing I know someone is shoving me hard from behind. The heels I was wearing were too high. I fell forwards, lost my balance and fell over the railing into the lake.' She looked at Josh. 'That's it. I don't know who pushed me, I didn't see them. A part of me thinks it was that creep Marcus, another part wonders if it was one of the girls who maybe don't like me that much.'

'Thank you for sharing that, it helps with our investigation a lot.'

'Why is there going to be an investigation?'

He glanced at her pale face; mascara trailed down her cheeks and flecks of glitter that had begun the night on her eyelids were now sprinkled across her nose.

'Tamara, someone tried and succeeded to push you into the lake. If we hadn't been on a boat in the area you could have drowned. Fortunately, you didn't; we managed to pull you out before that happened. At worst, it's attempted murder. At best grievous bodily harm. I'm not sure yet until we've ascertained the exact circumstances, but whatever it is, it's serious.'

She nodded. 'I can still taste the water in my mouth. I thought the cheap champagne they were serving on the boat was pretty crap. It turns out not as crappy as Lake Windermere.'

She paused. 'The third house along, with the wooden gates.'

He stopped outside a huge house set in its own grounds with wooden gates blocking access to it from the road. She opened the car door.

'Thanks, what's your name again?'

'Josh Walker, Detective Sergeant Josh Walker.'

'Well it was nice to meet you, just a shame about the circumstances.'

'Don't you want me to take you in and talk to your parents?'

She shook her head. 'They're not in, probably up at the golf club. I'm okay, just tired and cold. Oh, and I look a mess as well.' She began to dry cough into her hand. 'I'm probably going to catch a cold, but I'll live. If you need me for anything you know where I am.'

She got out the car and typed a code into the electronic keypad on the gate post. He waved at her, waiting for the gates to open and catching a glimpse of the huge house behind them. If he thought Beth's house was stunning, this was practically a mansion.

'Good night, Tamara. If you begin to feel unwell then ring an ambulance or get yourself to the hospital.'

She rolled her eyes at him, dismissing him with a wave of her hand. The gates began to close and she disappeared from sight.

A heavy feeling settled over Josh. He was sure she was okay, but he'd have preferred it if she'd let an ambulance crew check her over. Or at least if he'd been able to inform her parents. The fact that she was eighteen and capable of making her own decisions made it difficult for him to do anything more. He turned the car around to head back to the marina.

CHAPTER FOURTY-EIGHT

James, Marcus and Ethan had spoken to the police and given brief statements along with all the other passengers. When they'd all left, and police had finally gone, James opened a bottle of Jack Daniel's and filled three glasses with ice. Pouring generous measures of the whiskey over it, he then passed one each to Marcus and Ethan.

'What a fucking disaster.'

Ethan didn't speak. He wondered if James realised that most of this was the fault of Marcus and his wandering hands. If he hadn't tried to grope that girl, he wouldn't have had to challenge him and she wouldn't have gone back up on deck and fallen into the water. Ethan took a small sip of the amber liquid. He wanted nothing more than to go home to his cabin.

'What are you going to do?'

James looked at him. 'Not much I can do. The coppers said the boat was not to leave the marina. No more charters until there's been a thorough investigation. I'm going to lose my licence for sure, not that I'll have any customers after this. Might as well give it up.'

Marcus shrugged. 'Bloody stupid cow. What was she thinking going into the water?'

Incredulous, Ethan glared at him. 'If you'd kept your hands to yourself none of this would have happened. I don't think she intentionally decided to plunge into the lake.'

Marcus stood up. The glass he was holding slid from his grasp as he tried to balance but stumbled forwards. It smashed to the floor, spraying James and himself in whiskey.

'Bloody hell, Marcus, sit down, you idiot. You can't stand straight,' James yelled at him.

Marcus ignored him, taking a step closer to Ethan.

'You're just a jealous prick. She wanted me and you know it, you could see it in her eyes.'

He lurched for Ethan, swinging his arm. Ethan, who wasn't able to move fast enough in the confined space and was too drunk to duck in time, felt knuckles connect with his eye socket as a blast of hot pain shot through his brain. He stumbled back, falling onto the sofa he'd been sitting on, clutching his eye.

'Police! Stay where you are.'

Ethan looked up to see two police officers standing at the top of the steps that led below deck. He blinked his good eye and wondered if he was hallucinating. When he opened it three officers were coming down the steps towards him; one of them had a Taser drawn. He put up his hands.

'Not me, I didn't do anything.' He pointed towards Marcus, who was nursing the hand he'd punched Ethan with.

The woman with the Taser spoke as she aimed the yellow gun at him, and two red dots appeared on his chest.

'Marcus Johnson? You are under arrest; do not move or make any sudden actions.'

James also threw up his hands. 'What is this about? You have no right to come at me like this. My solicitor will have a field day with you lot.'

'You're under arrest for assault and the attempted murder, contrary to section 1 (1) Criminal Attempts Act 1981, of Tamara Smythson. You do not have to say anything, but anything you do say may be used against you in a court of law. Do you understand?'

'What the hell?'

Before Marcus could move, two officers had his hands cuffed behind his back. He began to laugh, and James and Ethan watched in horror.

James stood up. 'This is my boat, what's going on? He didn't attempt to murder anyone.'

The female officer nodded, and the other two began to lead Marcus towards the steps, where he stumbled, struggling to stay upright. He'd stopped laughing when he realised they were serious.

'We're taking him to the station. The best thing you can do for your friend is get him a solicitor.' She turned to Ethan. 'Do you want to press charges?'

'No, not at all. I mean he's an idiot, but we're drunk. It's been a pretty crap night.'

They watched as Marcus was led up on the deck and taken away. The officer turned around.

'Don't go anywhere in case we need to speak to you both as well.' She left them standing staring after her, mouths open in shock.

James ran his hands through his hair.

'I need to get off this damn boat and back home. I've had enough of it. You should go home too, Ethan.'

'How? Actually, can I borrow your rowing boat? I can row across the lake to my cabin.'

James shrugged. 'You can do what the hell you want. I'm going home to sleep in my bed for a few hours, then I'm going to shower, get dressed and go find that Chloe girl who works at the Hydro. I need a shoulder to cry on and a pair of breasts to lose myself in.'

He laughed, but Ethan knew he was being serious. Standing up, Ethan wobbled his way onto the deck and to the back of the boat where the smaller wooden tender was tied up. He heard James shout, 'Try not to drown, I'm in enough trouble as it is.'

Ethan smiled to himself; he hadn't drunk nearly as much as the other two. His eye was swelling shut, making it even harder to see in the rain and the dark, but he didn't care. He wanted to get home.

Clambering down into the boat, he picked up the oars and struggled to put them into the rungs to keep them secure. He leant too far and felt himself toppling backwards, landing on his back with a thud. As he lay there in the lashing rain, he stared up at the small motor and realised his prayers had just been answered. He didn't need to row; it had an engine.

CHAPTER FORTY-NINE

The sound of the front door slamming shut in the wind awoke Beth from her slumber on the sofa with a jump, all her senses on high alert until she heard Josh's voice.

'Sorry, I didn't realise how windy it was.'

He walked into the lounge where she was sitting up, rubbing her eyes. She did a double-take; he looked dreadful. There was two-day stubble across his chin, his eyes were bleary, and his shirt was crumpled.

'What happened?'

She didn't miss the glance he cast at the empty wine glass on the coffee table, then around the room to see where the bottle was. She'd already hidden the empty bottle in the recycling container, not that it was any of his business how much she'd had.

'Can I get you a drink?'

He shook his head. 'No thanks, I'm too tired.' He crossed the room towards her and she pulled him close. Beth wrinkled her nose; he smelt like the lake – the musty, earthy smell of someone who had been by the water. Instantly she was transported back to Friday night when she'd fallen in. She stepped away from Josh in alarm, and even though she told herself to let him have a hot shower and get some sleep, the words tumbled out of her mouth before she could stop them.

'What's going on, Josh? I know you were at Jodie's last night. I saw your car there this morning. Why didn't you come home?'

His pale face flushed deep red. 'Nothing, well not what you're probably thinking.'

'What am I thinking then? Because you haven't been home for two nights. I don't think I'm too demanding; the least you can do is be truthful.'

She didn't know whether it was the surprise of being caught out, embarrassment or anger but his voice was much louder than usual.

'Were you spying on me? I haven't lied to you about anything.'

'No, maybe you haven't. But you also haven't exactly been telling me the truth. Are you and Jodie back together? Have you been sleeping with her?'

Confusion clouded her mind; he looked so hurt and dejected.

'Is this you, or your friend Chardonnay speaking?'

She was speechless. He'd never mentioned her drinking before. Anger sparked inside her chest.

'What else is there to do? You're never here and when you should be, you're telling lies and sneaking around with other women. This is my house. If I want a glass of wine, I'll damn well have one.'

Afraid to face him, she ran towards the stairs and her bedroom, slamming the door behind her for good measure. She was angry with Josh, but also angry with herself for behaving the way she just had, and for reminding him he was in her house. She threw herself into the bed, pulling the duvet over her head and listened to him moving around downstairs. Eventually, he came upstairs, but he didn't open the door. Instead, she heard him go into the bathroom and the shower turn on. As she lay there wondering why she'd behaved the way she had, waiting for him to come to bed, the wine began to work its way around her brain and her eyes began to close. She was asleep before he'd even stepped under the shower head.

*

Opening her eyes the next morning, her heart tore in two when she realised that, once more, she was alone in her king-size bed. She lay there confused and blinking. It was still dark outside and the sound of the driving rain as it lashed against her bedroom windows was somewhat comforting. Josh would be in the spare room or on the sofa. She got up, pulled on her dressing gown and went to check, stopping in her tracks as she passed the bathroom and noticed his toiletries no longer taking up shelf space. Her heart began to race. She rushed to the spare bedrooms, checking all of them. He wasn't there. Opening up the closet, she realised his case was missing and felt a sharp, stabbing pain inside her chest. She ran down the stairs, praying he'd be curled up on the sofa and an anguished cry left her mouth when she realised he was gone. Rushing to the front door, she threw it open and was instantly drenched by the rain driving down. His car wasn't there, just hers. *Beth, what have you done?* she whispered into the rain, her words lost in the downpour.

Back inside, she didn't remember ever feeling this sad in her entire life. She didn't want to be on her own; she didn't want to have to wake up without seeing Josh's smile, the glint in his eyes. They just seemed to fit together like they were always meant to be. He made her feel alive again. She stepped into the kitchen, water dripping onto the grey slate tiles. She needed to get out of her wet pyjamas. Unbuttoning them, she let them drop to the floor and made her way naked to the bathroom. Josh was gone; she'd driven him away with her accusations and her drinking. She didn't even realise she was crying until she looked in the mirror to see her swollen, red eyes. There was nothing she could do, not right now anyway. Picking up a towel, she began to rub herself dry.

Back into the bedroom, she pulled a fresh pair of soft brushed cotton pyjamas from the drawer. They were warm and felt good against her skin as she climbed back into bed. She would shut her eyes and pray for a different outcome when she woke again to be on call from twelve noon onwards. Pulling her duvet over, she grabbed the pillow Josh used and hugged it tight to her chest.

*

A ringing phone woke her. Opening one eye, she reached out with her fingertips searching for it.

'Beth Adams.'

'Doctor Adams, it's Helen from the control room at Penrith. Sorry to bother you, we have a sudden death of an eighteen-year-old. Her mother found her collapsed on the bedroom floor, unresponsive.'

'What time is it?'

The question threw the voice on the end of the phone. 'It's, er, almost two.'

She opened both eyes. 'What's the address.' Sitting up, she grabbed the notepad and pen she kept purposely by the side of her bed.

'Thanks, Helen, I'm on my way.'

'I'll let the duty DS know you're on your way.'

Beth said goodbye. She'd almost asked who the duty DS was, but she already knew it would be Josh. At least she'd see him; maybe she could apologise if they got a moment alone. Although, that wasn't her style; once Beth was at a crime scene she would switch into professional mode and nothing would distract her from her work. *Not even Josh?* the voice asked inside her head. She replied out loud, 'No, not even Josh.'

CHAPTER FIFTY

Beth arrived at the address; the large wooden gates were open and inside were an assortment of police vehicles, an ambulance and now her. She glanced in the rear-view mirror, checking her appearance. She looked presentable; amazing what some concealer and foundation could do to hide the dark smudges under her eyes. Her ash grey hair was a bit of a frizzy mess, but she could blame it on the rain.

Josh's car wasn't here and she wondered if she had it wrong; maybe he wasn't on call. Getting out, she leant into the boot of the car to grab her case. Walking towards the house, she heard Josh's voice, simultaneously realising a police van was blocking his car from view. She pushed down all the feelings threatening to surface and switched into professional mode. It wasn't happening, not here, not in public. Josh looked up and walked towards her. She didn't think she'd ever seen him look so miserable. He nodded in greeting. No smile; she didn't smile back.

'What have we got?'

'A mess, a huge mess. Mother found her eighteen-year-old daughter collapsed on the bedroom floor around one p.m. Unresponsive, not breathing and rigor has set in, she's pretty solid.'

'Are there any underlying illnesses? Eighteen is very young for a sudden death.'

A loud sob caught in the back of his throat, and Beth felt alarm bells begin to ring inside her mind. He knew this girl, it was personal. Instinctively her fingers reached out to him, but he turned away. She realised he was composing himself and gave him a moment. When he turned around the threat of tears was gone, but the pained expression was still there, fixed across his face, making him look so much older than he was.

'Tamara Smythson. She was on *The Tequila Sunrise* last night and was pushed into the water. Me and one of the lake wardens dragged her out. I took her home when she refused all medical attention.'

'There wasn't much else you could have done if she refused, and if she's eighteen you couldn't have made her go to the hospital.'

He whispered, 'No, but I wish to Christ that I had. I would have dragged her there in a pair of handcuffs kicking and screaming if I'd have known this was going to happen.'

Beth didn't speak – what was there to say?

He led her up the stone steps into the spacious entrance of the house. An ornate, sweeping staircase dominated the entrance flanked either side by two huge marble panthers with amber eyes that stared at her. From somewhere inside the house she could hear the loud sobs of a woman and the hushed tones of a man trying to comfort her.

She turned to Josh. 'Is this a crime scene?'

He shook his head. 'No, the boat is the primary scene. I've asked the parents to stay out of the way until you've been and we've decided upon a course of action. We should get suited and booted. I only peered in through the bedroom door, I didn't go in. The first officer on scene did and the paramedics pronounced death. There's no actual evidence here, apart from her wet clothes.'

Even so, both went outside to dress in protective clothing. Beth looked up as she slipped on a shoe cover.

'I can manage if you would rather wait out here.' In all honesty, it would be easier for her if he did; she needed to concentrate on the body. He shook his head and she knew even though he was distressed he wouldn't be able to wait outside; he would want to be involved.

CHAPTER FIFTY-ONE

Dressed in white paper overalls, shoe covers, and double gloved, Beth stepped back into the house, and Josh led the way to the girl's room past huge oil portraits of what Beth assumed to be family members. She felt as if every pair of eyes turned to watch her, could almost feel them burning into the back of her neck. As they reached the last door on the left, the only one which was ajar, Beth felt her mind begin to focus. She was in full pathologist mode now as she looked around the huge pink room full of every modern gadget a teenager could wish for, including an enormous television that dominated the whole of one wall. On the bed was a MacBook still open, the screensaver spinning colourful wheels. Tamara's pyjama-clad body was curled up on the floor, her blonde hair matted and tangled.

'Shit.'

She heard Josh's sharp intake of breath behind her.

'I can manage if you'd rather take ten.'

'I'm good.'

She didn't question him further. He knew the drill: if he felt as if he couldn't cope, he was to get out of the crime scene and fast.

Stepping closer, Beth bent down to examine the girl, who looked as if she'd simply fallen to the floor. There was a small amount of vomit on the front of her pyjama top. Opening up her case, she took the girl's temperature and the ambient temperature of the room.

'She's in full rigor, which usually develops completely around twelve hours after death. I'm going to make an educated guess here, because you know how difficult it is to get this right.'

'But?'

'But, personally, I would put her time of death around eleven, no later than twelve last night. When was she discovered?'

He let out a sigh. 'Around one p.m. this afternoon. But time of death sometime between eleven and twelve, if that's right, means she'd been home less than an hour. I knew when I left her just after ten last night that I shouldn't have, but there was nothing else I could do. She refused help and insisted she was fine and just wanted to go home. What do you think happened?'

'I can't say for definite right now, but she went into the lake, right?'

'Was pushed off the boat into the water. She said it tasted like shit.'

Beth used a gloved fingertip to lift open one of the half-closed eyelids. The eyes were beginning to look milky, but there were no tiny red specks of petechiae which would have indicated asphyxiation by strangulation. But the girl *had* suffocated. 'I think that it's highly likely she died from secondary drowning.'

'What? How do you drown in your bedroom?' He went across the room to the ensuite, opening the door to a bath full of faded green water with specks of gold glitter forming a film on the top of it.

'She ran a bath.'

Beth joined him, took a cursory look around the room.

'She didn't get into it though, she never made it. There would be specks of that glitter on her body if she had. The glitter on her face is silver and I'm assuming from her eye make-up. Not only that, her matted hair extensions have bits of debris in them. She came home, ran a bath fully intending to get into it, only she never made it.'

'How, how could she drown? I don't understand it.'

'It's very rare and this would only be the second case I've come across since I became a pathologist. It's fatal if the warning symptoms are ignored. Inhaling the smallest amount of water into the lungs can irritate them and cause them to swell. If that is what happened, when I do her post-mortem I will likely find only a small amount of water present; but even the smallest amount of liquid is enough to hinder the lungs' ability to function as they should and provide enough oxygen for the bloodstream.'

She glanced at Josh, who was pacing up and down, shaking his head. He looked like shit. She knew he was taking this hard, and who could blame him? He'd had the foresight to take a boat out last night to make sure no one came to any harm. This girl had been pushed into the water and he'd saved her, only for him to bring her home and then to find out she'd died anyway. If things hadn't been so strained between them, she could have offered him some form of comfort, a quick pat on the arm, a squeeze of his hand. Only it didn't seem right. He'd snuck out of the house without saying goodbye, and she no longer knew where she fit into his life. She turned back to the body on the floor.

'You weren't to blame, and you really need to stop pacing, it's distracting.'

He ran his fingers through his hair, stared at Beth as if she was a complete stranger then turned and left the room.

Beth picked up the girl's hands to study her fingernails, wondering if she had any chips of paint underneath them as she whispered, 'I'm so sorry, sweetie, but I'll take care of you now.' She couldn't see anything, but to be sure she placed a paper bag over each hand to preserve any possible trace evidence. Someone had killed this girl. She didn't know yet whether it was linked to the other two victims but this didn't make her feel any better about it. All she could do was to make sure she did everything she could to get justice for their families.

CHAPTER FIFTY-TWO

James had watched Ethan take his motorised dinghy away then decided he was too exhausted to get home and was going to sleep on the boat. He had woken up less than twenty minutes ago and couldn't believe he'd slept all the way through to the following afternoon. He didn't have any further party bookings until December, which was just as well because after last night he probably wouldn't be able to anyway. Claudia Davenport would soon see to that. She had been so angry last night, and none of it had been his fault. The job was too bloody demanding and dangerous. It certainly wasn't worth the hassle it was bringing to him. His father would have a meltdown over this latest incident; any bad publicity was frowned upon. To bring shame on the family name wasn't worth the aggravation it caused. He'd learnt that at an early age.

He was about to leave the boat when he saw the blue flashing lights of a police van reflecting along Glebe Road. He groaned, muttering, 'What the fuck do they want now?'; of course they might be going somewhere else, but he doubted it. It seemed that his boat was a disaster magnet. He climbed off onto the metal jetty and waited with his arms folded to see if the coppers were heading his way. He heard the van stop nearby and felt his blood run cold.

'James Marshall?'

He turned to face the huge man standing behind him, as broad as he was tall.

'Yes. What now?'

'We need to secure the boat. It's a crime scene. You can't go back on to it until it's been searched by the crime scene investigators.'

'How is it a crime scene? I mean, it's a fucking disaster, I'll own up to that with both hands.'

Another officer had joined the first. They glanced at each other, and he realised that something bad had happened.

'The least you can do is tell me what's going on. I don't think I'm asking too much?'

The big guy shrugged. 'We also need you to come down to the station and give a statement. You'll be told more then. I'm afraid I'm not at liberty to discuss anything with you.'

'Am I under arrest?'

'No, you're helping with enquiries.'

He fished the keys for the boat out of his pocket and handed them over. 'Knock yourself out.'

The big guy took them from him, passing them to the other officer.

'I'll take him, you wait with the boat for Claire to get here.'

James walked briskly to where the van was parked. There weren't many people around. Still, he didn't want anyone he knew to see him get put into a police van. His father was going to go apeshit with him over this.

The copper opened the side door to the van and let him climb in. He supposed he should be grateful he hadn't made him get in the cage. Good job because the winding roads back to Kendal stuck in that tiny space with no windows would definitely have made him barf. He was glad they hadn't arrived as he was getting into his car; although he felt sober, the amount of Jack Daniel's he'd consumed last night might not agree with that diagnosis. If they'd got close and realised he reeked of whiskey they would have breathalysed him and he would be in the cage. He was grateful for that small mercy even if his whole life had gone to rat shit and was out of his control for the first time ever.

CHAPTER FIFTY-THREE

Josh rushed into the office, took one look at the whiteboard and began to clean it. Detective Chief Inspector Paul O'Neill was on his way from Barrow and would be here soon. He picked up the dried red marker, tugging off the lid and began to write the names of the three victims on the whiteboard. The pen gave out when he was writing Leah Burton's name. Sam, sensing his urgency, threw him another from her desk drawer. He then wrote the names Julia Bach and Tamara Smythson next to it. His stomach churned each time he heard Tamara's name; he could have saved her, he should have saved her. Underneath each name he listed what he knew about them.

Leah & Julia both from out of town.
Tamara, local.
All have blonde hair.
Aged between eighteen to twenty-four.
Found in Lake Windermere.
Two of them definitely came into contact with James Marshall.
Julia last seen on her way to the Marina to enquire about a job, possibly The Tequila.
Marcus Johnson was seen assaulting Tamara by Ethan Scales.
Marcus Johnson reportedly harassing Julia.
Ethan was also present when Leah was on The Tequila Sunrise.
Trace evidence found under both Leah & Julia's nails suspected match (not confirmed).

He wrote the number '1' by Julia, a '2' next to Leah and '3' next to Tamara's name, and Sam handed him a mug of coffee.

'Thank you. You were right to be so concerned about Grace going on that boat. Someone pushed Tamara Smythson into the lake during the party. I'm more than convinced the same person was responsible for the deaths of the other two victims.'

'You did everything you could; thank you for even going out on that boat. No one else would have done that, Josh. None of this was your fault, so don't go trying to blame yourself for it.'

'Thanks, but I should have made her get checked over.'

'Trust me, the only way you'd have been able to do that, if she didn't want to go, would have been to drag her to the hospital. She was eighteen; she didn't feel unwell and refused medical attention. There was nothing else you could do.'

He smiled at Sam; he knew she was right. It didn't matter though: he thought about the trickle of blood that had leaked from Tamara's nose in the car, the coughing fit. He'd never heard of secondary drowning, didn't know there was such a thing, but after he'd left Beth at the scene he'd done a quick Google search and discovered that Tamara had displayed all the symptoms. Had he known this he could have saved her life; a simple overnight stay in hospital on oxygen would have been enough. As it was, she was now in hospital, but not on a ward. No, she was in cold storage in the mortuary awaiting Beth to cut her open from her neck to her navel. He wanted to punch something he was so angry with himself. Instead he clenched the handle on the mug and walked out of the office. He needed some air and five minutes to get his head together before it exploded. He didn't have time to be kicked off the investigation, not now. He needed to find out who pushed Tamara off the boat, because it was highly likely the same person was responsible for the deaths of Leah and Julia.

After standing outside the back door taking deep breaths of the chilled air, he felt as if his head was a little clearer. At some point he would be interviewed by PSD because he was the last person to be with Tamara before she died. The professional standards department were a hard bunch to please.

'Morning, Josh.'

He turned to see the DCI strolling across the car park towards him.

'Morning, boss.'

'How are you? It's been a while.'

'To be honest, I've been better. This is a mess.'

'It might be a mess, but thanks to you we know there is a killer out there who is responsible for three deaths. I also believe we have three possible suspects ready to be interviewed, so it's not that big a mess. Well done, Josh.'

He followed Paul inside. If it hadn't been for Beth, they wouldn't have known any of this. He wanted to talk to her, to apologise, tell her everything that had happened and let her know that none of it was her fault. Because she was even better at blaming herself when things went wrong than he was. He pulled out his phone and sent a quick text.

I'm sorry. Xxx

Then pushed it back into his pocket. He didn't know if it would do any good; he didn't have time to go and see her: there were three suspects to interview and a post-mortem to attend, but before any of that a briefing to give to his team.

CHAPTER FIFTY-FOUR

Satisfied the body could be moved, Beth went downstairs and introduced herself to Tamara's grief-stricken parents. They were an older couple, much older than she'd expected. 'I'm so sorry for your loss.' She held out her hand, shaking both of theirs. 'I'm Doctor Adams, the pathologist. I'll be looking after your daughter.'

The woman, her head bent, didn't make eye contact. Her husband stared, his head moving up and down as he struggled to find a voice. He rasped, 'Thank you. We don't know what happened. She went to a friend's party then messaged Angela to say she was home, around half past ten.'

Beth made a mental note of the time; it was likely that Tamara had died not long after that message.

'Angela is always a bag of nerves until we know Tam is home safe, so when we got the message we relaxed and drank a lot more than usual. It was a friend's sixtieth birthday, so the champagne was flowing. We didn't get home until around three and the house was in darkness. We assumed she was asleep. She's our only daughter, we waited so long, all those years for her to arrive and now she's…'

His voice caught in the back of his throat and he took a moment to compose himself. 'She's eighteen you know and very independent; if we'd opened her door to check on her, she would have been furious with us. We stopped doing that a long time ago. If only we had.'

There was a long silence as he tried to come to terms with this. His wife began to sob.

'We should have checked on her, Bill, why didn't we? We let her down.'

He sat next to her, pulling her close. 'We haven't checked on her since she was eleven, Ange, why would we? She'd already messaged to say she was home and safe. You don't expect your teenage daughter to drop down dead; no one expects that.'

'I don't know the exact reason for Tamara's death at this moment. I'm afraid I'm going to have to do a full forensic post-mortem. I'll be able to tell you exactly what happened once it's completed.'

Angela was shaking her head. 'I don't want you to cut my baby girl up. It's bad enough she's dead.'

Bill kissed his wife's cheek. 'We don't have a choice. The doctor has to do her job. We need to know what happened. I can't bear the thought that she might have been lying there for hours needing help and we didn't hear her.'

Beth spoke, her voice gentle. 'I don't think that your daughter suffered too much. I think it was quite sudden judging by the way she is lying on the floor. It looks as if she collapsed, where you found her. If she'd lain there suffering, she would have tried to move, to reach a phone, to call out to you. The bedcovers would be messy where she'd tried to pull herself up. There is nothing to indicate that she did.'

She stood up, hoping this assumption was the right one. Secondary drowning was painful; inhaled water causes airway muscles to spasm. Fluid can then build up in the lungs, which causes trouble breathing. It would have been excruciating for a short time, but they didn't need to know that. Regardless of what she told them, they would spend the rest of their lives blaming themselves for not being there, when in reality even if they had found her straight away it was highly likely she would have been dead before she hit the floor. All the money or love in the world couldn't change what had happened.

'I'll be in touch; I really am so very sorry for your loss.'

There was an even older woman hovering around in the doorway to the lounge. At first glance Beth would have said grandmother, but then she realised the woman had a uniform on. A housekeeper maybe? Whoever she was, her eyes were as red-rimmed as Angela Smythson's and it was obvious she was very close to the family. As Beth passed her, she smiled and whispered, 'I'm so sorry.'

Then she was striding towards the open front doors, walking down the steps towards her car, inhaling the crisp autumn air and clearing her mind, expelling the emotions she'd just absorbed from the grief-stricken family. If she didn't, they would hang around inside clogging up her mind, and she couldn't afford to lose focus. A third girl had died as a result of being in that goddamn lake and Beth was determined there would not be another death.

CHAPTER FIFTY-FIVE

Beth made a detour on the way to the hospital; Josh had looked beside himself and she hadn't felt as if she could comfort him. It wasn't supposed to be this way: she loved him but would not be made a fool of. The only person who could answer her questions and put her mind at rest one way or the other was Jodie. She turned into her street once more. This time Josh's car was nowhere to be seen. It was likely that he wouldn't be leaving work for many hours yet. She questioned herself before she got out of the car. *Should you be doing this?* She didn't know. All she knew was that she wanted a straight answer. She could deal with the consequences once she knew what was happening. Wearily, she knocked on Jodie's door, a part of her hoping that she wouldn't answer, tempted to turn around before she could get the door opened.

'Beth, what are you doing here?'

'Sorry to bother you, have you got five minutes?'

The door opened further and Beth stepped into the narrow hallway. It smelt of vanilla cupcakes as she followed Jodie into the cosy kitchen and Beth couldn't help but envy how homely it felt. Painted pale lemon with cream shaker-style units, there were fairy lights and bunting everywhere.

'You have a lovely home.'

Jodie laughed. 'It's not much, but I like it. I've made the most of what I have I suppose.'

Beth smiled at her. 'That's all we can do, isn't it? Make the best of what we have.' She noticed the row of prescription bottles and the plastic container marked with days of the week.

'So, what brings you here?'

The question echoed in her head.

'I, erm. It's a bit awkward really. Things have been a bit strained between me and Josh. He hasn't been coming home and I wondered if he'd decided to come back to you.'

Jodie looked at her in wide-eyed horror. 'Oh, God. He didn't tell you, did he? He's such an idiot at times.'

'Tell me what?'

'It's my fault. I was the one who got in touch with him. I wouldn't have, but I really had no one else to ask. It's a bit sad when you have to ask your ex to give you a hand.'

'I don't understand. Are you two sleeping together again?'

'No, absolutely not. I – I have leukaemia and ended up in hospital after almost overdosing myself. They said I couldn't come home unless I had someone to keep an eye on me. Josh was the only person I could think of who wouldn't mind me looking a state and feeling sorry for myself. I didn't expect him to say yes. I did hope he would because I've spent too long stuck in hospital. I was being selfish. I wanted to come home. I don't understand why he didn't tell you though?'

Beth shrugged; neither did she. 'Oh, Jodie, I'm so sorry to hear that. That must be so awful for you to cope with all alone. Of course Josh should help you out. I'm so sorry, there was me thinking you were sleeping together…'

Jodie laughed. 'We didn't sleep together much when we were married and we're definitely not sleeping together now; his stuff is in the spare room. Go and see for yourself, there's nothing to hide. What an idiot.'

'He can be. Tell me, how are you doing?'

'I'm doing much better. I have a bad knee which gives me more pain than my bloody illness, but everything seems to be going the right way, albeit slowly.'

'Good, I'm glad to hear it.'

'Do you want me to find out what he's playing at next time I see him?'

'No, thank you. That's for me to sort out. I do appreciate the offer though.' She smiled at her and stood up. 'I have to go, I'm on call.'

'I don't know how you do it, cutting up all those dead bodies. I don't know how Josh does it either, working all those long hours to find people responsible for the terrible stuff you both have to deal with.'

'I wouldn't do anything else.'

At the front door, Jodie called after her as she walked down the path.

'You and Josh, you make a good team. A good couple as well, you're both suited to each other. Give him a chance. I made a mess of things, but he's a good man and I know he loves you. More than he ever loved me.'

She closed the door, and Beth felt her eyes prickle with tears. How strange to get relationship advice from the ex-wife of the man you were in love with. She was right though; they did make a good team and she loved him more than anything. She hoped he still felt the same way about her. When this case was over, she was going to make an effort to sort everything out. She didn't want to imagine her life without him in it. She felt better now she knew what was going on; she could focus all her energy and attention on helping to catch a killer.

CHAPTER FIFTY-SIX

Everyone who needed to be present for the briefing was present: Sykes, Paton, Sam, Bell and the DCI. Josh sipped from his mug of cold coffee and stood in front of the whiteboard.

'This started off as what we assumed was the accidental drowning of Leah Burton, found on Thursday morning by Ethan Scales, who was on the boat owned by James Marshall.'

The DCI asked: 'Marshall of Marshall estate agents?'

Josh nodded. 'The body of Julia Bach washed up the same day. The pathologist, who was the one to originally raise questions about the circumstances of both deaths, believes that Julia died first, due to the decomposition and bloating. She must have sunk to the bottom of the lake and got caught up on something. Once decomp was in full swing it caused the body to fill and bloat with gas from putrefaction and then to rise to the surface. We have trace evidence which although not confirmed yet suggests they both came in contact with the same boat – one that isn't *The Tequila Sunrise* – at some time before death. Finally, last night, Tamara Smythson told me she was pushed off the same boat Burton was on, *The Tequila Sunrise*; she fell into the water. I pulled her out along with one of the lake wardens. Tragically, she died not long after I dropped her off at home, and yes I did offer to take her to the hospital. Dr Adams believes she died from secondary drowning, but can't say for sure until the PM has been completed.'

There was a cacophony of gasps and sighs from around the room. Sykes spoke.

'What's secondary drowning? How do you drown when you're not in the water?'

'I'd never heard of it either until Beth mentioned it, and I asked Google. Apparently, it can happen up to twenty-four hours after someone has swallowed even the smallest amount of water. It goes into the lungs, making breathing difficult, and then it kills you.'

Paton sat up straight. 'Shit, that's terrible.'

Josh nodded. 'When I spoke to Tamara, she said she had felt someone shove her from behind, and she lost her balance in the high-heeled shoes she was wearing and fell into the lake. Response took everyone's details before they left the boat last night. However, none of the guests at the party had ever been on board before last night. But there are two, possibly three, people who have been on or around the boat at each drowning event: James Marshall; Ethan Scales, a school friend who sometimes helps him out; and Marcus Johnson, who was caught by Ethan sexually assaulting Tamara below deck. All three have been brought in and are currently waiting to be interviewed.'

Paul nodded. 'Excellent work. Have they been arrested?'

'Only Marcus Johnson. The other two have been brought in to give witness statements. I want to hear what they all have to say and take it from there. Personally, the person I'm most interested in is Johnson. He has the motive and the previous for sexual harassment according to one of his employees. Julia Bach worked for Johnson and had complained previously about his behaviour to colleagues. Again, that gives him motive and a connection to two of the victims. At this moment in time I can't say whether he knew Leah Burton, so we'll work on the evidence that we have. Sam and I will interview Marshall. Sykes and Paton, you can interview Johnson; Bell, I want you to take Scales. The other two will lawyer up straight away; they can afford to. Is everyone okay with that?'

They all nodded. Josh grabbed the black leather portfolio he used for interviews. Technically James and Ethan weren't under arrest and were helping with their enquiries, so they were free to leave whenever they wanted. He just hoped they didn't realise that too soon. He was hoping that by interviewing all three of them at the same time none of them could change their stories or come up with some watertight alibi. If they thought that each of them was singing like a canary, they were more liable to give away any pertinent information. He didn't want to rush this, he wanted to make sure that he had the facts straight and the right person in custody when the time came. He wanted revenge for the death of feisty, pretty Tamara Smythson. He'd taken a liking to her and her death weighed heavily on him. Until he found out who had killed her, he would live with the guilt as if he'd pushed her into the water himself.

CHAPTER FIFTY-SEVEN

As Beth walked into the mortuary she was glad to see Abe standing there holding out a mug of strong builder's tea in one hand and a chocolate biscuit in the other. He smiled at her.

'It's been all of almost thirty-six hours since I last saw you; how the hell are you, Beth?'

She grinned, took the mug and gave him a thumbs up. 'Truthfully, I've been a whole lot better but I'm alive, which is more than can be said for the poor girl who should be arriving anytime soon.'

'It's a bad one?'

She nodded. 'Very bad, tragic really as it could have been avoided. She went into the water from that stupid bloody boat *The Tequila Sunrise*.'

'Did she drown then?'

'Not straight away. It's a long story, but Josh was on a boat with a lake warden. They saw her go in and pulled her out. She refused hospital treatment, was taken home and collapsed and died not long after.'

Abe whistled through his brilliant-white teeth. 'Oh, that's sad.'

Their conversation was interrupted by the ringing of the back doorbell; it echoed throughout the mortuary, making both of them start. Beth laughed. 'Gets me every time.'

Abe grinned at her. 'I'll do the honours.' Then he went to open the double doors to let the private ambulance carrying the body back up to them so it could be brought inside discreetly.

Beth wondered if Josh was attending or if he'd send someone else.

As she was walking into the female changing room, she saw the double doors of the corridor open and Detective Chief Inspector Paul O'Neill walk through them.

'Beth, how are you? It's been a while.'

'I'm good, yourself?'

He shrugged. 'Apart from bloody awful indigestion I'm very good. Josh can't make it, he has three people to coordinate interviews for.'

She hadn't really expected him to come and felt relieved. It would have been awkward, and Abe, who was very astute, would have picked up on the atmosphere between them. It also wouldn't have been very nice for Josh; she knew he was blaming himself for the girl's death. He'd saved her; it would be too much to see her cut open and her organs dissected. It was okay for Beth, she got to work on people she didn't know, had never met. It didn't get personal for her, apart from with Robert and Charles had ensured she hadn't had to endure watching his post-mortem. For a moment she felt bad she'd been so pushy with the man; he'd only been doing his job and protecting her from herself. At times she was her own worst enemy.

She scrubbed and gowned up, hoping the duty CSI would be here soon. She didn't want to delay; she wanted to get this done and the results sent off. They didn't have to wait long; Claire came into the mortuary a few moments after Beth.

'Good afternoon, Claire, thank you for getting here so promptly.'

'My pleasure, Beth, I was only lying on the sofa watching *Star Wars*. I love being on call.'

Beth smiled. 'Don't we all. Are we ready to begin?'

A chorus of 'yes' echoed around the freezing cold room. The girl had already been identified at her home by her parents, which saved the hassle of waiting for someone to come and ID her. Beth pushed the pained faces of Tamara's mum and dad from her mind and got to work. She knew how important it was to capture any evidence and get it sent off; they couldn't afford for anyone else to die. This had to stop now. Beth took some comfort knowing that in the next few hours anything she could find would help to catch the bastard who had done this.

CHAPTER FIFTY-EIGHT

Ethan sipped at the plastic cup of water he'd been given by the custody nurse to help wash down two paracetamol. He had the sweats; it was too warm in this small room, his shirt was too tight and the taste of stale whiskey in the back of his throat didn't seem to want to go away. This was the second time he'd been in one of these rooms with a stinking hangover. He was through with drinking and hanging around with both his so-called friends.

The door opened and a woman carrying a clipboard walked in, smiled, then held out her hand. He grasped it in his, shaking it.

'Detective Constable Alison Bell, thank you for agreeing to come in for a chat.'

He smiled back. 'No problem, although I don't know what we're going to be chatting about.'

She sat down. 'It's just a witness statement as you were there on *The Tequila Sunrise* when Tamara Smythson went overboard. I just need to know the circumstances surrounding the event.'

He nodded. 'I was there, on the boat. I didn't see her go into the water though. I was talking to some of the guests, heard the commotion, turned around and she was already over the railings.'

'Do you know who it was you were talking to?'

He shook his head. 'No, sorry.'

'Can you talk me through what happened in the moments before she fell into the water?'

He began to feel uncomfortable. The tablets felt as if they were stuck in the back of his throat and the chalky, vile taste was making him feel nauseous.

'Do I need a lawyer?'

'Not unless you feel that you should have one. Do you think you should?'

She smiled again, and he felt as if he was being set up, like she was a spider weaving a big web and he was the unsuspecting fly about to get trapped inside it.

'Erm, I don't think so, because I told you I don't really know how she got in the water. It all happened so fast.'

'Before it happened did you go downstairs and see anything untoward happening with Tamara and anyone else?'

He squeezed his eyes shut. Christ, they knew about Marcus. He didn't want to grass him up, but what else was he to do? He nodded, feeling miserable even though he owed him nothing. She waited patiently while he sipped at the water.

'I went downstairs to get some more champagne and saw them.'

'Saw who?'

'The girl who went into the water; she was backed into a corner. Marcus had his hands on her, trying to…' He really didn't know what to say. What would be the correct terminology? Grope? Assault was far too strong; it was probably more of a drunken fumble.

'What was he trying to do, and what did you do?'

'I wasn't sure if they were, you know…'

She shook her head.

'Getting it on.'

'Did she look happy about the advances Marcus was making?'

He sighed. 'No, she didn't. She looked upset. I told him to get off her, and she pushed her way past him and went back up on the deck.'

'Then what happened?'

'I got the champagne, told Marcus he was an idiot and went back up. I didn't see what happened. The first I knew about it was when I heard a group of girls screeching followed by the splash. But she was okay; there was a boat nearby that pulled her to safety. Look,

I know it was a mess, but why don't you ask her what happened. She can tell you far better than I can.'

'We can't ask her. I'm afraid Tamara Smythson was found dead this afternoon.'

He wondered if this was some kind of sick joke. He stared at the detective's face, waiting for her to break into a smile. She didn't. Her face was like granite and the serious expression on it told him this wasn't a joke at all. The girl really was dead.

CHAPTER FIFTY-NINE

James Marshall was sitting back in his chair, his legs crossed and hands behind his head. He didn't look in the least bit bothered about being here, which infuriated Josh when he walked into the room.

'James, I'm Detective Sergeant Josh—' He was interrupted before he could finish his introductions.

'I know who you are, we only spoke the other day. I have a good memory. What is this about?'

Sam sat down. 'We need to find out what happened last night.'

He turned to stare at her. 'What's to know, that girl drank too much and fell into the lake. End of story.'

'That girl is called Tamara Smythson; she fell off your boat into the water. She told me that someone pushed her. I want to know who. I don't think that's too much to ask, is it?'

'I want a lawyer. You told me this was to give a witness statement. I don't like the tone of your voice, therefore, I won't be talking to you until I have legal representation.' He sat back and crossed his arms, glaring at them both.

'That's your choice. Do you have a preferred one you'd like me to contact?' Sam asked him.

He nodded then reeled off the number of the family solicitors. 'Ask for Oliver; I don't want anyone else.'

Josh stood up, leaving the room before he exploded; he didn't like the cocky, self-assured idiot. Sam followed him outside, closing the door behind her.

'It was worth a shot.'

'He's an arse.'

'Yes, and a rich one. You didn't really expect him to spill his guts, did you, Josh?'

'No, I suppose not.'

Sam went to make the call, and Josh went to find an officer to sit with James until the solicitor arrived.

Paton walked out of the interview room where Marcus Johnson was, and Josh hoped he had something more than he had.

'Anything?'

'There's some huge misunderstanding; he thought that Tamara liked him and now he wants a solicitor.'

'Crap.'

'Yes, it is. If it's any consolation, he's looking very uncomfortable in there and is sweating like a pig. He's asked for the heating to be turned off.'

'Guilty conscience?'

'That or he's got the beer sweats.'

Josh walked away. Why did everything have to be so complicated? For once it would be nice to catch a break and put this to bed before anything else happened.

CHAPTER SIXTY

Beth gave Abe the go-ahead to begin to sew Tamara Smythson's body back together. She'd been right: when she'd removed the lungs and measured the liquid inside them it had been less than twenty millilitres. The small amount of freshwater had inactivated the surfactant, leading to alveolar collapse and pulmonary dysfunction damaging the basement membranes, which then led to pulmonary oedema. The progressive neurologic failure through the swallowing of fluid had caused her to vomit a small amount of gastric content. The cause of death was indeed secondary drowning, only this time, from what Josh had told her, it wasn't accidental. Someone had pushed her into the water.

Beth wanted more than anything for Josh to catch the person who had done this. Someone had pushed her into the water, and whether they'd meant for her to drown or not, she had. There had been no trace evidence under her acrylic nails. She knew it was highly unlikely as Tamara hadn't had to struggle alone in the water and had been pulled out to safety pretty quickly.

Only herself, Abe and the body were in the mortuary.

Radio One played softly in the background; Beth thought that it was more fitting music for a teenage girl than the Smooth FM that she favoured. She watched as Abe carefully stitched the girl back together, knowing he was being overly careful; his way of making amends.

She looked so small lying there under the spotlight. Her matted hair extensions would be a nightmare for the undertaker to sort out when the body was released, which, unfortunately for Tamara, might not be in the near future. She would be kept in the mortuary longer than Beth would like because of the pending murder investigation.

Checking her phone, there were no missed calls from Josh. Paul had told her he was speaking to witnesses at the station. She wondered how it had gone; had they arrested anyone for these senseless deaths?

Abe finally stopped what he was doing, stretched then stood up. Beth looked at the neat row of stitches, all of them even. She liked that he hadn't rushed. She didn't know Tamara, but she felt that it was the least that she deserved. The phone in the office began to ring and she went to answer it; her mobile didn't always get a signal in the mortuary.

'Good afternoon, mortuary.'

'Hello, this is probably a long shot but I'm hoping to speak with Doctor Adams. Is she available?'

Beth didn't know this voice. 'Yes, speaking.'

'Really, wow. What a stroke of luck that was. I didn't expect anyone to be there on a Sunday tea time, if I'm honest. I guess death has no concept of time.'

She laughed, feeling instantly that whoever this woman was, she liked her.

'That's true, when death comes calling you answer the door. How can I be of assistance?'

'My name is Michelle Jones, I'm a research microscopist at the forensic science laboratory. I specialise in identification of small particles and small quantities of unknown materials. I've been studying the samples you sent in.'

Beth felt a surge of adrenalin rush through her. 'That's brilliant.'

'Yes, I'm a bit behind so came in to work extra hours today. I found both your samples very interesting. They both came from under two separate victims' fingernails?

'Yes, they did.'

'Are you aware of the process we use to identify them? Would you like me to explain?'

Beth had a rough idea but wasn't an expert. 'Not really, and yes, I'd appreciate it if you talked me through it.'

'The samples were only minute, so I had to use the infrared microscope which allowed me to examine them without any damage or having to prepare them. I then had to heat the samples up to a high temperature which made them decompose into a gaseous product.'

'So you were able to put them in a chromatograph?'

'Yes, that's right. A pyrogram was produced showing the chemical make-up of the binder, which is the same for both samples. I can confirm that both samples come from the same object. They both share the same properties and have an identical chemical fingerprint. I then ran them through the database, and it's come back as a wood stain and marine varnish. But, the bad news is that the test sample you sent in for comparison wasn't enough to match it with those taken from the victims. Sorry.'

Beth let out a sigh. She had been convinced the paint would match the boat tied up beside *The Tequila Sunrise*.

'Thank you.'

'I'm sorry it's not the result you wanted. Maybe you could get a better comparison sample, slightly bigger, and I'll run it through again?'

'Yes, I'll try. It's good that you've managed to confirm the evidence recovered from both victims was a match. At least that ties them together; now we just need to find where they were before they went into the water.'

'Yes, I suppose that's better than nothing. Anyway, I'll send everything over on official documentation. I just thought I'd ring on the off chance. What exactly happened to them?'

'One girl was found face down in the water next to the boat she'd last been seen partying on, and the other victim was last seen in the vicinity of the same boat. She went into the water first, but it took longer for her body to be discovered.'

'How sad, I hope you manage to find which boat it was. If it helps, I think you're looking for a wooden boat that hasn't been painted in a while.'

Beth closed her eyes, picturing the boat attached to the rear of *The Tequila*, though it had been too dark and wet for her to see clearly that night.

'Thank you for this. I'm so glad you called.' Beth signed off and put the receiver down. It didn't make sense; if they'd both come off a rowing boat, wouldn't it have been adrift, or wouldn't they have been with someone else? Someone had to have been in the boat with them, and she had no doubt that whoever it was had pushed the girls in and left them to drown. What kind of sick person would do that?

CHAPTER SIXTY-ONE

They regrouped in the office. Josh waited for Paton and Sykes to arrive before discussing how the interviews had gone. They all walked in looking sombre.

'Sorry, Johnson got all antsy and defensive when we asked him what had gone on. Asked for a brief,' Paton said.

'He's sweating buckets though, and looks shifty as anything,' Sykes added.

Josh looked at Bell, who smiled. 'Mine was lovely; Ethan Scales is hungover too. Very open, chatty, he was a bit reluctant to talk about what had happened below deck. That's pretty understandable though, he didn't want to be seen as grassing his friend up. He did though; he said he caught Marcus with his hands all over Tamara and she looked visibly upset. He didn't see her go overboard though.'

'What do you make of him?'

'I like him; he seems honest, didn't want a solicitor.'

Josh paused for a moment. 'Plus, he was the one to jump in and try to save Leah Burton. Right, get him to sign his statement and let him leave. It's Marcus Johnson I'm interested in. He has motive to push Tamara into the water. He saw red when he was caught groping her and saw an opportunity to get his revenge.'

Sam nodded. 'We also know Julia Bach was being pestered by him so much that she left her place of work, so he also had the motive to silence her permanently. We don't know how she ended up in the lake yet though.'

Josh agreed. 'James Marshall was the same, clammed up as soon as he realised the questions related to Tamara Smythson and asked for the family brief. I'm still not one hundred per cent he's clean. After all, it's his boat and he has a reputation as a ladies' man. We'll wait for their solicitors to attend and then we'll tell them things have taken a serious turn and they're now being interviewed. See what happens.'

Josh stood up. 'I'll go and tell Ethan Scales he can go home.'

*

He walked into the interview room. Ethan Scales was leaning on the table, his head on his arms. He jumped up as the door opened.

'It's okay, thank you for your time, Mr Scales.'

'Is that it?'

'Yes, you're free to leave. Can I offer you some advice?'

He nodded.

'Keep away from the marina, especially *The Tequila*. I'd probably give your friends a wide berth for a while as well. You might end up getting dragged into something you can't get out of.'

Standing up, he looked Josh in the eye. 'Thank you, you don't have to worry about that. I've had enough of boats, alcohol and my so-called friends for a lifetime.'

Josh opened the door and let him into the front office. When Ethan pushed open the heavy wooden door that led into the outside world, he didn't turn around.

CHAPTER SIXTY-TWO

Beth got out of her car, the darkening sky casting warped shadows all around the marina. She didn't know what being here could achieve; she only knew she had to try and locate the boat both girls had fallen out of.

There were still no messages or calls from Josh, which hurt. She knew he was busy, of course he was, but she'd sent him a text two hours ago saying they needed to talk and he'd only texted back 'sorry'. He would be furious with her if she told him about being at the marina doing her own investigating, but what else could she do? Someone had to put a stop to these senseless deaths.

She pulled the woollen hat down over her ears and zipped her coat up to her neck. The row of shops was all in darkness, closed signs facing the road, but she was thankful the pub was open, the light shining out through its windows casting a warm glow onto the side of the lake. No one was outside and she doubted there were many customers inside either. It was too cold and miserable; people would rather be by the fire watching the television in this weather. Into her pocket she'd stuffed a handful of blue crime scene gloves and several specimen pots. She figured that the boat both girls had come into contact with had to be near *The Tequila Sunrise*, so that ruled out most of the for-hire ones a good distance away along the promenade. Paul had said that Josh was busy taking statements, so that meant she wouldn't have to worry about bumping into James Marshall again. Did she have the nerve to go back onto his boat to get a better sample from the wooden boat he had tied up behind it?

She could use the excuse she was returning his boots and clothes. Without a search warrant the evidence would be inadmissible in court, she knew, but it could be the lead they needed to crack the case.

As she reached the jetty where *The Tequila Sunrise* was moored, a sinking feeling enveloped her: the dinghy had gone. Did James Marshall realise how serious and incriminating the evidence she'd almost got could be? He must have moved it somewhere else. Walking up and down, she realised that not only had that boat been moved, but there were no others like it in this part of the marina. Now what was she supposed to do? *Go home and have a glass of wine*, she laughed to herself, then spotted the welcoming glow of the pub behind her.

*

Inside, the television was on and there was an elderly couple sitting next to it watching a programme about buying a house in the country. She walked to the bar and sat on one of the stools. She hadn't been in here before and it was much bigger than it looked outside.

'What can I get you?'

The voice came from nowhere and she jumped. 'Do you do coffee?'

The man, who had a tea towel thrown over one shoulder, nodded. 'Cappuccino, latte, Americano?'

'Cappuccino, please. Is it always this quiet?'

He shrugged. 'Depends on the weather; there's a storm brewing. Locals don't come out in this weather and there doesn't seem to be many tourists around.' He pointed at the couple who were glued to the television. 'Well apart from those two.'

He left her and returned a few minutes later with her coffee.

'Thank you, have you worked here long?'

He laughed. 'Only since I was old enough to wait tables. My parents own the place, but I kind of run it for them now they're getting a bit past it.'

'Do you get a lot of boat owners in here?'

'Sometimes, more so in the warmer weather.'

'I was wondering if you knew of anyone who had an old-fashioned, wooden rowing boat they may keep moored here.'

His eyes narrowed as he thought about it. He began to shake his head. 'Not really, apart from the one the arse that owns the big party boat sometimes uses.'

Beth sipped her coffee. '*The Tequila Sunrise?*'

'Yeah, that's the one. It's the only rowing boat around here like that. There's plenty further around by the pier. You can hire them by the hour, although I wouldn't recommend it this time of year. It's too cold. It's terrible about those two women they pulled out of the lake, isn't it?'

'Tragic.'

'Rumour has it they came off the party boat. He needs his licence taking off him. If two people had died coming out of this pub the council would have shut us down in the blink of an eye.'

Beth couldn't agree more. Taking out her phone, she began to search the Internet for information on the owner of the boat, but her Wi-Fi signal wasn't strong enough. Finishing her coffee, Beth stood up; everything pointed to James Marshall. She needed to speak to Josh and tell him what she knew; hopefully between them they could put an end to these senseless deaths.

Her phone rang and she answered the private number.

'Doctor Adams.'

There was a slight pause and then a quiet voice said, 'My name is Jude Williams; I used to be Foster. I believe you rang the school wanting to talk to me.'

Beth had almost given up on hearing back from anyone.

'I did. Is it convenient to talk? We can chat on the phone, or I can come to you.'

'I'd rather speak now. I don't want to bother my husband with whatever this might be about.'

Beth realised that she probably hadn't told him she'd been in charge of a group of boys when one drowned. She walked away from the bar, tucking her phone under her ear and sat at a table as far away from the other couple as she could.

'Now is fine, I appreciate you phoning me back. I'm investigating three drownings in the lake, and when I was researching previous drownings a news article popped up about Tyler Johnson. I was wondering if you could tell me what happened?'

There was a sharp laugh on the other end of the line. 'I wish I knew. Did you read the article? There really isn't much more to tell.'

'I understand, but I'd really like to hear what happened in your own words. It really is just research; I can assure you it's nothing more than that.' There was a lengthy pause and for a moment Beth wondered if she'd hung up on her. The voice on the end of the phone began to talk, though now there was more background noise than before.

'Sorry, I've come out to the car. I don't want Michael to hear this; it's not my proudest moment. There were nine boys that day on the geography field trip. It was really just an excuse for a day out though; it was hot, they'd finished their exams and I'd had enough of sitting in stuffy classrooms. I thought it would be nice to have a little trip to Fell Foot, buy ice creams, let them mess around and burn off some of that teenage energy. I never told them they could go into the water. Even if they'd asked, I never would have given them permission. One of them just decided it would be a good idea to race across the lake and they all jumped in at the same time. I was mortified. You know what it's like, risk assessments until they come out of your ears. Well, there was nothing in place for nine fifteen-year-olds going for a swim. I screamed at them to get out of the water.'

'I'm guessing they never heard you, or didn't listen.'

'Oh, they heard me all right. I was frantic. There was so much splashing and noise it was hard to keep track of them all. Tyler and his twin brother Marcus got into a bit of a scuffle with another boy, James, in the water over some girl they'd all taken a liking to. Ethan said he'd tried his best to split them up, bless him. He took it very hard, almost as hard as I did. I never particularly liked James; in fact he was a bit of a bully. His parents were by far the wealthiest in the group and he wasn't ashamed of flaunting it whenever he could. He let his father buy him out of many a scuffle. It was a disgrace really, but back then I was young and very impressionable. I should have been much stricter with the boys; maybe if I hadn't let them walk all over me Tyler would still be alive.

'When they finally reached the lakeside and climbed out the other side, I counted them off one by one and realised Tyler was missing. I counted them again, praying to God I'd counted wrong. That was when I realised something terrible had happened.'

There was a loud sob, and Beth felt bad for making the poor woman drag it all back up again.

'It wasn't your fault.'

'Wasn't it? If I'd stayed at the school, it would never have happened. I've had to live with that day, and it hasn't been easy.'

Beth thought about the things she'd had to live with and felt nothing but compassion for the woman.

'Thank you, I'm sorry.'

'Yeah, me too.'

'How did the boys cope after that? Marcus, Tyler's twin, must have been in a terrible state?'

'I thought they'd all blame one another and distance themselves from each other. They didn't though, they stuck together. If anything, it brought them closer. James took Marcus and Ethan under his wing; those three boys spent all their spare time together. Look, I have to go. Was there anything else?'

'Just one thing, can you tell me the full names of the boys on the field trip?'

Jude began to recite the boys' names, though they meant nothing to Beth: 'Ethan Scales, Marcus Johnson…', until she said, 'and James Marshall.'

Her pulse began to race at the mention of James Marshall.

'That's very helpful. Thank you for your time. I'm sorry to have dragged up so many unpleasant memories for you.'

The line went dead, and she stared out of the window that overlooked the darkened marina, the rows of boats out there in the dark swaying in the wind. This was more than just coincidence.

CHAPTER SIXTY-THREE

Ethan left the police station; he had no car and was going to have to see if there was a bus this time of night to get him back home. It was doubtful on a Sunday night, but he didn't fancy the walk. He felt better now he was out in the fresh air, crossing the car park with his hands tucked in his pockets and head down against the wind. A car horn blared behind him, making him jump. He turned to give whoever it was a piece of his mind and was surprised to see the pretty girl, Grace Thomas, from last night grinning at him. She put her window down.

'Fancy seeing you here. Wait a minute, you're not a copper, are you?'

He shook his head. 'God, no. Definitely not.' He didn't want to tell her why he was here. She looked even lovelier today than she had last night. Her face was clear of make-up and her long hair was piled up on the top of her head in a messy bun.

'I lost my car keys. I came to see if anyone had handed them in.'

'Oh no, what a shame they don't do lost and found any more. You've had a wasted journey. Where is your car?'

'Back home, I was just passing anyway.'

'I'm just dropping something off for my mum. Where are you going?'

He felt bad when the lies tripped off his tongue so easily. 'I was supposed to be meeting a friend to grab a bite to eat, but he's messaged to say he can't get here now so I'm just going home.'

'Why don't you jump in? I'm starving so we could go get something then I'll give you a lift home. If you're not doing anything else, that is.'

Ethan couldn't believe his luck. 'That would be amazing, thank you, Grace.'

He opened the passenger door and she swept an empty crisp packet, handbag and a pair of headphones onto the floor. 'Sorry, it's a bit of a mess. I haven't had time to clean it.'

'You should see my cabin, it's not much better.'

She parked the car, but left the engine running with the heater blasting warm air onto his face. If there was a God then his prayers had been answered. He'd so hoped to see Grace again and never imagined for a minute it would be so soon.

Five minutes later she was rushing out of the doors back to the car.

'God, she's a complete psycho at times; she does nothing but moan about what I'm doing and who I'm with.'

He laughed. 'Who?'

'My mother, she works here.'

'I'm sure it's because she loves you.'

'It may well be, but she still gets on my nerves. Where should we go for something to eat?'

'What do you fancy?'

She looked him straight in the eye. 'You.'

He felt a rush of warmth flood his cheeks and laughed. She'd seemed so quiet last night. Wasn't alcohol supposed to free your inhibitions? Maybe she'd felt a little out of her depth with all the rich kids. He knew that feeling all too well. Looking at her, he didn't quite know what to say.

'I suppose we could get a pizza and go back to my place, but it's not up to much and according to my friend James it stinks.'

She laughed. 'James sounds like a right charmer. I'm sure it's not that bad. Pizza sounds great. I'd say we could go to mine, but my little sister is there with her friend and I can't take any more Justin Bieber YouTube video sing-alongs.'

He laughed too. 'I can't say I blame you; pizza and my cabin by the lake it is then.'

She reached out, patting his hand. 'Perfect.'

CHAPTER SIXTY-FOUR

When the phone on Josh's desk rang with news that James Marshall's solicitor, Oliver Millen, was here, he was seriously impressed. The Marshalls must have more money than even he'd imagined, for them to have a solicitor arrive so fast on a dreary Sunday evening. He'd gone downstairs and signed him in, then led him through to the custody suite. Both Marshall and Johnson had been taken through there to the formal interview rooms. Both had an officer waiting with them until their legal representation arrived. Johnson hadn't specified a particular one so he would get the duty solicitor, who would not be arriving here so fast.

Josh and Sam made their way through the station to where Marshall was being held. With a solicitor beside him, it would be 'no comment' from here on in from James, but they had to press him, nonetheless.

The door opened and the solicitor stuck his head out.

'We're ready now.'

Josh shook his hand and introduced both himself and Sam. He glanced over at James Marshall, who still looked as calm and cool about the whole situation as when he'd been approached at the marina earlier. All of them took a seat except for Marshall, who was already sitting down. Josh turned the tape on and did a full introduction. He then read James Marshall the caution. Marshall interrupted partway through.

'Hang on a minute, you said this was a friendly chat about last night. Why am I being cautioned; in fact, why have I been brought into here?' He threw his arms in the air.

Sam answered. 'We did want a friendly chat, but then you asked for legal representation. We had no choice but to make it formal. This is your decision, Mr Marshall. We are only following your wishes.'

Josh finished the caution. 'As we said earlier, at the moment we need to ascertain the circumstances surrounding Tamara Smythson's death.'

James jumped up, his hands in front of him. 'Whoa, no one said anything about her being dead. She wasn't dead last night when she was pulled out of the lake. I don't know anything about this. It's nothing to do with me.'

Millen clamped his hand around James's arm. 'Sit down, James, remember what we discussed?'

Josh knew what was coming next; the age-old dance between criminals and their lawyers.

'She was found deceased just after lunch; we believe it might be as a direct result of her falling off your boat into the water.'

Millen watched his client keenly. James glanced at him.

'No comment.'

Josh sighed, not missing the look of relief which passed over Oliver Millen's face. He continued to ask his questions, every single answer the same.

'No comment.'

After twenty minutes Oliver held up his hand. 'Look, DS Walker, I think you've got everything you're going to get. My client has nothing to say. He has no knowledge of the unfortunate events surrounding the girl going into the water. Until you have some evidence to say otherwise this interview is over.'

He stood up. 'Do you have any evidence to support my client's involvement?'

'No, like I said we are just trying to get to the bottom of how Tamara Smythson ended up in the lake.'

'Well he can't help you. Good evening.'

Before Josh could reply, James had been ushered out of the interview room. The custody sergeant buzzed the heavy metal door, and Josh tugged it open. He led them along the cold, white corridor to the exit where he then let them out.

Watching them walk across the car park to Oliver Millen's expensive Porsche – which was probably paid for by the Marshall family – Josh's shoulders drooped. He had wanted a better outcome than this, had hoped that Marshall would confess to pushing Tamara into the lake, as well as Leah and Julia. They still had Johnson though; hopefully Paton and Sykes would get a better result.

CHAPTER SIXTY-FIVE

After Oliver had dropped James off at his apartment, James had gone straight in to shower, and then dressed in a pair of faded Levi's and a black roll-neck jumper. It was cold and dark outside, but he needed a break. Then he smiled to himself. No, he needed a woman.

Oliver had had the audacity to ask him if he knew what was going on and why the police were so keen to pin something on him. He'd shrugged; wasn't that what they paid him extortionate amounts of money to find out? If his father got wind that he'd been formally interviewed by the police he would probably have a stroke. Best to keep a safe distance from his parents for the time being. Luckily, he had that longing in his groin that could only be satisfied by hot, lustful sex. Was it really less than a week since he'd brought Chloe back here? It felt like months. Smiling at his reflection, he sprayed a generous amount of Bleu de Chanel on his neck and went in search of her.

The Hydro was deserted, so he crossed the reception area and headed towards the bar. Sitting down, he ordered a glass of wine to be safe; he knew he could drink a couple of bottles and still perform to a satisfactory level in the bedroom.

'Have one yourself,' he said to the pretty waitress who delivered his drink.

She smiled at him. 'Thank you, I'm not allowed on duty though.'

He looked at her blonde hair which was slicked back in a neat bun. She was pretty, not as pretty as Chloe, but if he couldn't locate her this one would make a pretty good replacement. 'I'm looking for Chloe; I don't know her second name but I know she works here. She's French. Do you know her?'

She nodded. 'Yes, poor Chloe. She's been very upset since one of our colleagues passed away. They were close. Probably more so because they're both the same age and Chloe was staying with Leah in Devon on her exchange visit before they came here.'

'Yes, I suppose it is.'

Another customer appeared at the bar and the waitress went to serve them. He wondered how Ethan had fared at the police station. It wouldn't have surprised him if he hadn't sat there bawling like a baby because he was scared. He doubted he'd have been able to afford a decent solicitor either. Maybe he should check in on him, he thought, and then he caught a whiff of a soft, delicate fragrance behind him. Turning slightly, he felt a soft pair of lips brush against his cheek.

'I hear you were looking for me?'

He smiled at her; she was beautiful. The first few buttons on the top of her shirt were open revealing the soft swell of those magnificent breasts, and he wanted to drag her out of here and to the nearest bedroom now.

'I was, but you've found me first. How lucky am I? Would you like a drink?'

He remembered his manners; although he had nothing but sex on his mind he still knew that he'd get a lot more from her if he treated her right. After all, she'd been the first woman in a long time to give him the brush-off. It was time to make her pay for that mistake, but he wasn't in a rush. The girl from behind the bar smiled at him and he realised she'd probably messaged Chloe to tell her he was looking for her. He smiled back, ordered a bottle of champagne and slipped her a fifty pound tip.

CHAPTER SIXTY-SIX

Beth made it home before the storm broke. It was so gloomy inside the house she went through it switching on lamps both up and downstairs to make it cosy. Dressed in a pair of fluffy pyjamas, she opened the fridge to find something to eat and decided on cheese on toast. Quick and simple. She always kept the wine rack stocked up and for a fleeting moment she almost took a bottle out to pour herself a glass, but she resisted. It was a bad habit: work, home, wine, repeat. Instead, she took a carton of fruit juice and poured a glass of that. Things needed to change; she had to start getting out of the house for something other than work. She'd like to do more running, but it was dangerous this time of year when the roads were dark and not well lit. Swimming was out of the question after recent events. She walked over to the huge glass window that gave her views of the lake. She hadn't even walked down to the bottom of her garden since that day. Pushing her feet into the pair of boots she kept near the back door, she unlocked it and stepped outside. There was that definite chill in the air which October always brought, coupled with the heavy rain clouds that filled the sky. As a rule, Beth loved this time of year; she loved being able to wear warm jumpers, boots, covering her sometimes-wayward hair with a hat. The darker nights made it much easier to sleep longer, and she enjoyed watching the leaves on the trees turn firecracker red, orange and yellow before they fell to the ground. She hadn't really thought about all this for so long.

She pushed herself to walk away from the safety of the house. The entire garden was flooded with brilliant white light as the security lights blazed into life, banishing all of the dark corners and shadows until she was nearer to the lake. She looked around; there was no one here. The lights hadn't triggered; she was safe and secure in her own little slice of lakeside heaven. Reassured by this comforting thought, she walked down towards the water's edge. She'd forgotten how peaceful she found the sound of water lapping against the shingle. It had been the big pull of this house when she'd first looked at it. The seclusion, the security, the close proximity to the lake; just being able to sit by it and contemplate life had drawn her in hook, line and sinker.

As she stood at the water's edge, everything went black as the timer ran out on the security lights and, even though her pulse was racing more than usual, she felt as if she could cope. The urge to run back towards the safety of her fortress was there, but it wasn't as strong as it used to be. She had faced the monster in her life twice; fought it and won. It was time to begin to really enjoy what she had.

A wave of sadness washed over her as she thought about Josh. All relationships had their blips, and now she knew about Jodie's illness it was different. She understood his loyalty to her despite her betrayal; good old Josh, who wouldn't let anyone down.

As she looked out onto the lake at the boats in the distance, she thought about Leah, Julia and now Tamara. Three blonde beauties who had all died far too young. It hit Beth hard and she whispered to the lake: 'Three deaths makes you a serial killer. Are you aware of this, or do you not care? Leah's and Julia's deaths looked like accidents on the surface. What happened to make you push Tamara off the boat in a crowd? You like the excitement. You're getting brave and taking risks. So, does that make you clever, or a coward?'

A low rumble in the distance broke her thoughts. The storm was approaching. Turning, she rushed towards the house to fire up her computer.

CHAPTER SIXTY-SEVEN

He watched as Chloe drained the last drops of champagne from her glass.

'I could get used to drinking this.'

'Do you want some more, or would you prefer to go back to mine where we can relax? I have lots more back home.'

She paused to think about it. 'I think I would like to go to your boat.'

'Why? I mean you can, of course we can, but I would have thought you'd prefer to keep on dry land.'

'I'm feeling sad for my friend Leah. She died on there. I would like to say goodbye, to raise a toast to her.'

James laughed. 'I like a girl who knows what she wants.' He leant across and touched a wisp of her hair which had come loose. Stroking it, he pushed it behind her ear.

'The boat it is then.' He was glad the police had released it as a crime scene and returned the keys to him. There was something potent about her. She set his soul on fire and he suddenly wanted her more than he'd ever wanted any other woman. He phoned a taxi, definitely over the limit by now, and even though traffic police weren't around these parts very often he didn't want to risk it and get caught. Not when he had too many beautiful girls to attend to. Some people had notches on their bedposts, but he preferred taking a personal keepsake from his girls: the smallest snippet of their hair – a tiny lock he would tie with a piece of silk and hide away in his bedside drawer. Sometimes, if he was lonely, he would take them out to stroke them, each small piece reminding him of the girls he'd loved or lusted over. Some men liked silk stockings; he liked silky, soft hair. He'd had his fair share of redheads and brunettes over the years, but there was something special about a girl with blonde hair.

They went outside where the taxi was already waiting. He opened the door for her, and Chloe slid inside; he followed. 'Slow night?'

'You can say that again. Where to?'

'Glebe Road, the marina please.'

As the car sped off, he reached out and began to stroke Chloe's leg. Her hand reached over to him and caressed the ever-growing bulge in the front of his trousers. He had to stifle the groan which was threatening to erupt.

'There's a thunderstorm coming,' said the taxi driver.

That's not the only thing coming, James thought to himself…

CHAPTER SIXTY-EIGHT

The Internet was running unbelievably slowly. Another loud rumble in the distance echoed around the house and she wondered if the imminent storm was affecting it. Google loaded and she typed in 'Drowning Lake Windermere since 2011'. The first page of searches told her that, apart from the recent deaths she had dealt with, all of them female, it was only men who had drowned in the lake, so she continued searching. What did it mean? She sat back. So apart from Leah, Julia and Tamara it was very rare, if not unheard of, for a woman to drown in the lake. Cold fingers of unease crept along her spine as she read on.

After a couple of pages, she saw the headline:

LAST PICTURE OF SCHOOL FRIENDS BEFORE ONE DROWNED

Clicking on it, she watched as the fuzzy image taken from a tabloid newspaper article began to focus. She realised it was different to the one she'd read earlier. This one had more information and it named the boys. In the photo, a group of nine teenage boys were laughing at something. Zooming in to look at their faces, she thought she spotted one who was vaguely familiar: his face was rounder, but showing traits of the handsome young man he would become. How sad and tragic, she thought, as she wondered how much their lives had changed that day. Fifteen was a young, impressionable age to undergo such a traumatic experience. Was it traumatic enough to turn you into a cold-blooded killer though?

Her phone rang and she was relieved to see Josh's name. 'Hi, you.'

'Sorry, Beth, it's been a bit crazy here.'

'Paul said at the post-mortem you had three people in for interview. How did you get on?'

'Not as good as I'd hoped. The last one has just walked out of the station with his solicitor. We have nothing apart from the fact all three of them were present when or before two of the three victims went into the water.'

'Was James Marshall one of them?'

'Yes, along with Marcus Johnson and Ethan Scales. Why do you ask?'

'Those names are familiar. I think one of them might be a serial killer.' She paused.

'Go on.'

'Well I think we've been looking at it the wrong way. We've been thinking that maybe the victims were drunk and fell in or that they'd been pushed or it was some kind of accident. All three girls have long, blonde hair, all are young and pretty. Up to now, my suspicious mind aside, there isn't an awful lot apart from minute specks of marine varnish under two of the victims' nails to suggest the drownings were anything other than tragic accidents.'

'But…'

'Well for a start, I've searched pages and pages on Google. Women don't drown in Lake Windermere, at least not very often, and none in the last few years. It's all men and teenage boys. So it's unusual for a woman to drown. But we have had three drownings in one week. The trace evidence recovered from both Leah and Julia has been confirmed as originating from the same boat; I can't confirm which one, though. When I went to the marina to look at *The Tequila Sunrise* there was one of those old-fashioned rowing boats tied up behind it. But when I went back there this evening it had gone.'

'What were you doing at the marina, Beth?'

She could hear the concern in his voice. 'Just making some gentle enquiries. I might have spooked James Marshall a little on my first visit.'

'You spoke to him? Do you know how dangerous it could have been?'

She bit her lip. 'I was a little reckless.' She paused again; he didn't speak so she carried on.

'I thought the boat was empty, so I went on board to get a paint sample to send off for comparison. Only I realised when I was on board that the boat was fibreglass, but then I noticed the wooden boat behind.'

'What did you do, Beth?'

'I climbed down the ladder to get a sample. Then... then I fell into the lake.'

The sharp intake of breath was so loud her ear popped.

'Luckily for me James Marshall was on board, heard the splash and rescued me. When he asked what the hell I was doing I thought I owed him an honest answer. I told him I wanted a paint sample from his boat and then I left.'

'I honestly don't know what to say.'

'Well there isn't a lot to say. Luckily for me he was there to drag me out. I did get a sample but it wasn't a big enough one to compare, so I went back tonight but the boat was nowhere to be seen. He'd moved it, which kind of tells me he's guilty of something. Anyway, regardless of how good his alibi is or his lawyer, I think you should be watching him very closely. Whoever this is isn't in it for the glory, they're doing it for the thrill and now they've reached that level I don't think they'll stop. You also need to find out why they took such a risk to push Tamara into the water with so many potential witnesses around. Something must have happened to force his hand in some way.' She paused, but Josh was silent, taking it all in. 'There is one other thing. I found an article from eight years ago, with a photograph of a group of teenage boys on a school trip. One of those boys, Tyler Johnson, drowned after a race in the lake. James Marshall was there, and so were two others you said you interviewed today, Marcus Johnson was Tyler's twin and Ethan Scales. They were all there that day.'

'Thanks, Beth, but you need to leave the investigating to my team. What you're doing is dangerous and to be honest it's crossing the line. I don't want to have to be worrying about whether or not you're safe. Let us do our job, okay. I'll see you later.'

He ended the call, and she felt marginally better after confessing everything to him.

Only she couldn't settle. She wondered where Ethan Scales and Marcus Johnson were. Would they be willing to talk to her about the incident years ago? Not having the luxury of a police national database to do an address search, she did the next best thing; she logged on to Facebook, deciding to try and find Ethan first. It might be easier to speak to him rather than Marcus, given that it was Marcus's twin that had died that day.

CHAPTER SIXTY-NINE

Josh was furious with how reckless Beth had been, but he also held a grudging admiration. She'd make a bloody good detective and he'd have her on his team in a heartbeat. Though he was annoyed she hadn't told him about her near miss, he realised that she hadn't had the chance. He hadn't spoken to her properly for days, except for their argument the previous night. He rushed up the stairs back into the office, where the DCI was zipping up his coat ready to leave.

'Sir, there's been some developments. I think you need to hear this.'

Paul perched himself on the corner of the desk and everyone else looked up from what they were doing to pay attention.

'I've just spoken to Dr Adams and she told me the trace evidence from the first two victims is a confirmed match, and Dr Adams thinks it likely came from a wooden rowing boat. She also confirmed that James Marshall had such a boat tied to the back of *The Tequila Sunrise* only it's not there now. He has moved it out of sight.'

Paul spoke. 'The same boat?'

'Yes, I believe so. Which puts James Marshall back in the frame. We need to find that boat and keep a close eye on him. Dr Adams thinks he's doing this for the thrill and won't stop until he's caught.'

'Bollocks.'

Josh smiled despite the bleakness of the situation; it took a lot to make the DCI lose his cool.

'We need a warrant to search Marshall's addresses to find the boat. Sykes, can you do some background checks to see what properties, boats, houses, etc he owns or has access to?'

'On it.'

She bent her head and began to type on the computer.

'Sir, can you sort out the warrant?'

'Myself, Paton and Sam will go and see if we can find Marshall. Once we've located him, I'll request a POLSA team to come and take over until we're good to go.'

Josh didn't wait for Paul to say yes, he just grabbed his jacket and began to head out of the door, closely followed by Sam and Paton. It had only been a couple of hours since Marshall had left the station, so he would have either gone home or to his boat. At least that was what Josh hoped, though in reality he could be anyplace including Manchester Airport waiting to catch a flight to anywhere in the world.

He rang Sykes as he walked. 'Can you get a wanted marker put on James Marshall for me and make sure it's distributed to all the airports?'

He hung up, knowing it would be done before they'd even got as far as the marina. Next he rang Karen Taylor and asked if she could get Cal to meet them with the lake warden's boat at the marina. He didn't know if they were going to need it, but he was covering all bases. He just hoped they weren't too late, and that Marshall thought they were all too stupid to figure out what was really going on.

CHAPTER SEVENTY

Ethan opened the door to his cabin, sniffed, then stepped to one side for Grace to enter.

'Sorry, it really is a bit of a shithole.'

She laughed. 'I like it. You know what it reminds me of?'

He shook his head.

'Have you ever watched the movie *The Parent Trap*? Not the old black-and-white one? The one with Lindsay Lohan when she was a cute kid.'

He shrugged. 'No, I don't think I have. I'm more into superhero kind of stuff like *Batman* and *X-Men*. I'm also quite partial to a Teenage Ninja Mutant Turtle, but that's between you and me.'

She giggled and her face lit up.

He thought she was beautiful.

'Well in it she goes to a summer camp and they have to stay in these cute wooden cabins by the lake. I always wanted to go to a summer camp and stay in one.'

'Well your wish is my command. Welcome to autumn camp, where the accommodation has seen better days, but the views are pretty good and the company is even better.'

She followed him inside as a distant rumble of thunder erupted over the lake. 'I love a good storm. I bet you get amazing views from here.'

He nodded. 'I suppose we do. I've never taken much notice of them before. We'll be able to watch it from the window.'

He went to the kitchen area and put the boxes of pizza down, then he got some plates out of the cupboard. He began to fish in the drawers for cutlery, and Grace shook her head.

'Fingers are fine, pizza tastes better when you eat it with your fingers.'

Laughing, he picked up a slice and took a huge bite. Strings of hot, melted cheese dribbled down his chin and he scooped them up with his finger, shoving them into his mouth. 'Sorry, I eat like a pig.'

Grace tore a piece of the spicy meat feast off and took a bite. They ate in silence until there were only crusts left in the box. Ethan didn't have any nice wine glasses, just two chipped glass tumblers, which he took from the cupboard and rinsed under the tap. He opened the bottle of rosé they'd picked up at the off-licence and filled the glasses. He passed her one.

'Sorry, I don't really have company over often.'

She took it from him and clinked the glass against his. 'I'm not like the others, you know.'

He looked at her. 'What do you mean?'

'The other girls on the boat: the rich, bratty, spoilt kids. My mum and dad both work; we don't have money. Well, we have money, but not Claudia's kind of money.'

He nodded. 'Not many people do have Claudia's kind of money. I'm the same. I got a scholarship and met all my rich friends at school.'

'I met her through a friend of a friend; it's not really my scene to be fair. I mean, it's nice, the posh parties and stuff, but it's not my reality and it sometimes makes me mean and ungrateful about the things I do have.'

'Yeah, I guess it does. I'm the same.'

A huge flash of white light filled the sky followed by a rumble of thunder. Grace ran to the door. Throwing it open, she stepped outside. He followed, and they stood there looking up at the cloud-filled sky waiting for the next flash of lightning.

'One, two, three, four, five, six, seven, eight, nine…'

A burst of light flashed over the mountains in the distance.

Grace turned to Ethan.

'I wish we had a boat. Could you imagine being on the lake watching it? I'd be able to get some really cool photos for my Instagram page.'

He laughed. 'I think it might be dangerous to go out on the water in a thunderstorm. Especially armed with a mobile phone.'

'Why? You don't believe everything they tell you, do you?'

He shook his head, embarrassed. 'No, I don't. I have a boat we can use if you really want to, but don't say I didn't warn you.'

She ran inside to grab the wine and glasses. 'Come on, scaredy-cat, let's go out a little bit. If the storm gets too close for comfort, we can go back to your cabin. It's going to start raining. If we get wet, we might need to strip off and get dry.'

She winked at him, and Ethan decided being reckless and impossibly stupid might just be worth it.

CHAPTER SEVENTY-ONE

Josh and Sam went to James Marshall's apartment. Paton took the marina. The apartment was in darkness. They got out of the car and checked the area, looking for his car. It was parked in the underground car park. They could see it through the locked gates.

'What now, Josh?'

He radioed Paton. 'Any luck?'

'No, the boat's in darkness. Everything is in darkness.'

'Crap. We'll hang around for a while and see if he turns up. You do the same.'

Huge splotches of rain began to fall and the sky vibrated with a loud clap of thunder. Sam looked at Josh.

'I'm not getting fried by lightning, let's wait in the car.'

He threw the keys to her and she hurried back to the silver Ford Focus. Josh had a walk around the perimeter of the apartments. The rain began to bounce off the floor, huge drops that were soaking him to the skin. He ran towards the car, throwing open the door just as a loud crack of thunder filled the air.

'Shit, it's raining cats and dogs.'

Sam laughed. 'You don't say?'

She had the engine running and the heater was blasting warm air around the car. Josh's radio began ringing, and he answered to a hushed Paton.

'Boss, he's here at the marina. Just got out of a taxi. He has a woman with him.'

Sam put her foot on the accelerator and raced the short drive to the marina.

'Not too fast, we don't want him to get spooked by us speeding in there.'

'Why not?'

'Because if we screw this up, he can afford the best legal defence money can buy, and he'd walk. We need to get irrefutable evidence, something that can't be dismissed or glossed over by some smart-mouth lawyer.'

She slowed down. 'Let's hope she doesn't go into the water before we get there then.'

'Why?'

'Paton can't swim.'

Josh closed his eyes for a second, then radioed the control room.

'I need extra patrols to make the area of Glebe Road marina, but I want them to hang back and stay quiet unless you get a signal from me.'

The control room operator acknowledged his request and began issuing orders.

No more girls were dying in that lake, Josh would make sure of that.

CHAPTER SEVENTY-TWO

Beth scribbled down the address of the site where Ethan Scales worked. Courtesy of his Facebook page she knew he worked at the Freshwater Biological Marine Centre, that he lived on site there and was a keen fisherman. It couldn't hurt to talk to him; he might be able to tell her a little more about what happened that day eight years ago when he went into the lake and lost a friend. She'd left the house lit up, afraid to come home to the dark.

As she exited her front door, the huge raindrops turned torrential before she'd opened the car door. Even with her windscreen wipers on the fastest setting it was still difficult to see clearly, until a flash so brilliantly white illuminated the lake for the briefest of seconds. Her heart skipped a beat. Then thunder cracked so loud she jumped, even though she knew it was coming. She thought about going back inside and leaving her questions for tomorrow, but something told her to push on. Not least because the sooner Josh had the killer behind bars, the sooner he'd be able to come home to her.

As she reached the entrance to the marine site she saw the gates were fastened shut, meaning she was going to have to climb over the gates and walk down on foot. The storm was raging, and the whole driveway was surrounded by trees. She knew the chances of being struck by lightning were very low but still she double-checked that her shoes had thick rubber soles before she got out of the car and ran to the gate. She scaled it easily, but lost her footing jumping down on the other side because the ground was so wet and slippery.

Breaking into a jog, she kept to the middle of the driveway on the better ground and to avoid walking directly under the canopy of Scots pine trees that bordered either side of the narrow road.

As she rounded a steep bend, she thought she heard the faint sound of a woman's laughter carried in her direction on the wind, and she froze. When she heard it again, she followed the sound towards a row of wooden cabins. Looking around, she spotted a couple in the distance. The girl was inside the boat and the guy was untying it from its mooring. Waiting for a break in the thunder, she cupped her hands to her mouth and shouted as loud as she could.

'What are you doing out there? I need to speak to you.'

Her voice carried back towards her in the howling wind. So she had no choice but to push on closer to the water's edge and hope she could get their attention.

CHAPTER SEVENTY-THREE

Josh and Sam parked where they could see the ramp down to the lake, but the boat was out of view. Paton came running over to the car and leant through the window.

'They've gone onto the boat and straight below deck.'

'What's the plan of action, Josh?' said Sam.

Josh wasn't sure. All he knew was they couldn't afford to mess this up. That girl's life depended upon it.

'We'll find somewhere to take cover down by the boats. There might be one we can get on close by. We can't go barging in there and mess everything up or he'll walk.'

They got out of the car and hurried down towards the water, the driving rain lashing against their faces. There was a light on below the deck of *The Tequila*, but no signs of movement above deck. Josh pointed to the pub balcony that jutted out, giving a little shelter from the weather, and whispered, 'You two stand there; you can always pretend you've taken cover from the weather if they come out. Pretend to make out or something.'

Both Sam and Paton looked horrified but still rushed towards the small concrete balcony with a tiny dry patch underneath it.

Alone now, Josh walked onto the metal jetty which ran alongside *The Tequila Sunrise*, treading cautiously; it was slippery with the rain and he didn't want to go into the churning, black waters of Windermere unless he had to. There was a speedboat a little further down, the gate to gain access to it swinging in the wind. Deciding to take shelter there, he was just reaching out his foot when a flash of fork lightning lit up the entire marina; this was followed by a crash of thunder. Through the noise of the thunder he thought he heard a woman scream. He stopped and turned back around to make sure it wasn't Sam, but she and Paton were huddled together in the shelter of the pub. Another screech filled the air, and he lifted his radio, shouting 'Go, go, go,' as he turned and ran towards *The Tequila Sunrise* as fast as he could.

Sam and Paton were already close behind as he scrambled up the ladder to get on board. Sirens blared in the distance. *If he doesn't know we're here, he will now*, he thought to himself as his feet hit the deck, and he turned around to grab Sam's hand and pull her up, Paton right behind her.

All three of them rushed down the narrow steps and into the kitchen area, only to find it was empty. Pointing, Josh slammed his shoulder into the bedroom door and burst into the room. His mouth fell open as the girl who was naked on the bed screeched so loudly he wanted to cover his ears. James Marshall, wearing only a pair of black Gucci boxer shorts, walked out of the small bathroom.

'What the fuck are you doing?'

Confused, Josh looked at him, then the girl. 'I thought…'

'You thought what?'

His phone began to ring in his pocket and he snatched it out.

CHAPTER SEVENTY-FOUR

Ethan and Grace clambered into the boat, and Ethan began to row out towards the middle of the lake singing, 'Row, row, row your boat, gently down the stream,' into the crashing storm.

Grace giggled as the boat rocked from side to side. 'I wouldn't say this is the gentlest boat ride I've ever been on.'

He stared at her, wet hair slick to her face, eyes wild. She was perfect. Everything James Marshall liked in a woman, but Grace was interested in *him*. Oh, how he'd coveted the things James could buy without so much as even thinking about it, the lifestyle he lived, the women he chose. Ethan had spent the last eight years living his life through James and his money. He wasn't bitter that he'd been born into a poor family; he was furious. Everything was so easy for James, but that was all about to change.

The first time he had only meant to teach James a lesson – he hadn't meant for Tyler to die, just scare him in to focusing his attention back on to him. Scared by what he'd done, he'd sworn he'd never do anything like it again. But then he'd found Julia sobbing in the car park of The Hounds Inn.

He'd taken her to James's boat, moored only a short walk away from the pub. She began to tell him how much she hated working for Marcus and how she was going to go to the police about him. Ethan, who felt some misguided loyalty to Marcus, had begged her not to, and she'd slapped him, telling him he was as bad as the others. Angry, he'd pushed her away from him and she'd tripped and fallen overboard. He'd tried to grab her, he really had, but the rain had made everything slippery. Mortified, he'd watched as she slipped under, but the abject horror soon turned to excitement when he realised she couldn't swim. He'd watched from the shadows of the boat enjoying every last struggle until she'd gone under for a final time. It hadn't taken very long before the lake had taken her to her watery grave.

Then Leah Burton had blatantly turned him down when they'd been left alone on the boat. Telling him she didn't like him, she liked his friend with the cute, floppy hair.

Grace was staring at him. 'Ethan, are you okay?'

He looked at her, then nodded. 'Fine and dandy, you?'

'I, erm. Yes.'

A loud clap of thunder exploded above their heads, and she screamed.

He started to laugh.

'I think we should go back, this is dangerous and probably very stupid.'

'I think you're right. It is dangerous and extremely stupid. We should carry on.'

'I don't want to. Please take me back.'

He shook his head. 'No, I don't think so. We're here now. I wanted to ask you, what did you think of my friend who owns the big boat you were on?'

Grace paused. 'I don't really know him, he seems all right. Why?'

He shrugged. 'No particular reason. Do you think he's handsome?'

She turned to look around and see how far they were from the shore.

'Please, let's go back now. You're scaring me.'

'Am I? Sorry, it's only a simple question. You just have to answer and then we'll go back and get dry. Tell me, Grace, do you think James Marshall is good-looking?'

'I guess he is, I mean he's bound to be with all that money. Even if he was ugly he could afford to have himself made nice.'

'Ah, you know that's a shame.'

'What is?'

He dropped the oars and stood up, rocking the boat dangerously from side to side. Grace screamed as he lunged forward and grabbed hold of her shoulders. Then he gave her an almighty push.

As she tumbled over the side of the boat he shouted, 'Wrong answer.'

Then he started to laugh, rain pouring down his face, thunder crashing all around him.

CHAPTER SEVENTY-FIVE

Beth watched in horror as the boat lurched to one side when the man violently pushed the girl. She lost her balance, and the scream that erupted from her lips echoed around the lake. And then she was in the water with a loud splash. Taking out her phone, Beth pressed Josh's contact name, and he picked up immediately.

'Oh God, Josh, I think it's Ethan… he's pushed her in. At the Marine Centre. I'm coming,' she shouted down the phone, and the line went dead.

Beth had little choice. She unzipped her coat, throwing it onto the floor and kicked off the heavy walking boots. The girl was splashing around in the water which meant she was still alive, but not for long. Ethan was manoeuvring the boat back towards the girl as best he could in the wind and rain. Saying a silent prayer that Josh had heard her and was on his way, Beth tugged off her jeans, which would weigh her down, and ran into the lake.

A scream left her lips at the biting coldness of the water that washed over her – she didn't know how long she would last in the cold, but she had to try and get to the girl in time. Fully submerged, her limbs in shock and her teeth chattering, she swam towards the floundering girl as fast as she could. She watched in horror as Ethan reached the girl, calmly leant over the boat and reached out as if to grab her hand. For a moment Beth felt a surge of relief; it was an accident, he'd gone back to help her, it was all right, everything was going to be okay. But then his extended hand grabbed hold of the top of her head and he pushed it under the water.

Beth screamed 'No!' as panic filled her chest. She couldn't breathe. She tried to swim but her limbs felt like anchors dragging her down. She wasn't going to make it; there was no way she could get to the girl. Fear and frustration made her eyes prick with hot tears. She knew she had no choice, she had to keep on. The faint sound of a motorboat in the distance filled her with a sudden hope. Swimming as best and as fast as she could towards the drowning girl, she prayed it was coming their way before they both went under.

Beth pushed herself on and reached the girl. Trying to help, she lifted her fingers and scratched at the hands holding the girl under. The girl was strong and had managed to pull free from the grip on her head. Mesmerised, Beth watched as the girl swam closer to the boat instead of trying to get away; she reached out and grabbed his arm. Realising what she was about to do, Beth reached out and gripped the other, and between them they pulled him into the lake, screaming at him in anger.

Taken by surprise and wearing his outer clothes, he went under, dragged down by the weight of his coat and boots. Terror filled Beth's veins; what if he dragged her down and took her with him?

Finally, the engine of the boat was next to them, and a man and woman reached down. Beth had never felt such relief as when they took hold of the girl and hoisted her up into the boat. Then they headed straight for Beth. She was floundering, her arms too heavy. She was doing her best to tread water but her body was weak and tiredness was making it impossible to keep awake. Her eyes began to close as hypothermia began to set in.

She felt herself being dragged out of the water by two pairs of strong hands. The next thing she knew she was lying on the deck next to the girl who had almost drowned. They looked at each other; both of them had come close to death.

The woman was shouting at them. 'Huddle together, your bodies might warm each other up.'

Beth shuffled towards the girl and wrapped her arms around her, then the woman began to throw everything she could find on top of them: foil blankets, pieces of tarpaulin; she stripped her own coat off and threw that on top.

The boat was turning around, and Beth knew he was going to look for who she assumed was Ethan Scales. For a fleeting second she wanted to tell him not to bother. He didn't deserve rescuing. But who was she to make that judgement call? She wasn't God. Instead she clung on to the girl and whispered, 'You're okay, you're going to be just fine.'

And then she closed her eyes. It was far too difficult to keep them open. She needed to sleep.

CHAPTER SEVENTY-SIX

When Josh took the turning into the drive of the freshwater site, he saw Beth's car. The gates were locked; he revved the engine.

'Hold on,' he shouted.

Putting his foot down, he did the only thing he could think of and drove straight towards the gates. Sam screeched and he heard Paton swear from the back seat. They didn't have time to waste climbing over; he didn't know how far the lake was from here. It could be miles. The van hit the gates and there was an almighty crash. The windscreen cracked as a piece of white gate post smacked it and bounced off. He could still see though, and carried on driving fast down the narrow winding road.

When he saw the lake, he also saw the boat and two heads in the water nearby. Instinctively, he just knew that Beth was one of them. Abandoning the van, they all jumped out, but Sam was already streets ahead of them, screaming 'Grace!'

Paton looked at him in horror, yelling, 'I can't swim!'

Josh ripped off his shoes and coat, and was about to dive into the lake when he heard the engine of a motorboat coming close. Recognising the lake warden's boat, he had never felt such relief in his life as he watched Karen and her son Cal speed towards the girl by the boat.

Sam had a tight hold of Josh's arm. 'Oh, my God. What is she doing out here? Why is she here?' He couldn't answer that; he wanted to know the same thing about Beth.

They watched in relief as both of them were dragged from the water, then in horror as the boat turned around to go back for the person responsible for at least four deaths that they knew about, plus an attempted murder. The boat shone its spotlight onto the water as it circled around and around, to no avail. There was no sign of the man who had gone in head first.

After a few laps, Cal finally turned the boat around and headed to where Josh and Sam were waiting next to the landing dock along with two ambulances that Paton had requested. They rushed to the boat, and Josh held Sam back to let the paramedics get to Grace first. She was shivering, her lips were blue and her eyes were barely open – but she was alive. Once a paramedic had slipped an oxygen mask over her nose and mouth, Sam rushed towards her, hugging her daughter tight. Josh stepped back, giving them a moment. There were so many questions to ask, but they could wait until later.

Beth was brought off the boat next; she was barely conscious. Josh looked in horror at the paramedic who was dealing with her.

'She's okay, mildly hypothermic; it makes you sleepy. She'll be right as rain once we get her body temperature back up.'

As if on cue, Beth fluttered open one eye and looked at Josh. She tried to smile but faltered. He kissed the top of her head.

'You're so much trouble, Beth Adams, but I love you.'

This time she did manage to smile just in time for Josh to see it before she was whisked into the ambulance.

Josh turned to Sam. 'Go with Grace, we don't need you here.'

'What about you?'

'Beth will be fine. I'll come as soon as I can. You can keep me updated on the pair of them.'

Sam blinked and he knew she was trying to keep back the tears, then she climbed into the ambulance that Grace had been put into. The doors were slammed shut and it sped off, closely followed by the second one containing Beth.

Josh lifted his eyes up to the sky. The storm had passed, the rain had eased to a slight drizzle now, and the thunder had moved on beyond the lake. The faint rumbles getting quieter with every clash.

He bent down, pulling his shoes back onto his sodden feet and walked to where Paton was standing staring at the water, trying to see any sign of Ethan Scales.

'That was close, Josh.'

He nodded. 'Too close.'

'Do you think he's drowned?'

Josh shrugged. 'Hard to say, but it would be a turn-up for the books, wouldn't it? Talk about rough justice, a killer who died in the same way he killed his victims.'

'Grace had some balls, didn't she? Even though he'd tried to kill her she didn't give in and dragged him out of the boat. That's one tough cookie.'

He smiled. 'I suppose she takes after her mum; what an amazing girl.'

'Beth did good too; she figured it out before any of us, and we're supposed to be the detectives. The way she must have just dived right in to save her, makes me feel a bit of drip to be honest.'

'It's not your fault you can't swim.'

Paton shrugged. 'I'm going to learn. You never know what's next working on your team.'

Josh laughed, a little of the tension he'd been holding releasing with it. He'd been wrong about James Marshall, but on the right track. Ethan had them all fooled with his nice-guy act. All except Beth.

The boat came back towards them and docked. Karen and Cal got off. It was Cal who did the talking; Karen was speechless for a change. Paton began to relay everything that had happened on the radio to the control room to update them.

'There's no sign of him anywhere. He's either gone under or swum across the lake.'

'Surely we'd have noticed him if he was swimming across the lake?'

'I'd like to think so, but it's dark and the water is choppy. I'm not hopeful that he's made it out, but I do think there is a slight chance. It all depends on how good a swimmer he is. We're going to have to do a full search at first light.'

'Thank you, both of you. I don't know what to say. If you hadn't turned up when you did…'

The words were left hanging in the air. There was no need to say them out loud. All of them were aware that it would have been three bodies they were looking for instead of one.

A new-looking Jaguar parked behind where they were all standing, and Josh turned around to see the DCI get out and walk towards them.

'Josh.'

He felt a firm grip on his shoulder; it gently squeezed then let go. He knew this was Paul's way of asking if he was okay.

'Paul.'

'Well done, I got Paton's update. How's Beth?'

'Okay, mild hypothermia. She's gone to the hospital. Sam's daughter is the same.'

'Good, bloody good job. All round, excellent effort. I take it we're just missing the offender?'

Josh nodded.

'Well, I can't say that it's a loss to humanity if he doesn't turn up breathing, but that's between us. I would prefer to see him have his day in court, to hear him explain to those girls' families why he thought he had the right to take away their lives.'

'Me too, but we'll have to wait and see if we find him first.'

'You get yourself to the hospital, I'll take over here.'

He didn't argue with him; he was tired and cold. More than that he wanted to see Beth, to apologise for being such an idiot and explain what had been going on with Jodie.

CHAPTER SEVENTY-SEVEN

Beth had never been so grateful to wear a pair of clean, dry hospital scrubs. She lay on the bed in the cubicle in A & E wrapped in a special blanket to raise her body temperature, while the oxygen mask made sure she could breathe and there was no chance of her lungs collapsing due to the amount of lake water she had swallowed. She felt a pang of sadness for Tamara Smythson, who should have done the same and would still be alive to tell the tale if she had.

The curtain was pushed to one side and Josh stepped through; he was damp and his chin bristled with the beginning of a beard. He looked dishevelled, but so damn handsome. She smiled, and he rushed to her, pulling her close. Tugging down the mask, she whispered, 'Are you mad at me?'

He laughed. 'No, how could I be? You saved Grace's life. If it hadn't been for you, we would have been wasting time with James Marshall.'

Another face appeared through a gap in the curtains. Sam stepped through it, and Josh asked, 'How's Grace?'

She smiled. 'Thanks to you, Beth, she's alive. I'm still in shock about how she ended up with Ethan Scales, but it doesn't matter. Thank you. If you get fed up being a pathologist I think you should consider joining our team. Josh wouldn't solve half of his crimes without your help.'

'Where's Scales now?' Beth asked, blushing at the compliment.

It was Josh who answered. 'They haven't found him. I'm not ruling out the possibility that he swam to safety, so we've put a top wanted marker next to his name. But at first light the police underwater search team will begin diving to see if they can recover his body.'

Sam left them to it, and Josh pulled over a blue plastic chair and sat down next to the bed. He reached out for Beth's hand, and she clasped it tight. They might have obstacles to deal with in their lives, but she knew exactly what and who she wanted in her future, and Josh was a big part of it.

EPILOGUE

The autumn sunrise turned the sky above Lake Windermere into a glorious myriad of pink, red and orange. It was breath-taking and the woman who had left her husband fast asleep, tucked up in bed in their hotel room opposite the lake at the Water's Edge Hotel in Ambleside, was glad that she had. The only sounds were the gentle lapping of the water as it pushed against the wooden jetty and the quacking of some geese who were fighting over the few crumbs of bread she'd thrown in for them. She had walked along to the very end to take some photos of the lake in all its beauty before anyone else arrived to disturb the peace. As she admired the scenery of the lake set against the backdrop of the fells and mountains, a thud against the side of the jetty broke her trance. Turning around, she looked down into the glazed, open eyes of a man lying in the water. His very dead body thumping against the wood. Opening her mouth, she let out a scream so loud it terrified the geese, who all took off flapping and squawking. The council worker who'd arrived in his small truck to empty the bins dropped the bag of litter, which spilt all over the floor.

He ran towards the screaming woman, wondering what was wrong, pulling out his phone in case she needed medical attention. He reached her, and she pointed down at the body in the lake.

Holding his finger over the keypad, he pressed 999.

'I need the police. There's a man's body in the lake, by the second small wooden jetty opposite Water's Edge. He's dead.'

LETTER FROM HELEN

Thank you for reading this book. I was so nervous about Beth's first adventure, but you all loved it and took the time to let me know that you did. Which is quite amazing and I'm so thankful to you for sticking with me. This book was a little easier to write than the first, so I hope you enjoyed this one as much as I enjoyed writing it.

If you'd like to be kept up date with news about future books you can sign up for my newsletter here:

www.bookouture.com/helen-phifer

I'm very fortunate to live in a small town, not too far from the beautiful Lake District where Beth's adventures are set. Bowness, Windermere and Kendal are lovely places to visit if you ever get to this part of the country. Thankfully the crime rate is much lower than the stories in these books would have you believe.

Once again, I'm not a forensic pathologist although my ten-year-old self wanted to be one thanks to watching episodes of *Quincy* every week. If you are, please forgive any inconsistencies; they are all mine. I've tried my best to research and make the forensic procedures as true to life as possible. But at the end of the day it is a story and there may be some instances I've used my creative licence to bend the truth for the sake of the plot.

As always a huge thank you to my amazing readers for buying this book. Your support is truly appreciated. If you did enjoy it I'd be eternally grateful if you could leave a quick review. They make such a huge difference and are a fabulous way to let other readers know about my books.

Love always,
Helen xx

       🖥 www.helenphifer.com

       ⬛ Helenphifer1

       🐦 @helenphifer1

       📷 helenphifer

ACKNOWLEDGEMENTS

I'd like to say a huge thank you to my editor, Jessie Botterill. You took my story and turned it into something amazing. I can't thank you enough for being so supportive and so lovely, especially in times of desperation when a reassuring kick in the pants is needed.

I'd also like to say a huge thank you to the fabulous Noelle Holten for all her hard work promoting it. You're amazing. Also thank you to Kim Nash for always being there when hugs are needed by everyone. You both work so hard for your authors and I'm truly privileged you have my back.

Thank you to Oliver Rhodes for signing me and taking a chance; I'm so grateful I get to work alongside the fabulous team which is Bookouture. You guys all rock and you know how to party – you're my kind of people.

Thank you to the book bloggers who take the time out of their busy lives to read my books and support me. You are truly wonderful, and I can't tell you how appreciated you all are, there just aren't enough words. If I could hug each and every one of you, I would.

I owe a huge debt of gratitude to my fabulous readers, my number one fans, my inspiration. You have no idea how blessed I feel to be able to do what I love. I write these stories and you, my dear friends, buy my books and read them. Which is all a writer could ever ask for. This writer thanks you from the bottom of her heart.

A huge thank you to the Bookouture authors; I'm blown away by how talented you all are. Yet how lovely, down to earth and always there to offer advice when needed. I'm very privileged to be a part of this special group of writers.

Thank you to Paul O'Neill – I can't tell you how much I appreciate your surveyor's reports when it comes to the final read-through. You're my lifesaver.

A special thank you to Jo Bartlett for her never-ending writing support. A huge thank you to the rest of The Write Romantics: Jackie Ladbury, Jessica Redland, Sharon Booth, Deirdre Palmer, Helen J Rolfe, Lynne Davidson, Alex Weston and Rachael Thomas. You are my writing tribe and I love you all.

Thank you to my dear friends Sam Thomas and Tina Sykes – having coffee with you is still the best therapy there is. You're still in the book, sorry.

A huge thank you to my Wednesday night meditation ladies and gentleman: Helen, Jan, Val, Sam, Debbie, Tom, you are the highlight of my week and my life-savers. I still wouldn't want to fall asleep in public anywhere else. If anyone is still reading this, I can't recommend meditation enough.

I couldn't not thank the staff at my local Costa Coffee shops. You girls and guys are amazing and always there when I need you; well, when I need my coffee and the cheery smiles that go with it. A huge thank you to the Drive Thru for hosting my monthly book club as well, you guys rock.

Printed in Great Britain
by Amazon